Black Rabbit and Other Stories

Black Rabbit

&

OTHER STORIES

Salvatore Difalco

ANVIL PRESS ✝ VANCOUVER

Anvil Press Publishers Inc.
P.O. Box 3008, Main Post Office
Vancouver, B.C. V6B 3X5 CANADA
www.anvilpress.com

LIBRARY AND ARCHIVES CANADA CATALOGUING IN PUBLICATION

Difalco, Salvatore
    Black rabbit & other stories / Salvatore Difalco.

ISBN 978-1-895636-78-9

    I. Title. II. Title: Black rabbit and other stories.

PS8557.I397B53 2007   C813'.6   C2007-901757-6

Printed and bound in Canada
Cover and interior design: HeimatHouse
Author photo: Bruno Crescia

Represented in Canada by the Literary Press Group
Distributed by the University of Toronto Press

The publisher gratefully acknowledges the financial assistance of the Canada Council for the Arts, the Book Publishing Industry Development Program (BPIDP), and the Province of British Columbia through the B.C. Arts Council and the Book Publishing Tax Credit.

For Giuseppe D. & G. & the other ghosts . . .

ACKNOWLEDGMENTS:

Some of these stories first appeared, in various forms, in the following magazines and journals: *Armada Quarterly, Broken Pencil, Carousel, Collectanea, Dalhousie Review, dig, Fiddlehead, FreeFall, Grey Borders, Hammered Out, Johnny America Online, Kiss Machine, Malahat Review, Nashwaak Review, paperplates, Skive, Stationaery, subTerrain, Switchback, Transition.*

Many thanks to Brian Kaufman and Anvil Press; William Morassutti, Matt Firth, Kent Nussey, Carmela & Celestina G., Angela Difalco, Brandon Sunstrum, the PYC crew, and, of course, Alexandra Leggat.

stories

Black Rabbit

Uncle Toto took my hand in his and led me through the crowded parlor. The tail of his black scarf flapped in my face. It smelled of onions
and ashes. People touched me as I passed them, their hands falling
on my head, and murmured things I could not understand. A woman
I did not know with a long neck and red eyes pulled her hair and
started screaming when she saw me. Uncle Toto jerked me away from
her, squeezing my hand until I felt the bones. My father, in a tight
black suit, stood by a casket on wheels lighting a candle. He looked at
me and smiled. His eyes rolled back.

Someone had died. People wept. Three old women in black occupied a brown velvet divan against one wall, nodding and weeping as
they wolfed down tomatoes and tripe. One of them dropped a fork. I
stepped over it. Uncle Toto pulled me into an unlit back room, leaving
the door open. A wedge of yellow light spilled through, only to thin and
disappear as a draft shut the door. I stood still as Uncle Toto fumbled
with something in the middle of the room. I could just perceive his
outline as my eyes adjusted to the darkness, the large head, narrow
shoulders. He was talking to me or to himself, I could not understand a
word. It was too fast. He was dry, he sounded dry. His silhouette
thrashed. Then a naked bulb flickered on, shedding amber light.

Uncle Toto stood at one end of a heavy wooden table examining
the contents of a brown paper bag. He gestured for me to join him.

"Hurry up," he whispered. "What's wrong with you? Don't you
want to see?"

"What is it?"

"Come and see."

In the dim light Uncle Toto's missing eyeteeth looked like black fangs. His white forehead gleamed. I hesitated.

"Come on," he said.

"I don't want to."

"You're a donkey."

I tried to move my legs but could not. I slapped my thighs and felt nothing. What was this? Uncle Toto pulled at something in the bag. Then he turned to me and moved his mouth as though he were speaking. But I heard nothing. Was this some kind of game? I wondered. His wide-eyed, braced expression suggested that he wanted an answer to whatever he had asked me. But my tongue felt like a piece of paper and my vocal chords refused to issue any sounds. Uncle Toto struck the table with both hands and appeared to be shouting, but again I heard nothing. He hurled a shiny object in my direction. It missed me and struck the wall, shattering into silvery shards. Uncle Toto clapped his hands and brayed with laughter. Then he picked up another object and reared his arm, threatening to throw it also. I gathered myself, and with a great pull lifted my right foot off the floor and heaved it forward. The left proved more difficult. I found myself in a ludicrous lunging posture, my arms spread for balance. I tried to straighten myself out but my feet felt cemented in place, the left foot far back from the right.

His face hidden in shadows, Uncle Toto continued handling the contents of the bag, at one point punching it. Voices registered just outside the door. Cousins, perhaps, other mourners. No one told me who had died. My grandmother was still alive, I had seen her earlier in the bathroom, removing her dentures. I wondered where she was now. With all my strength, I forced my left foot forward and it flopped beside the right. The legs lacked all sensation. I sat down and stretched them out. Sawdust covered the floor and several empty brown beer bottles stood under the table, labels peeling. Uncle Toto appeared at my feet. He waved his arms and hoofed me but I could not get up. His lips moved but I heard only the rustling of the brown paper bag on the table.

Uncle Toto grabbed me under the armpits and lifted me to my feet. Then he guided me to the table, forcing my chest against the edge. I caught a glimpse of something dark in the bag before Uncle Toto's shadow covered the table like black cloth. I could feel his hot breath on my neck and his hands buried in my armpits, fingers wriggling. I pushed against the table, into his chest, and he released me, moving to my side. I glanced at the bag. It rocked back and forth a few times then rolled once.

"She's angry," whispered Uncle Toto.

"What is it?"

"I'll show you."

His hands reached inside the bag and removed from it what at first looked like a black cat. But then a floppy ear popped out and I saw it was a rabbit, its limbs bound in twine. Its upper lip looked torn, its choppers exposed and blood-streaked. Uncle Toto slapped the rabbit's haunches and it kicked some. He told me to touch it. I refused.

"Touch it," he whispered. "For good luck."

"I don't want to touch it."

"You'll die, then."

I tried to step back from the table but Uncle Toto's hand held my shoulder firm. The door flew open and a wave of sound—chattering, laughing, crying—flooded the room. Then the door shut with a bang. Uncle Toto laughed. He removed the scarf from his neck and formed a circle with it on the table. In this circle he placed the bound black rabbit. The rabbit twitched a little but had lost its will to fight.

"People have to eat," Uncle Toto said. "The tripe is almost finished. It's almost finished and what will the people eat when they come to pay their respects? They have to eat. Rabbit is the best thing. You like rabbit, I know you do, I've seen you eat it. You like the leg. Look at the leg. Do you like it now? Touch it. Touch the leg."

Uncle Toto grabbed my hand and pulled it to the rabbit, forcing my knuckles against the warm haunch fur. The rabbit stirred to my touch. I wanted to cry out but when I opened my mouth Uncle Toto's hand covered it.

"No screaming," he said. "If you scream I'll kill you."

His hand fell away from my face. He fished around in his pocket and produced a small curved knife. He held it up to the light, his shoulders shaking. He waved the knife under my nose. It reeked of garlic. Then he seized the rabbit's rear feet and lifted it above the table. The rabbit squirmed. I could hear it panting. Pink foam dripped from its jaws.

"Kill it," Uncle Toto said.

"I won't."

"You're afraid."

"I'm not afraid."

"You're afraid."

Without another word he jabbed the rabbit in the abdomen with the tip of the knife. The rabbit bucked like a fish. Blood trickled from its wound. Uncle Toto jabbed it again, this time in one of the legs. He turned to me with glittery black eyes, a smile twisting his lips. Then, while the rabbit was still alive, he started skinning it, cutting a slit along its spine. Just before he tore away the black fur he held the knife to me again. I took it and without hesitation pierced one of the rabbit's eyes. Blood spewed. The creature yelped once and fell silent. Uncle Toto grabbed the knife from me and plunged it into one of the black haunches, working with a sawing motion until the right rear leg came free. He held it out to me, blood dripping off his knuckles.

"There's a leg for you," he said.

"I don't want it."

He slapped me. "You think you're smart, eh? You're not smart. You did a good thing though. In the eye. Nice."

"Shut up."

He slapped me again, harder. I could taste blood. He slapped me a third time across the ear and I felt something pop and then I heard nothing from that ear but a roaring sound. Uncle Toto now flayed and quartered the rabbit carcass. He pushed aside the black fur, scooped up the watery blood with his hand and licked it off his palm. He ordered me to do the same but I refused. He went to slap me again but stopped in mid-motion as the door flew open. My grandmother stood there, dressed in black with a black veil covering her face, tiny, severe.

"Come here," she said.

I thought she was talking to me but when Uncle Toto stepped toward the door I relaxed. He walked with his shoulders hunched, shuffling his feet. He kept some distance from my grandmother, shaking his head as she addressed him. I could not hear what she said. When Uncle Toto started speaking, rubbing his hands together and bowing his head, she lunged at him, slapping his face so hard she knocked him backwards over a stool.

My grandmother now called for me. But I could not move. Uncle Toto stood up and brushed sawdust off his trousers. My grandmother called me again, and with great effort I shifted my legs and dragged my feet toward the door where she stood waiting with her hands on her hips, her face hidden. She cupped her hands and stirred them before her breasts. I stopped well out of reach, but she insisted I come closer.

"Are you afraid of me?"

"Yes."

"Don't be afraid of me. Did Uncle Toto hurt you?"

"He slapped me."

"Did he kill the rabbit?"

I looked at Uncle Toto who leaned over the table. He winked at me as he picked up the scarf from the table and draped it across his shoulders.

"I killed the rabbit," I said.

"Don't be afraid of him," she said. "He'll pay for what he did. He'll pay. Come with me."

My grandmother took my hand and led me to the bathroom. She told me to wash the blood off my face. I washed my face and toweled it dry.

"Are you afraid?"

"No, I'm not afraid," I said.

She took me back into the parlor. We passed the three old women sitting on the divan with their legs spread and their hands on their swollen bellies. My father still stood by the casket. This time he held

a wreath of red flowers at his chest. With his mouth wide open and
his eyes shut tight, he looked like he was singing but I heard no song,
only the rumble of the people, some weeping, many eating from
steaming plates.

"Are you hungry?" asked my grandmother.

"No," I said. "I'm not hungry,"

Two Cups

On the morning of his sixtieth birthday, Mike Crea got out of bed early and shaved off his moustache. Except for the time he shaved it to remove a growth on his upper lip, he had sported some sort of moustache since he was twenty. When he went down for breakfast, his wife Mufalda noticed nothing out of the ordinary. She wished him a happy birthday. He thanked her. Then, after a moment, she realized what he had done.

"Jesus, Mike. You shaved it."

He said nothing. Truth was, he felt self-conscious about it. His upper lip looked too long. It was one of those lips that suited a moustache, that invited one.

"You look ridiculous," she said.

"Oh, be quiet."

She bared her teeth and let out a laugh.

It wasn't right, her reaction. How could she laugh at him? He didn't laugh at her the day she plucked her eyebrows and pencilled them back in. He didn't say anything.

"You'd better grow it back," she said.

"Never."

Her laughter reverberated in the kitchen.

He went upstairs to the bathroom, but though he sat on the toilet for half an hour he couldn't perform. Mufalda had sunk him like a bloated porpoise, and his bowels weren't moving as they should have been after breakfast. He stood up from the toilet, did up his pants, and looked at himself in the mirror. He wasn't going to grow back the moustache, not under any circumstances. He didn't look bad; he looked younger, yes. But of course he had doubts.

He went to visit his mother Filippa that morning. She was eighty-three years old, crude and pungent. When she noticed the missing moustache she let fly the pepper.

"You were never good-looking. Not like your brother. He took after my side. You took after your miserable father."

Indeed, relatives in private joked about how much Mike looked like his *mother*. The two were virtually twins, said some. Like mother like son, said others. He himself didn't note the resemblance, and perhaps not much should be made of it, but Mike's upper lip had been inherited from his mother and not his father, as evidenced in every family photograph. Mufalda had long ago stopped caring that Mike looked like his mother, though it must be said the moustache had much to do with this. Free of the moustache, the lip cried out its provenance.

"Ma," Mike said. "Leave it alone. I don't need this today."

"What you need is a good slap in the face to wake you up."

"Ma—"

"You want coffee?"

"Okay."

"Make it yourself. You know where everything is. And grow that damn moustache back. You make me regret you. That's the problem these days. People are vain. Even men. Men more than women these days. You're vain. You were never vain, and now that you're an old sack of shit you're vain. You think that you look younger without the moustache. But without the moustache you don't look younger. You look like a jackass. My son, the jackass. Go make the coffee, jackass. Go now."

Mike walked away grumbling. He made coffee. He saw his reflection in the mirror over the kitchen sink and, turning his head this way and that, thought, I don't look so bad. I don't. I look good. Not bad at all for my age. My mother is senile. She doesn't know what she's talking about.

When he brought his mother a cup of coffee, she was laughing, her toothless mouth open and wet. Tears erupted from her small hard eyes and trickled down her leathery cheeks.

"Ma," he said. "Enough."

"Shut up."

"Enough."

"Shut up. Don't talk to me like that. Not to the woman who bore you without the assistance of a doctor. Dio, you had a head like a Sicilian eggplant. I don't know how I did it. And you talk back. Bend over here, let me slap your face, come on."

"Ma—"

"You're a jackass."

"I'm leaving."

"Leave then, go on." She smiled. "By the way, Happy Birthday. Happy Birthday, Mikey."

✝   ✝   ✝

After a week without the moustache, Mike got accustomed to the naked lip and ignored Mufalda's hectoring. Who did she think she was? He didn't bug her to let her leg hair grow, though he thought of it. He liked the hairy legs of a woman. He was sitting at the kitchen table one afternoon, eating a pear with a hunk of bread. Mufalda stared at him with her dark, dry eyes.

"What is it?" he asked. For a moment he thought she was about to riff on the moustache again. She'd been merciless. But by mocking him she just solidified his resolve. Nothing in the universe could make him grow it back, nothing.

"Joe Garzo passed away."

"Joe?" The news startled him. He felt as though someone had punched him in the stomach.

Mufalda trembled and began weeping.

"My God," said Mike. "I just talked to him the other day." Joe had been in hospital several weeks with a diseased liver. Mike had visited twice, the last time three days ago; he'd found Joe jaundiced and

bloated, but in good spirits, joking about the nurses and such. Mike
couldn't believe it. His jaws arrested. He couldn't believe that Joe was
dead.

Mufalda sobbed; she had been close to her cousin Joe, though he
was almost twenty years her senior. He had always been more like an
older brother to her than a cousin. How unexpected. How utterly
unexpected. Joe was one of the constants of Mike's circle, one of
those people you assume will always be there. They've always been
there. Mike shook his head. Joe was a fine man, a gentleman; he had
been most respectful to the Creas over the years. His loss would be
deeply felt.

"He'll be at Friscolanti's," Mufalda said, wiping her tears.

Mike stared off into space.

"Did you hear me?"

"Yes," Mike said, distracted.

"Go get your dark blue suit on. Visitors will be received after two
o'clock."

Mike nodded. Dead. Dead. Just like that. One moment among the
living, then death, then nothing. He took a final bite of pear and
gathered up his napkin and scraps.

✝   ✝   ✝

At Friscolanti's they were seated in the family section with a few
other relatives. Joe's wife, daughters, and sisters occupied chairs
adjacent to the casket, all of them in black. Vince, Joe's son, a small,
neat young man, stood behind his mother, weeping.

How awful to lose your father, thought Mike; especially when he
happened to be a good man. His own father had died at the age of fifty,
a hard death, enduring stomach cancer for a year before succumbing,
venting invective on his family. No wonder Mike's mother was the way
she was. The man had dummied her, shaped her into something like
himself. Mike was twenty then, engaged to Mufalda, but with no
prospects. He recalled the black shroud that seemed to flutter around
them. Nothing was right back then, and he hadn't been able to see

beyond that dark fabric. Such was life in Racalmuto, their hometown in Sicily. He believed that coming to Canada had saved his life.

Mike's son Che Che showed up after a while without his wife Rena. The two never appeared in public together. She was a cross, dumpy little woman with big haunches. When Che Che first brought her around Mike was taken aback. He thought his son could have done better. Che Che wasn't a brain surgeon but he was tall, hard-working. Probably like the old man in the bed, Mike thought. Anyway, he wouldn't suffer from jealousy. Mufalda had been a looker when she was young—Mike's jealousy had been tested on more than one occasion because of that. He wasn't considered in her league, and perhaps he wasn't, but he had been determined. And back then Mufalda had pitied him to some extent.

Che Che wore a pale blue suit that looked inappropriate, insubstantial. His wife must have chosen it. Further, he had grown a goatee that made his face look long and sombre. Che Che stood almost two metres tall. He was a mule of a worker and provided well for his wife and three children.

After he paid his respects to the Garzos, Che Che joined his parents.

"Sad, eh, cousin Joe?" Mike intoned.

"What can you do? Ma, how are you?" He leaned down and kissed her cheeks.

"I'm fine, son," she said, peering at him. "That hair on your face is not you. Shave it off. A moustache, okay. But that stuff. Your father shaved his off. You didn't notice?"

Che Che's eyes widened.

"Pa—"

"Shut up."

His son's mouth clacked shut, but his eyes widened further.

Mike felt like belting him. He wasn't too big to be belted, that big salami.

"Che Che, are you coming Sunday for *pranzo*?"

"No, Ma. I told you we were invited to Rena's mother's."

"When's the last time you came, ah?"

"Leave him alone," said Mike laughing to himself. "He has responsibilities."

"Who asked you, you harelip?"

They were interrupted by the appearance of Grace, Mike's daughter. She was with her husband Lillo, a three-hundred-pound obstacle to Mike's felicity. Grace had always been ample, but perhaps encouraged by her obese and gluttonous husband, she had let herself go. Mike grimaced whenever Lillo came around; he held his tongue to maintain peace, but in his view Lillo was a pathetic slob of a man. Pathologically lazy, he had been on Worker's Compensation three years running for a variety of questionable ailments.

"Mind yourself," Mufalda whispered.

"What?" he said. He glanced at his son, standing there with his mouth agape. "What are you gawking at?"

"Nothing, Pa." Che Che blinked. Then he put his hands in his pockets and pretended to admire the ceiling.

Mike endured an entire hour seated next to the fat slob Lillo. He reeked of sweat and garlic. He bored Mike to death yapping about his sciatic nerve, irritated due to a bulging in his spine, how excruciating the pain was, how the codeine pills he took constipated him and he hadn't shit in two weeks, *two weeks*. Mike bolted to his feet.

"What is it?" Mufalda asked.

"I have to go to the bathroom."

"Well then go, for crying out loud."

"Dad, you shaved your moustache!" Grace cried from the folds of her fat face.

Mike ignored her and his wife's dry cackling, and made his way to the bathroom. He ran into Domenic Carbone in the foyer. The insufferable old codger was bawling like a child.

"Poor Joe," he blubbered. "Poor, poor Joe . . . "

Poor you, thought Mike. His number was almost up, and he knew it. The man had already survived three heart attacks. It was only a matter of time. Yet he wasn't ready for death. How sad. Mike wondered if *he* was ready, if he would be ready. He wasn't afraid of it, like Domenic. But what could one think? If Mike were to die now would his life have seemed worthwhile? His children were doing well—except, of course, Grace, though her two children were beautiful. Che Che was spanking, three kids, nice house, and so on. Francesca had married a barber on the dwarfish side, but he was a solid little fellow, respectful, honest; they had a gorgeous daughter, and a son. Carmela had married an opera baritone and lived in Milan, at the moment pregnant with her first. What more could a man want? He and his wife were fine, as fine as two people could be after thirty-five years of marriage. Thinking about all this gave him a headache.

In the washroom he tried to pee, but had no desire or need. He washed his hands and wet his hair a bit. His roots showed. His upper lip looked fleshy. So what could you do? he thought. You get old, you get ugly. What could you do? At least he wasn't fat. Mike had worn size thirty-six pants for thirty years. Not bad considering how much he ate. Walking did the trick, kept him fit. For thirty years he walked to and from the Otis Elevator plant on Burlington Street where he toiled as a janitor. He never got his driver's license, never felt the need. He still walked, though not as much. Yes his pants were a little snug, but so what? If he had to buy a bigger size, so be it.

So many people, he thought, when he sat down again. Joe was popular, well-liked. Mike knew his own funeral wouldn't draw this kind of turnout, no sir. And he didn't care one way or another. He sat away from Lillo this time, under the pretense of exchanging a few pleasantries with Mimmo Sinicropi, Joe Garzo's brother-in-law. Mimmo didn't care much for Mike, and Mike knew it. But he liked to talk to him, just to get under his skin a little.

"Mimmo," he whispered.

"What?"

"That suit?"

"What about it?"

"Is it brown?"

"Brown?" Mimmo wore a look of annoyed puzzlement. Obviously his suit was black. He crossed his arms on his chest and raised his chin.

"Sorry," Mike said. "It looked dark brown. Like a chocolate. Nice."

"Mike, your voice carries." Mimmo nodded at the assembly of mourners.

"Of course, sorry."

He turned around and faced the casket again. Then he felt his thigh being pinched. He had to swallow a yelp. Mufalda. Was she crazy? Her face was a black-eyed mask of evil.

"What?" he said, bewildered.

"Quit making a fool of yourself."

"But what did I do?"

"Ssst," she said, crossing her lips with a finger.

Mike shook his head and felt his ears reddening. Sometimes he hated that woman, hated her sharp senses, hated her righteousness. He retched inwardly, containing his bile. That's what life was—at least for a man—containment. If you were not a rich man, you were measured by containment. A rich man could shave off his moustache and suffer no one to bother him about it, and perhaps silence anyone who did bother him about it.

Mike's eyes grew heavy and in short order he dozed off. He dreamed he was eating fruit with Joe Garzo and Domenic Carbone, both of them toothless, muttering things to him that he didn't understand. What? he kept asking. What?

He felt a pinch again, and this time he almost fell out of his chair. Jesus Christ!

"You disgust me," hissed Mufalda. "Come on, get up. Get your carcass up. It's time to go. Unless you want to sleep with Joe."

"Okay, already."

"Never mind okay. Never mind."

And on the way out of the funeral parlour, and on the whole way home Mufalda didn't let him forget his indiscretions. He didn't bother defending himself. If he was guilty, so be it, let her rail. He simply thought of other things, like the mule he used to have back in Sicily. The mule was stubborn; the mule was rude. But Mike liked the mule because it refused to be anything but itself. That mule spoke volumes with its eyes, with its brays. Thinking about little scenes like this made the nagging nothing.

At home Mike found a slab of leftover lasagna in the refrigerator. Glutinous and so cold it made his teeth ache, he still ate it with gusto. Mufalda entered the kitchen grimacing.

"You didn't even heat it up?"

"No."

"What do you mean, no?"

Mike didn't answer. Mufalda snorted and exited the kitchen. He finished eating and retreated to the bathroom where he applied dye to his hair, restoring the dark lustre he so fancied. One of the reasons he had shaved his moustache: it had become difficult to coordinate the hues. I'm a simple man, he thought. I'm not a complicated man. I don't need complications in my life, not now.

The next morning he went downstairs to the kitchen, loaded up the espresso pot, and put some milk on the stove to make cafe latte.

He stared out the window: it was a sunny day, the birds out in force, the trees greening. It was nice, a happy scene. But not more than a minute passed before his chin trembled and his eyes moistened and, despite his efforts to stop himself, he found himself weeping. Mufalda entered the kitchen and seeing the milk sputtering from the pot started shouting at Mike. He regained his composure and tuned her out.

✝   ✝   ✝

Mike took Francesca's son Norbert to the park one morning. He was a four-year-old with blubbery arms and legs and a rather sullen disposition. He lacked the spark of Mike's other grandchildren, dragging his thick legs around and kicking up sods.

"What are you doing?" Mike barked.

"Nonna . . ."

"Never mind Nonna. Behave."

The boy looked at him with large brown eyes positioned close. The cheeks dew-lapped over the jaws, the upper lip was elongated, almost unnatural.

Mike started.

He decided right then to grow back the moustache. He should never have shaved it off. What a can of worms its absence had opened. It wasn't fair.

Mike visited Grace that afternoon, hoping to avoid Lillo, who was supposed to be at the physical therapist. But after only an hour at Grace's, Mike's espresso half-finished, the big slug showed up limping and whining. Mike gnashed his teeth. It wasn't fair.

"My back, my leg."

"What happened?" Grace asked.

"At the therapy—"

"You injured yourself?"

"I did, I really did this time. I'm fucked, Gracie, I'm fucked."

"You want to go to the hospital?"

"They can't do anything for me!" he shouted.

"Honey, I was just saying."

"Well don't! Hey, Mike, what brings you here?"

"Just visiting my daughter and grandkids."

"More and less than what you bargained for, haha."

"The kids will be home soon, Daddy," Grace said.

"Good, that's good," Mike said.

Lillo hobbled to the refrigerator and opened it. He took out a stick of *sopressatta* salami and began gnawing.

The kids came at last and Mike spent time with them while Grace cooked a meal and Lillo took a nap on the chesterfield. That fat bastard, thought Mike. Could a man get luckier?

"Daddy's got a boo boo," said Pina, the littlest one. She had warm blue eyes like her mother.

Her sister Antoinette, the dark one, said, "Daddy always has a boo boo."

"Yeah," Mike said. "Daddy's a big boo boo."

The children chuckled.

Grace whipped up a fabulous *pasta a la carbonara*. She made a kilogram of pasta for them and yet at meal's end Mike was still hungry. Why? Simple. Lillo ate about half of it himself. Mike tried to load up on bread and apples afterwards, but it was no use.

"What do you mean, you're hungry?" Mufalda harped later, when she saw him rooting around in the refrigerator. "Grace called and said you guys demolished a kilo of pasta."

"Lillo," he said, barely able to tongue the name out. "Lillo, the pig that he is, was in form today, yes. He was in form. He could have been filmed. Genius."

"What are you talking about?"

"Genius."

Mufalda shook her head. "Eat, eat all you want. Don't let me get in your way."

"Don't you worry about it."

"I won't."

"No you won't."

His wife looked like the ugliest woman in the world at that moment. And no doubt he looked like the ugliest man in the world to her, judging from the expression of revulsion that made her so ugly. Mike lost his appetite and sat at the kitchen window for a time, gazing out, content in his way. So long as you didn't think too much you could float through it like a turtle in a tub.

"Mike? Are you okay?" Mufalda asked.

"What?"

"Are you okay?"

"I'm fine."

She huffed, turned around, and marched out of the kitchen.

I'm fine, thought Mike. We're all fine.

But what were these tears? Staring at the trees made him cry. Staring at the blue sky made him cry. The birds. That's all.

✝   ✝   ✝

Life is odd, Mike thought the next morning as he washed up. One day you cry. One day you laugh. You have kids. They have kids. You die. They mourn, then they die. But that's okay. If that's what it is, so be it. Why kick and scream? Why be afraid like Domenic when no matter what, you wind up like Joe? And why give yourself headaches by dwelling on things too deeply? It's easy to blubber and bow. But here we are. It's not as if we have many alternatives. He didn't want to think about it beyond that; maybe it was too painful. No, not painful: unnecessary.

He put coffee and milk on and stared out at the trees. He stared at the trees a long time. The milk boiled over.

Mufalda entered the kitchen. She didn't say anything. She cleaned up the mess and said nothing while Mike continued staring at the trees.

Mike went to visit his mother the following morning. She was in coruscating form. Today she targeted Mufalda with her vitupera- tions. Mufalda hadn't visited in weeks. What was the problem? Was she avoiding her for some reason? Nice thing, a daughter-in-law avoiding her mother-in-law. There's no more religion, people are pigs.

"Ma—she's been . . . her cousin Joe died. You know that."

"Joe? And I'm next. Joe didn't die alone. He didn't die like a dog. One day you'll come, son, and you'll smell the stench of rotting flesh and that stench will belong to my maggoty corpse. And then what will Mufalda say?"

"Ma, you're being ridiculous."

"Ridiculous? This morning I had blood in my stools. Black blood. You know what that means, don't you? Black blood?"

Mike bristled. "I'll take you to the doctor."

"Doctor? What will the doctor do? He'll put a glove on and stick it up my ass and then tell me I've got a few months to live. Nice job. You should have been a doctor, Mikey, heh."

His mother's eyes gleamed like onyx pebbles. Who was this woman? he wondered. I don't know her. Why am I trying so hard? I can't win. And then it seemed so amusing to him, the entrapment, the hopelessness, and he started laughing. He covered his mouth. His shoulders shook. You couldn't alter the variables by much in the final analysis. And it was funny, a grand joke, the grandest conceit.

"Why are you laughing?"

Mike regained his composure, wiping his eyes with a handkerchief.

"Idiot," said his mother. "I gave birth to an idiot. Go home, Mike. You're boring me."

"How about I make us a coffee first?"

"You think I need you to make me a coffee?"

"Fine," he said. "Fine. I'll go home."

He left his mother there, her mouth open and her eyes closed and her hands balled into small grey fists. He walked home with a nice chopping stride, swinging his arms. Before he reached his front door he felt a pain in his chest. He put his hand over his heart. Maybe he was being called up, maybe the ticker was ready to conk out. But maybe it was just stress: visiting his mother stressed him right out. He mounted the porch stairs, wishing she would just die already.

But no, once inside he hated himself for thinking of her death. She had suffered plenty in her life, and perhaps had every right to be the way she was. He hadn't been the most dutiful son. And if she were to die, wouldn't he miss her, even at her cruelest? Yes, he would miss her. Nothing could ever change the fact that she was his mother, that he had sprung from her loins. That's everything I am, he thought. Something that fell out of her, something she voided.

He sat by the kitchen window and stared at the trees.

He was lucky. He was lucky to have the house around him, and the trees outside, green against the blue of the sky.

Mufalda quietly entered the kitchen. She put on a pot of coffee.

Then she put her hand on Mike's shoulder. He turned to her. He was surprised at how soft and gentle she looked. She smiled. How rare for her to smile these days. His chin trembled. His eyes welled with tears. He didn't want to weep. He fought it; but then Mufalda's eyes moistened and she hugged him around the shoulders. Mike couldn't help himself. The tears fell. They held each other for a time. Then the coffee came up and Mufalda broke from Mike to pour it into the two cups she had positioned on the counter.

Pink

"This is crazy," the girl says. She sits at the kitchen table in a pink tank top smoking a cigarette. A white plastic bowl full of red pistachios rests in the middle of the table. I'm tempted to take one, but I resist, I'm feeling a little bloated. Behind the girl hangs a copper plate with horses hammered onto it, muscular, masculine figures. Sunlight knifes off the doubled haunches, the hooves. Several silver bracelets tinkle as the girl taps the cigarette over a glass ashtray the same blue as her large eyes. She tilts her head to the right. "I told you," she says, "Eddie won't be back for a while. Trust me on this."

A ginger cat enters the kitchen and freezes, glaring at me with yellowy eyes. What is it, cat? Ducking smoke, I look at the girl. Since I quit smoking it bothers my sinuses. But everyone smokes in my circles, everyone. It comes with the turf. We don't choose our calling. It chooses us. I studied philosophy in university. But it wasn't my calling. My black leather jacket makes menacing sounds as I stir in my chair and flex my biceps and chest muscles, but the girl seems unaffected by my posturing. What is her story, I wonder, and how did she come to be here for my arrival? No one alerted me to her existence. She looks young, though not undeveloped. The cat thumps its ginger head against my shin and with some force. I used to have a cat. Sheila. My mother didn't like Sheila. I shake my leg and the cat recoils. Sunlight pours in through a window facing a spacious backyard. It's very warm in the kitchen. Sweat trickles down my spine. I endure it.

"What's the matter?" asks the girl. "You're making faces."

I wave my hand.

"You are," she says, "you're making faces. Tell me why? Do you have a stomach-ache or something? Hey, are you going to freak out? You're not an epileptic, are you? My cousin Rudy is an epileptic and, when he goes off, first he makes faces and then he starts foaming at the mouth like a rabid dog. Ever seen a rabid dog? I saw one at my Uncle Harry's farm. Bingo. Bingo was a big black lab. Nice pooch. Got bit by a raccoon or something. Should have seen him. Uncle Harry had to shoot him in the head. That's not you, is it? You're not going to foam at the mouth, are you? Are you going to hurt me? Because if you're going to hurt me I'll start screaming, swear to God. I haven't screamed up till now but I will."

I tell the girl to relax. I'm not like that. I have no beef with her. This is between Eddie and me. Actually between Eddie and my con-tractors. Just business, in other words. I'm a little warm. "Mind if I have a glass of water?" I ask her.

"Help yourself," she says, drawing on her cigarette with volup-tuous zeal.

I quit smoking a year ago and watching her suck on that filter with her eyes half-shut and her lips pursed like two wet cherries makes me want to ask her for a drag. But I stay strong. I owe it to myself. Smoking would have killed me before my enemies did, the way it was going. Two packs a day. I never did other drugs, except for a little blow and maybe a popper or two when partying with friends, and I never drank much, a Scotch now and then or vino with the pasta, you know, that's it. But with the smokes I was a fiend. My uncles said I smoked like a Turk, whatever that meant. They tried to call me the Turk for a time but that name belonged to Tony the Turk Celestino, my second-cousin, God rest his soul, who passed a few years ago. I didn't want a nickname like the Turk so that was part of the way I reinforced myself to quit for good. I didn't want it. I didn't want to be called the Turk. I quit smoking and so far so good.

I rise from my chair, sidestepping the stupid cat licking its ass-hole by the chair leg. What the fuck is that? I want to say, because I've always wanted to say that to an animal licking its own ass, but I say nothing. I'm not one hundred per cent today. This morning my mother made me a three-egg frittata when I told her I only wanted two eggs. Two eggs, Ma. Two, Jesus Christ. My mother worries about me. You need a wife, she tells me, and a family of your own. You're not getting any younger. I don't have the heart to tell her what I really need. But I ate the entire frittata anyway and she had chopped up the onions too rough or something because this massive heartburn in my chest started up, and the repeating onions, and my own breath blowing back in my face—even a mint isn't helping right now.

I find a tall glass on the steel rack by the sink and run the tap for a minute before I fill it with water. I drink some, top up the glass, and return to the table. The girl asks me how old I am. I tell her it's none of her business.

"I'm going to be eighteen this Sunday," she says, twirling her studded tongue.

"Great," I say. "You can vote in the next election."

She looks at me blankly then pulls another cigarette out of her pack. She offers me one. I hesitate but accept it. Touching my hand she lights my cigarette with a pink disposable then lights her own. I take a puff and hold it in my lungs so long I start seeing spots and stars and almost pass out. The girl smiles as though she knows exactly what just happened. She knows. She's one of those people. I let my head clear before I try another puff. Then it's nice. Smoking in the kitchen with the soon-to-be eighteen-year-old girl, puffy lips and ice-blue eyes in pink.

"Why are you here again?" she asks.

I tell her it's just business.

"Whatever," she sniffs. "Just business. Like, what does that mean? Are you opening a sub shop or something? Be real for a second, eh." She has straight white teeth with a tilt to her smile and she knows how to lower her eyes when addressing a male.

I crush my cigarette in the ashtray and get up again despite my bad knees. I refill my glass and drink it down completely.

"I think you should leave," she says.

"I don't think so," I say.

"What if I call the cops?" she says.

"I don't think Eddie would appreciate that," I say. It goes back and forth like this for a while then the girl takes a big drag of her cigarette and falls silent. The cat fucks around in the corner with a crumpled piece of aluminum foil. The kitchen could use some air. I get up and try the window but the girl says Eddie never could open it. Then I notice the thick nails riveting the frame to the sill and return to my chair. I should remove my jacket but I am vain and with my paunch well-hidden behind my leather I am a lion; without it I am not. A svelte young man like Eddie gathers girls like a squirrel gathers chestnuts, I imagine. He's suave. I once met a fellow in Acapulco who looked just like him. When I first saw Eddie I . . . why make myself feel worse than I must? In leather I impose, I know I do. I come off as a big tough man, not a fat soft man. It doesn't matter perhaps. But it does.

"You're sweating," says the girl.

I brush drops off my forehead and force a smile.

"What was that?" she says, almost coming out of her chair. "Did you smile? Oh my God! The man smiles. For a second I thought you had no sense of humour. Like you weren't human or something. Like when Eddie was fucking me up the ass the other day he was so serious. You'd think *he* was being corn-holed! Would you like another cigarette?"

Her frankness appals and amuses me. Then it saddens me. Things being what they are. I refuse the cigarette. It's amazing how thirsty I am. But if I drink too much water then I'll have to pee. My bladder isn't what it used to be. It would be embarrassing to have to excuse myself, so I suffer.

"Are you in the Mafia?" she asks.

"Well," I say, swallowing. "That's an outdated term. I'm contracted by an agency, and I happen to be of Sicilian heritage, but I am not a *mafioso* in the traditional sense. I'm university educated and perhaps a little more refined than my predecessors."

"Hmm."

A long silence follows. I've been reprimanded more than once for venting to my superiors about some matter that concerned me, for speaking out when others thought it more prudent and life-affirming for me to swallow my tongue and sew my lips together and keep my feelings, my true nature, closeted. Well, perhaps that explains enough, or not enough, but enough for now. While I'm garrulous, I don't like to make things too clear. It softens the blow. The girl jangles her bracelets. She asks me what my favourite position is.

"I beg your pardon?" I say.

"Your favourite position, when you're fucking."

I clear my throat, feel myself blushing. She's rather enjoying this. "When did you say Eddie was due back?" I ask.

She shakes her head.

I look at her face. I notice the freckles now, on her cheeks, and her long neck. She stops smiling only when her teeth dry, then she wets them with her pink tongue and smiles again, gummy, her nostrils dilating. She's mocking me. You're mocking me, I want to say.

She shrugs. "I was going to dump Eddie today," she says.

"You were?"

"Yeah. That's why he went out. He knew it was coming. I told him we needed to talk and that I wanted to tell him the truth about where I was the other night. He refused to hear it, so like he raged for a while and then split and I figured he'd be a couple of hours tops before the jealousy got to him and then when he got back I planned to tell him to fuck off and die, that I hated him, and that it was revenge for him fucking my best friend Patricia a month ago. She confessed it to me when we got drunk the other night. She said he came on to her at a party and then offered her coke. Well, she did the coke of course, and coke makes her crazy, so then he took her to her mother's house and banged her right in the living room. Right on the sofa. Can you believe that? She said it hurt. Eddie has a big dick."

Mercifully, she falls silent again, her breasts heaving. Ignoring her digs and my thirst for a moment, I ogle the pistachio bowl. One would not hurt. But who am I kidding? One. Just try to eat only one pistachio. Perhaps annoyed with my lack of interest, the girl spreads her arms and asks if she has nice breasts. I tell her I think so.

"You *think* so," she says, crossing her arms under them.

Whatever. I look at the copper plate, the hammered horses, buttocks glinting, and wonder if Eddie purchased it or if a friend gave it to him as a housewarming gift or some such thing. How long has he lived in this house? A little shabby, but in a solid neighbourhood. She asks if I want to see them, to see her breasts. Eddie paid for them but he thinks they're too big. Are they too big? Are they? No, they're not, I lie, jerking my eyes away, the balloons in question galling under the circumstances. What is the fucking cat doing? I look for it, my cheeks burning. It has leapt to the top of the counter and watches me thin-eyed, motionless, even the tail, coiled behind it like a felt rope. What? Is it going to jump at me or something? That would be embarrassing.

"How much money does he owe you?" asks the girl.

"It's not a question of money, sweetheart," I say.

She smiles. "You just called me sweetheart. That's so nice."

I should say something more but my mouth, too dry to open, remains shut. Not that I had anything to add—sweetheart was a manner of speaking. How awkward. When I finally think of something to continue the conversation, to be amiable despite everything, the moment is gone. The timing would have been wrong had I asked her, for instance, what she planned to do for her birthday. Her birthday. Poor girl.

"Do you like pink?" she asks, staring at her fingernails. I like pink. I like it a lot. In my aesthetics class—"

"You studied aesthetics?"

"Yes, at beauty school."

"Oh, oh, *beauty school.*"

"I learned that pink is a colour made by mixing red and white. There are many different shades of this colour. You've heard of hot pink, eh?"

The cat reappears at my feet. It's purring. You'll live, I think, because words fail you.

"So you went to university," the girl says.

"Yes. I studied philosophy."

She blinks.

"I wanted to be a professor."

"What happened?"

"Well, things, things."

She locks her fingers together and bangs them lightly on the table. What does the gesture signify? Her fingers, quite pale and long. Her pale wrists, blue-veined, fragile. Her fingernails painted pink . . .

What's this? She doesn't have a clue. Look at her, I think. She must have been strawberry shortcake before Eddie got his greasy paws on her.

"Are you going to kill Eddie?" she asks.

I reassure her that I don't plan to kill him, exactly.

"Is there anything I can do?" she wonders, licking her lips, trying in her way, trying.

But it would have made no difference. I'll save her the indignity.

"Pink was not a colour known to Shakespeare," I say. "It was invented in the seventeenth century to describe the light red flowers of pinks, flowering plants in the genus *Dianthus*, named pinks because the edges of their petals appear to be cut by pinking shears."

"You're definitely not in the Mafia," she says. "Who do you work for again?"

"That's not important," I say, reaching for the pistachio bowl.

In snooker the pink ball counts for six points. They call blue movies pink in Japan. Pink cherry blossoms abound in anime. The Giro d'Italia leader wears a pink jersey, not a yellow one. Feminists used to decry the colour pink. In Roman Catholicism pink symbolizes joy and happiness. Years ago my mother went to Rome and brought me back a pink Versace shirt that was a size too small. I wore it anyway. My uncles laughed at me. They associated pink with homosexuals.

Alicia

She regretted eating the second helping of shepherd's pie but it was her favourite and she rarely got home for dinner anymore. She spent most of her time after school and on weekends with her boyfriend, Joe. Her mom disapproved of Joe because he was twenty years old and Alicia was only fifteen, but she could do nothing about it. The age of consent was fourteen. Alicia knew her rights. As long as she didn't get kicked out of school and didn't catch anything or get pregnant, her mother had no say in the matter.

Alicia looked at herself in the full-length mirror in the hall and thought the red and white striped sweater she had borrowed—without asking her sister Mattie—made her look fat. Her belly bulged even when she sucked it in and stood up as straight as she could. But it didn't bug her that much, being fat. She had a pretty face and big breasts and this helped. Guys at school said she was hot. Joe said he liked his girlfriends with some meat on their bones.

She couldn't wait to see him. She planned to be nice no matter what. They'd been arguing a lot lately. She tugged at the sweater but this didn't help. Mattie would kill her if she saw her doing that; she spent a lot of money on her clothes. Alicia wondered if she had left for work yet. She stripped at a club in Niagara Falls. Their mother didn't care. Mattie was eighteen, old enough to make her own decisions. Not to mention the fact she pulled in over a grand a week. It was crazy money. Alicia thought she might want to strip some day. She was a good dancer and it wasn't as if you had to sleep with all those bozos.

Mattie said they'd never hire a butterball like her, but maybe she'd thin out by the time she turned eighteen.

In the bathroom she argued with her younger sister Jen about the broken blow-dryer. Jen insisted the thing just blew up in her hand; Alicia suspected she had tampered with it. Jen had a reputation for fucking with things. She got away with a lot of shit because she was only twelve and the baby of the family. She took medication for a mood disorder but that didn't help her much. Jen raged whenever it suited her. She grabbed a fistful of Alicia's hair and yanked her out of the bathroom.

As they scuffled at the top the stairs their mom didn't intervene; she knew better than to get between the sisters when they locked horns. Alicia freed herself and almost knocked her sister down the stairs, catching her at the last moment and then regretting it when Jen took a final whack at her and fled to her bedroom, the little bitch. Alicia returned to the bathroom and combed out her tangled blonde hair. Scratch-marks striped her neck. She covered them with foundation. She tugged the comb through her hair. The blonde came from a box, but it suited her ice-blue eyes and fair complexion. She looked ordinary with brown hair. She applied makeup to her face, blue eye shadow, and a dark red lipstick that Joe said turned him on.

In her bedroom she called Joe but got his answering machine. It was the end of the month; welfare cheques were cashed. He was probably still out hooking people up with smoke or coke or whatever else they needed. He made a lot of money dealing drugs but Alicia worried about him getting busted. She said she'd wait for him if he ever went inside, but in her heart of hearts she wasn't so sure about that. Joe wasn't always nice to her. Back in August, on her fifteenth birthday, he didn't buy her a present; he said it slipped his mind and promised he'd make it up to her. He never did make it up to her, though she never reminded him, fearing his reaction. He could be pretty touchy.

Downstairs her mother and Mattie sat on the chesterfield, smoking a joint, Mattie in her red coat having one for the road. Their mother, a pothead, said she'd rather see her girls smoking dope than doing harder drugs or drinking. Their alcoholic father nearly killed her, so booze was as bad as crack in her eyes. Alicia didn't like drugs, not even pot. It made her sleepy. She liked drinking. Joe liked drinking too, but he smoked pot from morning to night and liked doing lines now and then. He let her do coke with him once but it made her nostrils burn and her throat hurt and when he rubbed some on his penis and told her to suck it, she almost puked because with her throat numbed she took too much of him down. He had a big penis, with a purple head. It smelled sometimes. Whenever she sucked him off she thought she was going to puke. She didn't like the taste of his cum, it was bitter. She had sucked off a few boys before and almost always refused to swallow. She didn't see the point of it. One time she swallowed her ex-boyfriend Tony's cum and it tasted lemony. Mattie yelled something at her about the sweater. Their toothless mother laughed; without her dentures her mouth looked like a black hole with smoke spewing out of it. Alicia peeled off the sweater and whipped it at Mattie. Then, wearing just her black bra, she put on her bomber jacket. Her mother laughed so hard she started coughing, hurling phlegm. Mattie kept yelling at her even as she went out the front door.

Alicia walked to King Street, busy for a Tuesday evening. People had money to blow. Drunks thronged the taverns. Crackheads and potheads and junkies searched the streets and alleyways for dealers. Everyone was getting high or making money. It was cold out, the skies clear and flecked with stars; Alicia's teeth chattered and her torso shook uncontrollably. She wanted to hop a bus out to Joe's place. She didn't have a key, and he'd probably get pissed off if she got there before him, but she didn't care. When he saw what she had on underneath the jacket he wouldn't care either. Joe always said she was the best pussy he'd ever had. Not that she was very experienced. He told her what to do and she tried her best. She even let him do anal, and though he used this lube from Europe it still hurt. But she never mentioned this to him. She wanted to make him happy. One time her doctor asked about the blood in her panties but she played it off. She changed doctors after that.

As Alicia waited for the bus at the stop near the fire-station, three teens approached her, a girl and two guys. At first she didn't recognize them. The guys had hoods pulled over their heads, their movements jerky. Then she recognized one. His name was Justin Royal and he had done time at the youth detention centre for beating and robbing an eighty-year-old woman. Put her in the hospital for a month with a fractured skull and a broken leg. Justin wore the hood in a way that concealed his acne-scarred and cratered cheeks. He couldn't hide the nose though, and the ripe boil bulging the end of it almost clownishly. She recognized the other guy now too. Danny Orr, a crack dealer and an asshole. He had tried to come on to Alicia one time at a party and when she told him to go fuck himself he slapped her across the face. She was drunk or she would have killed the bastard. She never told Joe about it or he would have done it for sure.

The skanky redhead with them didn't look familiar. Then she said, Hey, it's me, in this raspy voice and right away Alicia knew it was Jessica Ferris, a girl from the group home. When Alicia was ten, her father beat up her mother and threatened to kill the lot of them. After the cops arrested him, Family and Child Services moved in and put the sisters into foster care until their mother recovered from her injuries and got her life back together. Her father went to Kingston Pen for aggravated assault and was still there, as far as she knew. Anyway, her sisters landed in good foster homes but she proved harder to place, rebelling at every instant and treating her foster families with contempt. They finally stuck her in this shit-hole group home near the old steel mill, run by a bunch of perverts, and she hated every minute of it. She never liked Jessica; she was sneaky and dirty and used to give the boys blowjobs in the washroom for quarters. Man, she looked rotten, her face red with pimples and little scabs, her eyes bloodshot and puffy, her lips blue. Only two years older than Alicia, she must have been sucking the pipe pretty hard to get her face like that. No telling what else these punks were doing with her. A pocketful of crack gives some people a sense of power. Danny felt pretty cool, standing there smiling with his faux-platinum gate and his neck weighted down with shiny chains. He crossed his arms on his chest and checked out Alicia from head to toe. Then he sucked his teeth and nodded, as if in approval. Jessica said something. The words came out slurred, delayed. She was high as a kite, her eyes half-closed, her head lolling. Justin stuffed his hands in the pockets of his camouflage pants. He seemed bashful, evasive. Alicia didn't know him that well; she wondered what had driven him to beat the shit out of an eighty-year-old woman. Was it just the money?

Danny sparked up a joint and passed it around. When it came to Alicia she refused but Jessica insisted. For old time's sake, she cooed. Alicia took a few light tokes that tasted like sulphur. She wondered if they'd laced the weed with something. She passed the joint to Justin. He took it with blunted fingers, nodding and mumbling under his breath. His eyes looked odd; one sat lower on his face than the other, and as he smoked the joint the higher eye closed while the lower one stared off into space.

Alicia stood up on her toes hoping to see the bus, but it was running late. Jessica asked her if she wanted to party with them. Alicia told her she was on her way to her boyfriend's place. What's his name? Jessica asked. Joe, Alicia answered, Joe Moffat. The Priest, Danny said under his breath. Alicia knew people called Joe the Priest but she didn't know why. She wanted to ask Danny why but his sneer discouraged her. He puffed on the joint and held it out to her but she refused. He spat on the sidewalk and hauled on the joint again before handing it to Justin whose face popped out from the hood like a snapping turtle's. Alicia looked for the bus *again*.

Jessica started talking, rapidly, but more to herself than to anybody. She was fucked. Alicia almost told her to shut up, but not with those two snakes standing there. She didn't trust them. Then Danny said something. Alicia told him to repeat it. I hear the Priest's into kiddy porn, Danny said. Despite the cold air Alicia's cheeks heated up. But the weed buzz creeping up her spine and gripping the back of her head dulled her anger and suddenly she felt anxious, short of breath. Danny stood there grabbing his crotch and leering. Jessica continued talking, her face contorting, her voice like sandpaper. She asked Alicia if she had any smokes. Alicia stumbled for words and drew a toothy grin from Justin, rocking back and forth on his heels. Look, Danny said, she's all fucked up. Yeah, Justin said, all fucked up. Relieved to the point of peeing herself, Alicia saw the blue-lit bus approaching and readied her fare. Danny swung his head around and also saw it coming. He jumped to the curb and waved his arm for the bus to pass. It whooshed by without slowing down and continued to the next stop. Danny and Justin screeched with laughter. Another bus wasn't due for an hour.

Enough of this shit, Alicia thought. She'd just walk to the variety store at the corner, withdraw money from the ATM there and cab it to Joe's. She started down the street, moving quickly, but Jessica caught up to her, the boys in tow. Leave me alone, Alicia told her. Don't be mad, Jessica said. I didn't do nothing. I love you. We're sisters. Where you going now? To the store? Buy me some smokes. Alicia continued walking. But Jessica kept on her heels, stumbling as they neared the corner. Danny and Justin hung back, still laughing.

Alicia entered the store and took out her bank card. Jessica came in behind her but stopped to look at the magazines. Alicia just wanted to take out some cash, hail a cab, and get to Joe's. She withdrew her money and exited the store, leaving Jessica at the magazines. The two boys waited outside with their hands in their pockets.

When Alicia hurried by them Danny said, I'd like to come in your face, baby. This stopped Alicia cold. She turned around, walked up to Danny, still laughing, and slapped him across the face. She slapped him so hard her hand stung when she dropped it to her side. Danny did nothing at first. His chin quivered and his lips twitched and tears welled in his eyes. But he didn't cry. He cocked his fist and punched her in the mouth with a crack. She dropped to her knees, her eyes glazed. Then Justin appeared before her, smiling, bowing, and reached out his hand— not to assist her, but to balance himself as he flung his leg and kicked her in the face, pitching her backwards. Hot salty blood gushed from her sinuses, filling her mouth. Someone grabbed her legs and then she felt her arms and her hair being pulled. They dragged her into an alley and threw her against a dumpster. They stretched her out on her back, spread-eagled, and she could see the sky above her, cold and star-filled.

Justin jumped up and down above her, his boots landing on her head, but she didn't lose consciousness. She kept her gaze focused on the sky and the stars. Her jacket came off—Look, the fucking ho is only wearing a bra!—and then her bra fell away, baring her breasts to the cold air. A hot mouth descended on one of the nipples and for a moment it almost felt good, not sexual, but comforting, human. Then teeth clamped down on the nipple and the stars grew brighter in the sky and Alicia felt herself lifting off the ground, away from her body, away, until she seemed to float above a doll of herself, plastic and silent, eyes shining in the smashed face. Justin's trousers came down. Danny let him go first.

Sirens sent the trio scrambling out of the alley. Jessica's turned her ankle, but daring not to stop, she limped behind the others. The sirens passed. Alicia stirred. Blood poured from her mouth. She tongued chips of broken teeth behind her torn lower lip. She had no idea how badly hurt she was. She looked at her bloody breast, and then saw the bra twisted up beside her. She pulled up her pants, found her bomber jacket by the dumpster and, blood flowing in ribbons from her mouth and nose, put it on. She touched her skull, where she thought it might be fractured. She didn't feel any pain, just a tingling sensation. A light came on in a window above her and then went out again.

She hailed a cab on King Street and when the driver got a good look at her face he wanted to rush her to the hospital, but she gave him Joe's address and quietly pleaded with him to take her there. Feeling pity for the beaten girl, the driver relented and said he would drive her. He even offered her a handkerchief. Afraid of what she'd see, she avoided looking in the rearview mirror as she cleaned herself. She wondered what Joe would say, what he would do when he saw her, what he'd do to them. She'd tell him the truth; she couldn't keep this from him. He wouldn't allow it. And he wouldn't let them get away with it. Joe would take care of it, he'd fix it somehow. The driver dropped her off, refusing to take her money. Watch yourself, little girl, he said. She climbed out of the cab and staggered to the front door of Joe's apartment building.

She rang up. After a moment Joe's voice came over the speaker and asked who it was. It's me, Alicia said, and he buzzed her in. She took the elevator up to the fourth floor. Smells of pan grease and marijuana smoke permeated the dimly lit hallway. Indistinct sounds of crying, a woman or a child, issued from one of the units. When Alicia knocked on Joe's door a shadow crossed the peephole. A latch clicked. The peephole remained covered. She stared at it. What was he doing?

Joe? she said, pressing the blood-soaked handkerchief to her mouth. Her front teeth were loose, her tongue scratched. Her crotch burned and ached. Joe, she said, please. She could feel him standing there behind the door. Her legs trembled. She tried the doorknob but it was locked. She spat a clot of blood into the handkerchief and rested her forehead against the door. Joe, she said again, but more to herself this time as she felt him retreating.

Miss Alligator

Wendy Kovach wasn't shocked to hear that her nephew Connor had beaten up and robbed an old man. Mugging a senior was right up his alley. He snatched an old lady's purse at the mall last summer, dislocating her shoulder. She was the aunt of a police sergeant, so the cops took care of the matter themselves. After they were done with Connor, he couldn't talk for a month, what with the jaw wired shut and his throat bruised—but they never pressed charges.

This time they issued a warrant for his arrest. Two cops came by that morning asking questions. When Wendy told them Connor hadn't been around for days they traded little cop smirks and said they'd return. Wendy wondered what they had in mind this time. She knew he needed to be taught a lesson, but prayed they didn't go too far. He was blood after all. But mugging seniors never won you any friends. Maybe a beating wasn't the worst thing for him.

When Niagara Family and Child Services came snooping around a week ago, Wendy told them she could not control Connor's behaviour. She urged them to make him a ward of the state, but they refused.

Away for a two-month stretch of court-ordered rehab, Connor's mother Kim had it easy by comparison. Connor no longer concerned her. And he no longer concerned his father, Ronnie, Wendy's brother. Ronnie had begged her to take custody of Connor, just until he got flush. She agreed but knew what awaited her. Connor, a sixteen-year-old thug, followed his own rules. He only came around when he was hungry or needed a place to crash or money for smokes. Wendy gave him just enough coin for smokes but never more. She knew what he'd do with any extra.

"Stop it, Donna," she shrieked at the loudest of the seven-year-old triplets.

"It's not me, Mommy!"

"Stop it or I'll tear your fucking head off!"

The other two, Doris and Deb, hiding smiles, waited for Mom to finish scolding the sister. Little differentiated the three: blonde hair, blue eyes, and identical pixie attitudes. When they gathered in a room people stared; and people stopped and gawked in malls and on the street, especially when Wendy dressed them up the same. Sometimes she found herself gazing at them with wonder, and not just because she was their mom; she saw nothing of herself in those faces. They looked exactly like their father, the prick.

Donna burst into tears and in seconds the others joined her. A wave of stomach cramps bent Wendy over. Usually they passed in a few seconds.

The girls stopped crying. "Mommy's sick," they said together.

Kind of creeped Wendy out when they did that. Never pulled that shit as toddlers. Sometimes she overreacted. She took the wooden spoon out one morning, as she readied them for school. They'd been acting up, confusing her, making her feel bad. She snapped right out. Hurt Donna bad, in the face, told her to say she fell down the stairs if anyone at school asked about it.

Bracing the filthy toilet, Wendy puked her guts out, the last of it coming up green. She had eaten almost nothing that week. Her bones ached. That morning after the cops came by she went down to the methadone clinic with the girls in tow—thank God school started up in two weeks—but barely got a buzz from the juice. Now her stomach was fucked up.

She washed her face and put on lipstick. The bathroom smelled like cat shit. The girls kept the kitty litter behind the door, knocking it around when they entered, but they refused to move it anywhere else. They were stubborn, like their father. Maybe that trait would help them more than it had helped him.

She pushed aside a green plastic alligator on the edge of the sink, and it clattered into the bathtub. She started brushing out her tangled, bleach-scorched hair but gave up after several painful tugs. So, she looked like hell. What else was new? Not that she needed to get dressed up for anyone—her ex-husband was doing time in Kingston Penitentiary. She had almost lost the girls because of that fucker, bringing contraband home, not to mention all the blow. But Chris never owned up to any of his crimes; not even to punching out Wendy in front of the girls on their third birthday. He blamed the booze for that, or was it the cocaine?

She opened her tea-stained bathrobe, glanced at her arms, then retied the belt. She still had a soft spot for Chris, no matter how she tried to hate the man. She'd even gone up to Kingston for visits. He had abused her, fucked around, taken away her youth—but he had fathered those triplets and they were nothing short of life to Wendy. And Chris was cool; no one could short him on that. Not a big talker. He did most of his talking with cool baby blues and narrow hips. Any time he and Wendy showed up to a function or a bar the ladies eyed her with envy. People said he looked like Patrick Swayze, but Wendy thought Chris had it all over Swayze. Yeah, Chris was very cool. He'd stand in a room wearing blue jeans and a T-shirt, sucking on a beer, blonde hair all crazy, and he looked cool, exuded cool, and he knew it. She wondered how cool he felt sitting in his prison cell.

She opened the medicine cabinet and removed a plastic vial full of Percodans. They helped dull the aches and pains. Connor had scored this batch for less than a fin a pop. He was good for that, the kid. Technically, this breached her court orders, but if no one knew, no one could rat her out. She downed four pills with a gulp of tap water. The doctor had ordered her to eat better and to exercise. She chuckled at the last suggestion. Exercise.

In the kitchen Doris had Deb by the hair. The third sister watched with an impish smile.

"Let go of her fucking hair!" Wendy yelled, but half-heartedly, she didn't want them crying again.

Doris let go, but not before Deb's chin started quivering. Wendy grabbed three lollipops from a canister on the counter and handed a red one to Deb. The other girls, offered yellow lollipops, demanded red ones. Some remained in the canister but Wendy refused to budge this time. The girls had to learn to take what they were given. Life offered few handouts. She ordered them out of the kitchen. "March!" she cried, but the Percodans had come on, smoothing the fray in her nerves and filling her chest with a numbing, radiating warmth that took her breath away.

She stretched out on the chesterfield and watched a muted television show with pregnant women shouting at skinny, goateed men who looked sheepish, broke, and stupid. Why do women fall for scum like that? Wendy wondered just before she dozed off. She dreamed she rode a horse across the countryside, a tiny pinto, with ink-blot markings. It kept looking back at her with sad brown eyes as they clopped over the green terrain. Then the terrain gave way, the pinto dissolved. One of the girls had mounted her. Doris. She jumped up and down on Wendy's thighs. Wendy grabbed her hand and squeezed until she stopped.

"That hurt, Mommy."

"Did not, now get off me."

"Mommy, I'm hungry."

"We're hungry, too!" chimed the others, floating around the chesterfield.

For a moment Wendy couldn't tell them apart. That happened once in a while. They aped each other on purpose to confuse her. She rarely dressed them the same for that reason.

She found hot dogs in the refrigerator, a carton of milk, and not much else. She needed groceries but hated leaving the house. People stared at her and the girls like they were from Mars. When triplets had shown up on Wendy's ultrasound, she demanded to know their sex. She would have terminated the pregnancy had they all been boys. She liked males fine, but three boys would have killed her. As it was, three girls were doing a pretty good job.

As she put a pot of water on the stove, she thought of her dream. She had ridden horses before, but didn't enjoy it. She thought horses were stupid, too highly-strung. Once, while riding an old mare in Virgil, they came upon a tiny creek, and the horse freaked out and threw her. She landed on a big rock and wrecked her back. Later the trainer admitted that running water spooked the beast. What a fucked up thing. She had never dreamed of horses before. She wondered what it meant.

While the hot dogs boiled away, the girls sat at the kitchen table rubbing crayons over colouring books and nibbling cheese-sticks with expired due dates. Seeing no mold, Wendy figured the cheese-sticks were fine. Just then the doorbell rang. The girls jumped up and raced to the door, almost trampling Tatters, one of two Siamese cats sharing the flat with the humans. Max, hiding somewhere, only ventured out at night. Tatters raised her head and wailed. The cats were bizarre, but they had cost Chris a grand, and had grown on Wendy.

When she opened the door a big man stood there with a clipboard and a poised silver pen. Sunglasses hid his eyes. At first she mistook him for a traveling salesman or a canvasser—he looked too buffed to be a Jehovah's Witness. Swarthy, with big arms and broad shoulders, he cut quite a figure. His white shirt seemed just-pressed despite the humid weather, his black silk tie clipped with a red-jeweled silver bar. The man smiled and nodded.

"Hello," he said. "My name is Felix Torres, I'm with the Ministry of Child and Youth Services." He glanced at the sheet on the clipboard. "Is this Connor Kovach's residence?"

Wendy nodded. "Yeah, but he hasn't been around."

"Connor's probation officer referred him to me for cognitive programming. Anger management, anti-criminogenic thinking, and so on. I'm here for an intake."

These words came at Wendy in a whirring, incomprehensible stream. She didn't know what to say. The guy's smile started creeping her out, the teeth too white or something.

Felix glanced at the clipboard again. "Legal guardian listed as a Wendy Smith."

"That's me,"she said, involuntarily touching her hair. "I'm the aunt. His father's sister."

"Okay," he said, winking at the triplets huddled around Wendy.
"Girls," she said sharply.

They squealed and retreated.

Felix continued smiling. "I understand Connor has no contact
with his father."

"No, and his mum's in rehab at Collingwood 'til October. Connor
never calls or anything. They aren't close like that." Ashamed to
admit this, Wendy looked down at her small, bare feet—a further
embarrassment—chewed up like meat from years of bad shoes, .

Felix frowned and ticked off a box on the sheet with his shiny
pen. "This program falls under the umbrella of extra-judicial
measures—initiated recently as a consequence of the revised Youth
Criminal Justice Act."

Again, the man's words whirred by in a stream of guttural gasps
and clicks that made no sense. But she noticed that Felix wore no
wedding band, and warmly smiled at him, so handsome in his way, so
strong and sure, and he returned the smile.

✝   ✝   ✝

Ronnie came by in the morning, screaming about being killed, that
they were going to kill him. He stared right through Wendy as he
screamed, waking up the girls, who scrambled from the bedroom to
the bathroom in their pink pajamas. Twitching and drooling, Ronnie
looked deranged, likely fucked up on crack cocaine. Crack fries the
central nervous system, triggering frenzies and hallucinations.
Wendy knew all about that. She'd had her time with crack.

"Just keep your voice down," she whispered. She hated Ronnie
barging in whenever he felt like it, the fucking tool. She hated all
these weak and stupid men. Her father was the same. An asshole
through and through. If not for Mom, the family would have ended up
on the street. As it was, working all kinds of nasty jobs, never saying
no to anything, no matter how degrading, she eked out enough for
bare necessities, while Dad drank beer and porked their slutty neighbours whenever he could get it up.

Tears welled in Ronnie's ruined eyes. "Listen—listen to me. If they come here—no, don't say anything. Say you haven't seen me."

Wendy glanced down the hall and saw Doris's head pop out of the bathroom. Not Doris—Deb the little bitch, playing games again, grimacing like Doris did when something scared her. Deb didn't scare so easy. Wendy laughed, almost proud of how clever they were. But she'd call Deb on it later and see what the little lady had to say for herself.

"Tell them you haven't seen me," Ronnie said. "I don't want you involved."

She felt like kicking him in the nuts for saying that. "What's going on, Ronnie?"

Elbows together, he cringed. "They'll fucking kill me!" He rocked on his heels, wheezed, his asthma acting up. Luckily, he had a puffer and took a few hits. But while this relieved the chest congestion it did nothing for his state of mind.

Wendy seized his arm. "Get it together for a sec, man. Who the fuck is going to kill you? Ronnie, look at me. *Look* at me."

He turned up his face with wide, terrified eyes, tilting his head as if appealing to her humanity. Tears streamed down his cheeks. He mumbled something, then abruptly bolted for the door. She heard it open and slam shut. A car engine turned over. Tires squealed. Then she heard nothing but the girls bawling in the bathroom, and the cats bawling in the hall.

✝   ✝   ✝

After that night, Ronnie disappeared. He left Wendy with no money to care for Connor, no forwarding address, nothing. A week passed and he didn't call. He didn't even send a postcard like that time he split to Vancouver for a month. Wendy still remembered that card, a shot of mountains, oceans, and whales. Was it really like that there? She doubted Ronnie was checking out whales this time.

Ronnie was hard to love, maybe harder to like. When he first pre-sented Kim to her, Wendy almost shit herself. Kim was a looker,

Ronnie no Romeo. It all made more sense when she learned of Kim's love of cocaine.

Connor called one afternoon.

"Auntie Wen," he said. "Is my old man around?"

"Nah. This guy came here looking for you. This Felix dude. Says you have to call him right away. He left a card. Sounded like he meant business."

"Whatever. Tell him to smoke my bone next time you talk to him. Fucking fag."

"He's just doing his job, Connor." Wendy wanted to hang up. "Your old man stopped by a few days ago and I haven't seen or heard from him since."

"He was supposed to leave some money."

"He left nothing."

"That motherfucker." Connor hung up.

That just about summed up everything. Late for her methadone fix, Wendy had a hint of the bugs. The bugs used to plague her when she was using hard. Got so bad she started carving up her arms. She butchered her left arm, cutting right into the bone. The doctors warned they'd have to amputate it from the shoulder if she continued cutting. But the arm healed on its own. Wendy considered it divine intervention. She went to rehab after that, cleaned herself up as much as she could.

When the girls first saw the scars they cried and cried and hugged her. Wendy told them they were old wounds, healed over now. They didn't need to worry. Took some convincing, but they came around. After that, whenever she exposed the arms, they'd gently mock her. *Look at Miss Alligator!* Doris would cry and the other two would join in a taunt.

Miss Alligator! Miss Alligator! Mom-my is Miss Alligator!

The plastic alligator in the bathroom entered the scene only after Doris first made the comparison. It didn't bother Wendy, though sometimes it did. As for Connor—fuck him if he was jammed up. She had her own problems. In the bathroom she popped four Percodans. Fuck everyone, she thought.

She promised to take the girls shopping for new school clothes. Cash-strapped and maxed out on her only credit card, she worried about keeping that promise; if she bought the girls nothing, they'd be bummed out. She dressed them up in matching white outfits with pink lace trim, white socks, and white shoes. She tied pink bows in their hair—Doris complained that it hurt—and looked at them. Pretty as dolls. Sometimes after a fix she had trouble keeping up. But they knew the routine, and behaved on Wendy's "medicine" appointments.

Not far from her flat, near Silver City, the clinic skirted a cluster of squalid tenements and skeletal factories. The overcast sky pressed on Wendy's temples. Then the Percodans came on and she flowed across an intersection with the girls trailing her like cotton candy faeries. A man in a silver Buick with a grey beard and bullet-grey eyes rolled down his window and yelled an obscenity. Happened all the time. Maybe the way she dressed or looked provoked it, or maybe something deeper tagged her. They never ever let her forget who she was. Never.

"Mommy, what did that man say?" Donna asked.

Wendy said nothing and led the girls to the clinic. Junkies crowded the entrance. Many knew the girls by name and traded greetings perfunctorily. The nurse in the bulletproof dispensing booth, a pleasant, ruddy lady called Cheryl, always shot out of her seat when she saw the girls, and handed them granola bars. The girls despised granola bars but took them graciously, and saved them in a shoe box for—as they put it—another rainy day.

That they had lived through many rainy days, and expected more, broke Wendy's heart. So unfair. But what was fair? She neared the glass shaking in her shoes. The nurse gave her the juice in a small plastic cup. Wendy drank it down while a security guard joked with the triplets. Old and kindly, a hint of the molester shaded his profile. You couldn't trust anyone these days. Simple as that.

On their way out, Wendy noticed a wall calendar with a picture of a pinto—the bloody source of the dream horse. What a disappointment. Outside she lit a cigarette. She smoked less than ever these days. Her uncle Norm had just died of lung cancer. He looked freakish after a

lung removal, wheezing like a torn accordion. Probably better to die
of an overdose than go out like that. But after a fix she loved a smoke.
You smoked it slow and felt every fibre of tobacco and paper crackling
and burning and sending its dark whisper through your body. The
girls watched, rapt. She had caught them once with cigarettes in the
bathroom; they had dropped the matches in the toilet bowl and never
lit up. She beat them for an hour after that, bursting Donna's
eardrum. Boy, did she howl. She howled so loud at the hospital they
never got around to asking her how she hurt the ear; Wendy told them
she fell from a swing. The other girls confirmed this.

They walked to the mall, a thirty-minute hike from the clinic. It
felt like hours to Wendy, but she savored every moment—beside herself to see the girls so well behaved and pretty, what angels—and didn't
want it to end. The girls sang and skipped along. They were off to get
clothes, something to make any girl happy.

The foul and humid air washed over Wendy like warm water; and
the hard, rough facades of Silver City yielded to a smudged blue-grey
tranquility, an exquisite ballooning that even swooping seagulls could
not burst.

✟   ✟   ✟

She outfitted the girls on the cheap, by stealing, risky given modern
security measures. But Ronnie had given her pointers. He excelled at
ripping off shops. The trick was finding one with a faulty security system—flawed, or in disrepair. Of course, stores never alerted the public
to breakdowns—please don't rob us while our security system is
kaput!—but they happened.

So Wendy sniffed around the mall and tested several systems until
she hit the jackpot at a tony children's boutique. The silly young
salesgirl, flattered by Wendy's compliments about her fucked up blue
hair, noticed nothing untoward, and Wendy managed to lift three
outfits, in three pretty colours, right from under her pierced nose.
She also purchased a few inexpensive accessories to further dodge
suspicion; and the girls, hiding smirks, played along.

When they emerged from the boutique, they looked like cats after a canary feast and hurried down the street, unable to contain themselves. Even Wendy got caught up in the excitement, losing some of her buzz, but still feeling good. That it took an episode of shoplifting to make their hearts beat faster and their blood race saddened her, but for now she put that aside.

They found Connor at the flat—petting a reluctant Max—with some other boys dressed in black clothes. They looked far too serious for teens. They occupied the living room like pirates, dark and sardonic, their smiles masking malice. Wendy smelled it on them and felt her stomach muscles tighten. She recognized the boy on the chesterfield with the red bandanna tied around his head, Ryan Clair.

"What are you boys up to?" she asked.

"Just chilling," Connor said with an unfamiliar drawl.

She stared at him and he reddened, dropping the cat with a thud. Auntie Wen was embarrassing him.

"How long do you plan to just *chill*?" she asked. "I've got things to do around here."

"Nice little girls you got there, miss," said a boy in a wicker chair by the window.

"You're too heavy for that chair," she said. "Go sit somewhere else." When he didn't move she said it louder. "Go sit somewhere else, or get the fuck out of my house."

"Auntie Wen," Connor said. "The chair is fine."

Wendy stared at her nephew.

"I mean, it ain't breaking or anything."

"Get out of my house," she said in a quiet but firm tone. The girls got up on their tiptoes and cupped their mouths. They recognized that tone, understood its seriousness.

Connor fumed, rubbed his hands together. His posse, five strong, adjusted themselves. The boy in the wicker chair found a stool by a small bookshelf with an empty fish bowl on top of it. Tatters the cat had dined on Barney the escaped goldfish a few evenings back. The girls mourned the passing with feeling. It bothered Wendy to see that moron near the fish bowl.

A stocky fellow with a shaved head and tattoos on his neck stepped over to Connor and said something in his ear. The others exchanged glances.

Wendy sent the girls to their bedroom. When they hesitated she said, "Go to your bedroom now or I'll put you to sleep forever."

This drew smirks and sniffs of laughter from the boys.

"Hey, Auntie Wen," Ryan said, handling a rag doll robed in red gingham. "That sounds like abuse to me, see what I'm saying? I mean threatening the children and all, not nice."

"Mind your own business," Wendy snapped.

Ryan flung the rag doll against the wall. He grinned at her through clenched teeth. She could sense his willingness to smash her face, put the boots to her. Chris used to work himself up like that when he couldn't get his own way. Like Chris, Ryan was all about beating up a woman. You could tell with some males. You could see it in their eyes, that bottomless gaze looking right through things. And it wasn't Ryan's friendship with Connor that held him back. Something else explained that.

"Connor," Wendy said. "Do your girlfriends mind if we talk in private for a sec?"

"Bitch has some mouth on her bro," said the short stocky guy.

"Connor, I'm talking to you," she said, her voice cracking.

He rolled his eyes. Then his expression darkened and he stood up. "Auntie Wen," he said. He glanced at his crew and fought a grin as he continued, keeping his chin tucked down and averting her gaze. "My dad said he gave you a bunch of money before you took custody of me, in case of emergency. I know he did because he said it."

"What are you talking about, Connor? Your father's a deadbeat. He never gave me a dime, not even for emergencies, if that's what you're wondering. Nothing. Not one penny."

"She's lying," Ryan said, "I can tell. My dad taught me how to tell when someone's lying. Their eyes—it's all in the eyes, bro. I can tell the bitch is lying by the way she keeps looking down the hall."

Wendy almost burst out laughing. She kept looking to see if the girls had come out. She fought the urge to slap her nephew's face—

they'd kill her. The living room reeked of their pomade, cologne and sweat. And they still might, she thought.

"Auntie Wen," Connor said. "Listen. If you don't tell me where the money is, someone's gonna get hurt. See what I'm saying?"

"Yeah, Auntie Wen," Ryan chimed. "You're in *danger.*"

Wendy noticed one of the boys standing at the living room entrance, arms folded across his chest, just daring her to make a move. The buzz from the methadone and Percodans had all but worn off; her head ached and nausea fingered her tonsils. She also felt the bugs coming on, wriggling over her arms, neck, and shoulders. The boys gaped as her head and arms shook.

"What the fuck!" cried one.

"Bitch is psycho," remarked another.

Connor had seen his aunt suffer the bugs before and felt a pang of sympathy as she writhed and contorted. Horrible to watch. He turned his face. The others found it hilarious, laughing and hacking. Connor did nothing to silence them. He must have known that his aunt had no money, but he did nothing to help her.

The fellows stirred, scraping boots across the hardwood floor, flexing muscles. Ryan removed something from a pocket of his combat pants. A knife with a serrated blade. Wendy held her breath as he flashed it and affected a manic Joker's grin. As he twirled the knife, the stocky guy stepped on Max's tail and the cat somersaulted across the room, thudding down on a Persian rug by the closet.

"What a fucking athlete," someone said. "Let's see it again."

"Yeah, encore," chirped someone else.

Ryan neared Wendy and held the knife so close to her throat she could feel the cold of the steel. "What do you say, junky mama? How about I hook you up right here, right now. I've got some killer China smack just off the boat, and I mean killer. Not recommended for amateurs. But you and Mr. Brownstone go back a long way. My old man used to sell to you. Jacky Clair, remember? That's right. Jacky Clair, my papa, the King of Horse they used to call him in the old days. The King of Horse—you know, like the King of Beer. Like the King of Beer, only heroin—*horse.* That's what they used to call it in the old days. These bozos don't know what I'm talking about. But you do, don't you Miss Junky? Yes, you do. Jacky's doing a dime in Kingston now because of cunts like you." Ryan stopped talking and withdrew the knife.

Wendy heard the girls scream in the bedroom. Panic filled her chest like a cold white liquid and for a moment she couldn't breathe. She stepped backwards as Ryan came again, waving the knife, the blade glinting. She raised her hands and waited.

"Stop it!" Connor cried, jumping up and rushing Ryan. But before he got very far the small stocky guy decked him with a sucker punch. Two others joined in and started giving Connor the boots.

Ryan grinned at Wendy, swivelling his head to watch the beating. "Looks like your boy there forgot who his friends are."

"You're nothing but a scumbag," she said quietly.

"Maybe I am," Ryan said.

When the blade slid across her cheek Wendy felt nothing unusual, just a cold edge glancing the skin. Then she touched her cheek and looked at her fingers: wet with blood. The other boys stopped beating Connor. He lay on the floor moaning. A moment passed where no one moved, no one breathed. Then the doorbell rang, and it resounded through the flat with the clear, pure tone of a gong. All eyes looked to the door.

Ryan pocketed his knife. The others shuffled around, unsure of themselves.

"The fire exit's blocked!" someone cried from the back. Then someone blurted that a cop was at the door, and the panic set in.

"I'll fucking smoke him," Ryan said.

"Yeah," said the small stocky guy, "with that penknife you're going to smoke a cop. Get serious. We're fucked."

"Hold it!" someone cried. "I don't think it's a cop. Never seen him before."

The doorbell rang again.

"Answer the fucking door," the small guy said. "Tell Connor to answer the door. When the guy comes in we'll jump him."

"Connor's fucked up, bro," Ryan said, twitching.

"Then I'll answer it, tell him I'm a cousin or something. Keep the bitch quiet."

Ryan and another of the boys dragged Wendy to the bathroom. She went without a fight.

They threw her against the tub and left her there, bloodied and stunned. She wondered if Ronnie had come. Or cops. She who hated cops prayed it was cops this time.

Something crashed against the door and she cringed, drawing up and hugging her knees. The glare of the bright ceiling lights pierced her eyes and she recoiled, blinking, wiping away tears and blood. The commotion continued and she wondered about the girls, but they seemed far away, safe and sound somewhere else—not here, they could not be here. She draped herself over the bathtub and saw the green alligator jammed in the drain.

She heard hitting sounds and sounds of people falling. She shut her eyes and prayed it would stop. But she knew that when it stopped worse would follow. She had seen things escalate before, in her father's house growing up, in her own house, mayhem fueled by booze and drugs but often something in itself—violence as its own thing. She rocked back and forth as the fighting continued, eyes shut, fists clenched. Then she made her mind black, black as a pool of ink, blacker, and leaning closer, closer, let herself fall.

✝   ✝   ✝

And then quiet. It took a moment to focus. She tried to stand but her legs felt flimsy. Blood streaked the floor and the side of the tub, and dried blood crusted her face like a mud mask. She waited and listened, hoping to hear something, anything.

Then she heard the doorknob jiggle, and the door opened. Felix, the counsellor, stood there with a grim expression, white shirt bloodied and torn, one of his hands wrapped in a dishtowel bright with blood. He shut the door.

"Wendy," he said.

She couldn't believe it was him, this big man, bigger than life, filling up the bathroom like an apparition. He didn't seem real. And then he smiled that smile and her entire being felt relief. She wanted to get up and hug the man, kiss him on the lips. His dark eyes studied her with empathy and tenderness. She wanted to ask about the girls but her mouth wouldn't open; yet she knew they were safe—now that Felix had arrived they were all safe.

"You're hurt," he said.

Wendy pointed to her cheek.

Felix touched the wound. She winced.

"Not too bad," he said. "You'll live." His smile returned, bright and white and perfect. "The ambulance is here. They're attending to the others first." He stopped smiling and grasped Wendy's wrist. "Hey, if you're wondering about the girls—they're okay. They're in good hands now."

Wendy tried to ask where they were but her words came out garbled. Felix looked at her strangely and shook his head. Then his smile returned.

"Maybe you want to know what happened out there," he said, lifting the toweled hand. "I'll give you the short version. When the punk who opened the door refused to look me in the eye, I knew something was up. I used to work in detention. I'm a martial arts expert."

Felix paused. People shuffled around the flat, moving things. A vacuum cleaner screeched on. Wendy wondered what was happening. She tried to get up but couldn't.

"Anyway," he said. "After I took care of him, I dealt with the others. Then the biggest, oldest looking one—pulled a knife. Imagine. So I disarmed him, and turned the tables, so to speak." Felix roared with laughter, nodding and wiping his eyes.

Again Wendy tried to get up but Felix barred her with his arm.

"You don't want to hear the rest of my story?" he asked.

Wendy shook her head. She noticed how hard he was breathing, his chest heaving in and out. Sweat streamed from his temples, bending round his nostrils and blood-smudged lips. She could smell his body, its heat. She tried again to get up but his arm pressed down.

"Uh-uh," he said. "You're good right there. Trust me. Don't move."

Wendy remained still.

Felix smiled. He wiped the sweat off his brow with annoyance and shook his hand. "You have beautiful daughters, Wendy—mind if I call you Wendy? I hate formalities. As I was saying, the girls are beautiful, and three of them identical to the eye, my goodness, what a gift, what a gift from God. I envy and admire you, Wendy. I do. I think it's great how you've maintained a household for them despite all your barriers. You are my hero. Yes, well. I have news about your daughters, and I hope you don't take it the wrong way."

Wendy sat up straight and pushed against Felix's thick arm. It didn't budge. Felix pressed himself closer, smiling.

"Your social worker said she'd find good placements."

Wendy's mouth fell open.

Felix stopped smiling. "What I mean is that I don't think you're fit to care for them in your condition, do you?"

Wendy shook her head. She felt his hot breath in her eyes, his hand pushing between her legs. She tried one final time to get up but Felix pushed her shoulders down, and she sat back and shut her eyes, feeling nothing above or below her, nothing at all.

The Dream
of Giraffe

Francois Giraffe pressed his hands against his flanks to keep them
from shaking. He clenched his jaws to keep his teeth from chattering.
He said he was calm, but he wasn't calm.

They spooned him cherry syrup before bedtime and it helped him
sleep for a while. He dreamed he was crossing the blue-green water of
the Niagara River, hanging over with his legs hooked to a wire. A
breeches-buoy operated by an ape in white overalls winched across the
river to save him. A ticker-tape parade ensued. A huge billboard illuminated by a golden sun portrayed his triumphant visage. Then he awoke
to the sound of scraping. A man in a yellow tunic stood at the window
with a metal scraper, scooping out filth from the sill. His shoulders
rocked as he worked. The back of his head looked like the face of a beast.
Francois wanted to ask him what he was doing but before he could, the
man put the scraper in his pocket and sauntered out of the room, the
back of his head barking. Francois returned to sleep.

✝   ✝   ✝

Someone brought him yellow flowers and they looked lovely against
the bone white wall. Who brought them? A little man with big hands
and big feet. Someone else brought a book with a black cover, written

by a man with a black beard and beady eyes. Francois tried to read it that morning, in the early light, but the words bored him and his eyelids closed. Then he dreamed he was dancing with a long-necked woman wearing a gown with black flowers and yellow stripes. The top of his head nestled under her chin. She asked him where he had learned to dance so well and he said Morocco. When she reached down and bit his ear, he awoke to the sound of a train rushing through his room. He pounded the bed and screamed but the train drowned him out. Then a green gas hissed from the vents and filled the room. He could barely see the walls. What rotten luck to miss another sunrise. He took his pills, blue and white. He took them under the presumption that they helped.

He pulled out a blue velvet sack from the bed stand and removed from it an orange. He peeled the orange and separated its segments. Oranges held sunlight in their core. Sunlight powered the world, fueled its slow green lifeblood. Otherwise all would be mud and rock, inanimate and sterile. Francois liked to watch the sunrise on occasion. He put an orange segment in his mouth and sucked the juice from it without chewing. Then he spit the mush into his hand. The orange tasted warm and too sweet for his liking, so he stopped eating it and chucked it into the trash.

His feet sweated under the blanket. He rolled it off his legs. His feet looked like aubergines, his toenails like chips of charcoal. Good thing the doctor planned to visit him that afternoon. If he failed to come Francois would hold him accountable. Last time he came late, he blamed traffic, the tourists, and so forth. Why did Francois have to suffer because of a traffic jam or because of some bloody tourists? What did he care about tourists? He had seen a hundred million of them in his life, more, more.

"Don't argue with me!" someone yelled in the hallway.

"Get baked, you fucking retard."

"Say one more thing!"

Sounds of scuffling and slapping erupted and Francois sat up in his bed and listened. They had worked better before, his ears, in the past, when it mattered. Now he heard the sound of rushing water all the time. Was that okay? He had lived in the Falls too long. The cataract and its incessant din had nearly deafened him, among other things. He had once dreamed of going over in a barrel. The idea of it made him smile. Going over in a barrel! Maybe he still would. That would draw the crowds. Maybe they'd erect a billboard with his smiling face on it. The light looked rough this time of day—what time of day was it? Other people passing talked in street tones, cursing and dragging their feet like zombies. Francois had no tolerance for retrogrades and drug addicts. Were it up to him, he would command a score of marksmen to load their rifles and open fire on anyone who vaguely fit the description. But Francois knew that this would never happen.

✝   ✝   ✝

A woman in a pale green tunic wearing her hair very short handled his wrist and looked at her watch. This wasn't the first time she had done this. Indeed she often came. Sometimes another woman came, wearing pink, her hair not short. Her teeth reminded Francois of the gorge. The one in green never showed him her teeth. She never said a word, breathing calmly through her small black nostrils.

No one said a word, sleeping through the endless days with open eyes. Violins whined and oboes moaned and nothing made Francois sicker to his stomach than tepid music. Why not drums? Give everyone a heartbeat. Thump a little. Trash the joint. Francois smiled as he imagined all the noise.

"Let's go see the scow!"

"Fuck the scow, it ain't nothing."

"It won't hardly stay there."

"Fuck the scow."

Francois recalled the day he went down to see the steel sand scow near the Falls, and its rusted condition depressed him. He could hear the voices: "We're going over, we're lost!" People rushing to and fro. Never a dull moment in the Falls. Daredevils flocked to these parts, testing nature's fury, seeking acclaim and infamy, sometimes dying but dying well, as it were. He had read of people fishing bodies out of the Whirlpool to harvest the organs. Other bizarre schemes for making money. Often, it was all about the money.

✞　✞　✞

He spent the rest of the morning in the resident lounge reading the black book, making neither head nor tails of it, and coughing up black phlegm. Then everyone came to play in the euchre tournament.

They huddled round the table cracking their knuckles and grimacing. The dealer wore a red velvet tux for the occasion, but his sleeves kept catching on the felt of the card table and he misdealt at least ten times. Finally they gave him the boot and brought in a liver-lipped woman wearing a yellow turtleneck with black designs. Hands squeezed. These people knew their euchre, even though they lived inside their heads now. They filled up on grape juice and counted their cards, then recounted them, then again. They slapped trumps on the table top with skill and fury. Someone steeped English breakfast tea and served it with stale biscuits. All good.

"He's cheating!"

"No, I'm not."

"Take him out."

Someone took Francois by the arm and led him out into the hall and to his room. After yesterday's fall his face looked like road kill. He felt no different, though.

✞　✞　✞

He sat in his room and counted the cows he could see on the nearby farm. Twenty-four. No, twenty-five. A little black one gamboled away from the herd. Had a wolf appeared, great harm may have come to that calf. But later, the cows huddled under a tree, shading themselves from the sun, yet so crowded their rising vapors propelled a white-tailed hawk into the heavens.

Where was Francois then? For a time he sat there by the window thinking of nothing at all. Then he thought of how much time had passed when he had not been thinking but quickly lost his thoughts entirely. He stalked around his room in a paper hat he made that afternoon in crafts class. Once a week a lady from Niagara College came and gave them little projects. Francois talked a lot to her, but she never more than nodded. Her aloofness bothered him, but then that is the way with artists. They while away the time, crucify themselves to their work with nothing but fire in their souls and steel in their hearts.

A splash of cognac would have served him well in the dense afternoons when his eyes refused to open and his limbs felt like molten lead, spreading over his bed and pooling in its folds and wrinkles. But where could he get cognac now? It was an impossibility.

"Shut the fuck up!"

"I'll shank you, motherfucker!"

"Go ahead and try!"

Someone screamed.

Then a herd of antelope clattered down the hall, cleared out the obstructions, and it went quiet again. This happened now and then. These little bursts of violent sounds. Francois shut his eyes and listened. He heard something creeping through the vent. Was it his friend, Maurice? Maurice, a wee man, came to visit him on occasion. He was different. Never stayed long.

"Francois!" cried a squeaky voice from the vent.

"Maurice! You are here again! I am delighted."

"You're delighted? No, I am! I am!"

"How are you doing?"

"Simply superb! And I must say you look very fit! Well, must be leaving, the little lass and so forth."

"Won't you stay for tea?"

But he was gone. Francois had never actually seen Maurice, but he knew he could trust him with his life if need be. You can tell with some folks. Civilization itself depends upon the efficacy of these human bonds. A blue jay flapped by his nose, just missing. It vanished into the mirror over the sink. The brain is but a tool, Francois reflected. Manifold in function true, but a tool nonetheless. People go to school for years to sharpen their tool. The same holds true for people who better their minds living life directly. Never rule that out as a viable alternative to years in dusty libraries and lecture halls listening to professors bark like seals.

People lose their marbles all the time and don't know it. But sometimes sadness gets mistaken for madness. Francois understood his heart had blown a tire. It was a long story that he could no longer remember. His life was going reasonably well until . . . See, he could not remember. But the truth was that happiness had eluded him and this made him blue, not deranged. Still, they ignored his turgid letters of complaint and they tolerated his phlegm—and forgave him for the fire in the belfry.

All this. All this.

True or not, he killed a bird the other day while gardening. Knocked it from the sky with a hoe, a bird with golden wings and blood-red eyes. One of the other fellows started whistling like the dolphins at Marineland when he saw the bird. Then he started hitting himself in the face. *Whap, whap, whap.* This fellow often hit himself in the face, he was always looking for a reason. Francois wept when he realized what he had done to the bird, but his tears made no difference to the world. Nothing altered for their falling. And everything must die; no one gets away from the chap with the scythe. Scream all you want.

After a moment, a man in yellow pajamas arrived with a portable blue blowtorch. He fired it up and put on a pair of goggles. He aimed the rushing flame at the yellow flowers on the windowsill, carbonizing them in an instant. Francois wanted to ask the man what business he had torching his flowers, but he didn't want to make a fuss. The man killed the blowtorch, removed his goggles, and, without acknowledging Francois, departed. This gesture, or lack of one, offended him to the quick.

☦   ☦   ☦

Two giant pandas escorted Francois to the yard for recreation. They were new to the facility, or at least he did not recognize them. He liked to walk in circles until he fainted. The pandas watched him while he wheeled around the yard, pumping his arms. I feel alive, he thought, for the first time in . . . again, like a vapor, his thoughts were gone. But he didn't have to think to keep walking, left right, very nice. He felt alive. This was fun! Then he ran into a tree stump and his fun came to an end. The purple skin of his feet burst, releasing a yellow goo that reeked like cheese.

They wrapped his feet with iodine-soaked bandages and suppressed his screams. He watched the sky outside, indigo through the tinted glass, the mist from the cataract whirling like a cyclone. Be cool, they said. Be cool. He tried to hide but where? Every corner held a camera. A camera over his bed had been filming him from the beginning. He could hear it swivelling as someone with a remote made adjustments.

✝   ✝   ✝

We believe what we want to believe, that's what Francois believed. The concrete of reality had nothing to do with it. If you drove your head hard enough into the wall, it would come out the other side or be crushed. In the lavatory a man with a very long neck was shaving his creamed face. He scraped a razor along his bristles and shook it over the sink. Scrape, scrape. Blood flowed from his nostrils in two red stripes that carved into the foam covering his upper lip. Francois frowned and entered a stall. He squatted but maintained separation between his cheeks and the toilet seat. When he finished, he noted the long green banana jutting out of the bowl.

The shaving man now toweled his head. He stood there waiting for something to happen or something to end. Francois wanted to tell him to fuck off but reconsidered. He padded back to his room. On his bed he spread the down-filled comforter, smoothing out the corners. As night fell, Francois felt bizarre. He glanced out the window and noted the moon, almost full but not quite. He could see the face of it, cheerful, serene, and smiled.

At dawn dark blotches whirled around the room. Francois blinked his eyes hard but the phenomenon continued. It frightened him. He huddled under the comforter. He heard water rushing, and voices, *We're lost! We're lost!* Then a siren started wailing. Was there a fire? Francois sniffed for smoke. A man down the hall had set fire to his hair. He ran out of his room screaming, turning and turning in circles.

The House

They were sitting at a kitchen table doing cocaine. It was evening. Eric struck a match and lit a candle even though Jack said no fucking way, not yet. But a flame beautified the moment; later, Jack would agree. Eric watched the flame as Jack cut the cocaine with a razor blade. He had scored an ounce of it that afternoon, for a box of jewellery they found under the bed in the master bedroom. Neither the jewellery nor the house belonged to anyone they knew. The owners were vacationing in Florida.

Eric fancied the vintage silver pocket watch in the box for himself, but Jack balked at the idea, reckoning they'd get a couple of ounces for the stuff, but not without the watch. Eric said nothing when Jack returned with only one ounce of cocaine, but it bothered him. It would have made no difference had he kept the watch. Jack would have scored an ounce with or without it. But after Eric snorted a few lines, his bitterness abated. What would he have done with a watch like that anyway? he thought.

The house felt cold to him. The people who lived in it were cold, he imagined: the gruff, moody father; the mother, stiff as a board; the bland children, underachieving and overfed. The candle-flame flickered. They would never understand. It would hit them down there, in sunny Florida. They'd be on beach blankets, reeking of coconut oil, bronzing their doughy skin, sipping fruity drinks, and the news would hit them like a tidal wave. Who would do that to us, to our house? Who wishes our family harm? But no one wishes them harm, Eric thought.

Jack was bent at the table snorting a thick line of coke with a rolled up twenty-dollar bill. Half the line went in one nostril, half in the other. Wiping tears from his eyes, he rose from the table, his low-crotch jeans sliding under his hipbones. He peeled off his T-shirt, exposing a hairless, sallow torso and an abdomen bearing the scars of DMT-induced self-immolation. He claimed he had come face to face with the fabled little people of DMT hallucinations, and they were not friendly. A tattooed skeleton in top hat grimaced from his left pectoral—a cartoon, the needlework slipshod. Jack moved his mouth and Eric heard his voice, but it seemed to come from elsewhere, from another part of the room.

Eric lit a match and stared at it, but Jack continued talking, scrolling his tongue between his teeth. Eric heard only the hissing of sibilants, and intermittent sighing. He let the match burn down to his fingertips, savoured the sulphurous smoke, then looked at the sunburst clock above the sink. Time was passing. The candle lessened by the moment, though the flame burned as lovely as ever. It spoke to him, languid, feminine. He understood the language of the flame. Jack walked over to the china cabinet against the wall and slammed it with his forearm, shattering its glass panes and delicate contents. Plates and glasses chimed and crackled, glinting shards sprayed across the floor. Jack stepped back, bent his knees and planted his feet. He sprang out of the stance and rammed his left shoulder into the side of the china cabinet, knocking it over with a dreadful crash. He sustained a shoulder gash that bled profusely. He smeared his tattoo with the blood then licked the palm of his hand. His mouth moved: more words. Eric snorted a line of coke into his right nostril. It went in roughly. His eye started blinking and his sinus cavity burned. He could taste the cut and it so numbed the right side of his face, his eye sagged and his cheek slackened. He slapped his cheek but felt nothing, as though a dentist had shot it with Novocain.

Jack, meanwhile, opened the refrigerator and removed a bottle of ginger ale. He uncapped it, drank some down, and scowled. Then, gripping the bottleneck, he whacked it against the refrigerator with little effect, the bottle still intact. This enraged him; he whipped open the refrigerator door and kicked it off its hinges. Then he switched on the burners of the stainless steel gas stove and waved his hand over the leaping blue flames. This gesture made Eric euphoric. The warmth, the light, the destruction, all equal parts of the pleasure. He banged a spoon on the tabletop. *Bravo! Bravo!* But if Jack only knew. If Jack only knew how beautiful the fire could be, how beautiful it *could* be. And what was this? Eric's eyes widened. Gritting his teeth, Jack held his hand over one of the burners until it started smoking. Eric's nostrils flared as the smell of burnt flesh filled the kitchen, and he hoped for more, more, but Jack awoke to the pain and the stench and began whirling around like a dervish.

Eric studied his reflection in the spoon: convex, concave, monstrous. Monstrous, perhaps, to occupy the house, given his intentions. But for now it was a place to rest, a place to reflect. And something could change by Saturday morning, no one knew for certain, conscience could get the better of him for instance, though it didn't look good. Jack recommenced his task, dashing a porcelain figurine against the cupboards. Then he opened the cupboards and started on the plates, the mugs, the cups and saucers. Irked by the noise, Eric retreated to the stodgy living room. The ornamental fireplace—faux-brick finished and copper-screened—offended him. No fire there. If these people deserved everything they had, then they deserved everything coming to them. But it was confusing too. These people. Who were they? He didn't care. And yet he thought about them. He flopped on the green chenille chesterfield, lit a match and stared at the orange flame while Jack took apart the kitchen.

A friend had told Jack about the house, said the owners went south for a month. A lady came on Saturdays to check things out but otherwise the house sat empty. On Tuesday, Jack pleaded with Eric to break into it with him. Eric refused at first but when Jack promised him total freedom, he gave in. Total freedom. Eric knew what that meant. He could barely contain his excitement. And just when things had gotten stale. It was a chance for a real stroke, a statement. This is who I am, it would say. Accepting who you are is half the battle; proclaiming yourself is victory. So on Tuesday evening they rode bicycles to the house. It sat in an isolated enclave by the canal, the property landscaped for privacy and comfort. These people had coin. Jack's Uncle Tommy, a professional thief, had taught him how to disable conventional alarm systems. It took just a snip of a wire. Then they jimmied a side door and entered.

It was weird at first, being in there, walking around, admiring, detesting. Eric had entered strange houses before, to rob them, or to set them on fire, but that meant hurried exits with little time for reflection. This was different. He had time to get close to his subject, to gather it up from inside. While he walked around the house, mentally noting his observations, Jack attacked the liquor cabinet, downing whisky and rum, and soon passed out on the living room rug in a gurgling stupor. Eric puffed a joint and chilled on the chesterfield, resting his feet on a glass coffee table. The moment was good. He found a candle and lit it. He gazed at the flame. Lovely. He switched on the television and watched a nature show, some cheetahs chasing down a gazelle. Cheetahs couldn't help themselves. They did what they did very well. As long as you did what you did very well, nothing could touch you. That wasn't necessarily true, but he wanted to believe it.

In the master bedroom Eric found some photographs on a chest of drawers. People. Old, young. A nice-looking blonde framed in gold. Something glittered in her hair, a tiara; festively dressed people posed in the background. Eric picked out a candle-lit cake, ribbons, and balloons: oh, a birthday party. He glanced at the other photographs. Family memories. Eric thought about his own memories, how he tried to forget them but couldn't. He blew some dust off the photograph and returned it to the chest. These weren't people he'd ever want to know. They looked dry, annoying. A real family. He had never belonged to a real family. His fourteen-year-old mother, pregnant by rape, gave birth to him in a basement. The rapist later died in prison from shiv wounds. Eric never met the man, knew nothing about him except what he'd read in a newspaper clipping, and that wasn't flattering. His mother gave him up for adoption right after he was born, committing suicide a year later.

Eric spent most of his youth being moved from foster home to foster home, absorbing his share of mental and physical abuse along the way, and learning how things really were in the world. If you weren't fucking somebody up then somebody was probably fucking you up. He lived with the Macleans now, Mary and Bill, both of them like milk, except Mary was earnest, and Bill liked little boys. Eric hated the Macleans. He kept breaching his curfews, but they never called the cops on him. They disapproved of his friendship with Jack, but never openly complained, reasoning that at least they knew the company he kept. When their double-garage went up in flames, they suspected Eric but never said a word to him. They were so lame they made him want to weep. He wondered why people like them were alive, why they bothered to keep living. What was waiting for them at the end of their journey? Flowers and cherubs and harp music? He knew what he would do to them in time, and not just because he hated them. It was necessary. Balance had to be restored.

Jack often ribbed him about his parentage. You into raping girls and shit like your old man? he asked him one day on the telephone. He said he had a thirteen-year-old virgin in his bedroom if Eric wanted to come over and try his luck. He was getting her drunk and stoned and planned to fuck the shit out of her. Come on, she's yummy, he said. Eric almost went to Jack's on that day. Turned out the little girl got so wasted she puked on his duvet and then shit her pants. She actually shit her pants.

Something flew out of the kitchen and crashed against an antique armchair. Eric looked up and saw a microwave oven in the middle of the floor with its broken door dangling open, wires popping out of it, and a chair leg jutting from its chassis. Jack swaggered in, brandishing a giant knife, thrusting it to and fro like a fencer. He attacked the velvet curtains and the furniture fervently, bright-eyed. But how misplaced, all that energy. Eric had tried to convince him to focus his fury. People reacted when you broke *them* up. The cringing, the crying, the writhing brought a body chill. A chair did nothing.

Tomorrow was Saturday and if that lady came by to check the house she was in for a surprise. They planned to exit by morning.

Eric tingled with anticipation. Jack would let him do his thing. He promised. Jack looked unapproachable now, plunging the knife into a green silk pillow and stabbing it until the stuffing sprang out. Then, smeared with sweat and blood, the muscles of his scrawny back striating, he thrust the knife into an embroidered ottoman, striking something hard, the knife stopping cold. He angrily pulled the knife free and returned to the kitchen. After a moment he screamed for Eric to join him. Eric sat for a time with his head back and his eyes closed, swirling in the vortex that was his mind, before he went to the kitchen.

Jack hunched over the table, snorting directly from a pile of cocaine. He gestured to Eric and flipped him the rolled-up twenty. Eric stooped to the table and took a hoot from the bluish pile, but it caked in his nostril. He tried to catch the spilling crumbs with his fingers, sniffing up what he could, but much of it fell to the floor. For a moment he considered getting on his knees, but just then Jack jingled a key-chain in front of his eyes. Buddy, he said, keys to the family car, a big-ass Buick. He wanted to go for a cruise. Eric didn't think it wise for them to be out driving in their condition: they were a heat score. Jack picked up the knife and waved it at Eric's head. You're afraid to go out, he said. You're fucking afraid. You'd rather just stay here, wouldn't you? You love this stinking place. What the fuck are we doing here, anyway? What are you doing, Eric? Answer me. What's going on in that head of yours? Jack leaned in to him. Eric, he said, I need to get out of here for a while. I need to get out of here before I kill you. I'll kill you, Eric. You creep me out. Are you listening? Are you listening, you fucking psycho?

Eric dipped his head and flattened his hands on the kitchen table, his shoulders shaking with laughter. The table belonged to someone, he thought. It belonged to a family. They had eaten hundreds, no, thousands of meals on it. A heavy, sturdy table, something passed on from generation to generation. It smelled of them, bore their grease, their human stain. It would burn so beautifully. Fire would relieve the table of its memories and chase away the ghosts of all those happy moments around it, fire would. And this saddened Eric. Yes, it did. His eyes welled up with tears. He wanted to weep. He wanted to hurt himself, to stop himself. But he did not want to stop himself. He wanted to see the flames engulf the house; he wanted to warm his hands in that fire.

To some extent, Jack understood Eric's state of mind, he had listened to his stories and knew him insofar as someone like him could be known; still, Jack saw destruction as sport, as gymnastics, not as redemption or fulfillment, and certainly not as achievement. He did what he did without forethought, without blueprint or map. He acted on impulse. He was stupid, primal, easily angered, easily pleased, and easily distracted from the truth.

What is it? Jack said. You wanna drive, Eric? Is that what this is about? Be honest. I'll let you drive, man. But Eric didn't want to drive, he didn't know how, and he didn't want to go out in his condition, vulnerable, choked, and black inside, so black—something would alter his course, something would obstruct or delay him. Jack didn't care, thrusting the steel of the blade to Eric's throat and gently pressing. If you're gonna do it, Eric said, get it over with, and he imagined the blade breaking skin and sinking into his oblivion. It made him smile; it warmed him, the thought of hot blood spraying from his throat and drenching Jack and the room, painting everything red, bringing everything to life. Fucking do it, Eric said.

Breathing heavily, Jack withdrew the knife and let it fall to the floor. Okay, you sick bastard, he said, okay. We'll chill for now, we'll stay put, but later we're going out. We'll score more blow and maybe get some pussy over here tonight. What a waste of a house. We'll have a fucking party. That's it, a party. I'll make some calls. He continued talking. Eric nodded but stopped listening. Nothing Jack said mattered anymore. But Jack needed dialogue to pass the time. Without it he suffered. Without it he lost his sense of reality, he floundered. He snorted another line, the only remedy for his affliction. Meanwhile, Eric slipped off into the house with his matchbook, the only remedy for his.

Country Road

Presley Banyan climbed into the black pickup truck and nodded to the driver, a heavy, bearded man with gold hoops in his ears and tat-tooed forearms. He said nothing to Presley, didn't gesture, didn't even blink. He adjusted his rearview mirror, put the truck in gear, and roared out of the parking lot. They were on their way to score a sizeable quantity of hydroponic marijuana at a local grow house. Presley's old man had made the arrangements, but he was on the road with his rig, probably in California by now, or some place like that, so he wanted Presley to handle the introductions. He didn't mind doing things for his old man. He saw him so rarely these days it offered a way of maintaining a connection with him, of gaining his approval. Besides, if everything went well there was a hundred bucks in it for Presley.

The driver of the pickup truck, an old biker buddy of his dad's, planned to buy the weed off the Dacunhas, three Portuguese brothers who owned a farm just outside of town. They too had biker connec-tions, but different ones. Presley's old man used to run weed south for them before crossing the border got too hairy. The money for the weed must have been stuffed in the bulging manila envelope resting between Presley and the driver. His name was Bart or Bert, Presley wasn't sure, and he wanted to say something to him, just to be socia-ble, but held his tongue. He had learned long ago to keep his mouth shut around these biker dudes unless they asked you a question, and then you answered with the fewest words possible.

Stars glinted in the asphalt-black sky like specks of pelletized glass, and the moon resembled a huge white dinner plate. Trees flanked the road, spectral and black, their lost leaves swirling in the headlamps. The pumpkin fields lay bare and black except for grotesque swollen stragglers, rotting remnants of an overabundant harvest, abandoned to crows, voles, and whatever else could stomach their foul, stringy flesh. Winter loomed; Presley dreaded it. He hated the cold. He wished he could join his mother in Jamaica. She wintered there these days with her boyfriend, Trevor, a dreadlocked Rastafarian. But she laughed when Presley suggested it. Said she didn't want him smoking all that evil Jamaican weed and fucking up his brain. Like it wasn't fucked up already.

It smelled like ass in the truck, and to avoid this unpleasantness Presley breathed through his mouth. Bad smells disturbed him. He used to go off in the detention centre when the other youth smelled bad. He had punched out a score of them for farting in his presence or failing to shower after recreation time. Presley was doing time for beating up this dude who owed him money. He'd accused Presley of selling him bad blow and refused to pay, maybe betting that he'd do nothing about it, that he'd forget about it—after all, he was a fucking fourteen-year-old. But Presley caught up to him one day outside his garage; took a tire iron to his head, mucked him pretty good. That it was over blow never came up in court. The dude said that Presley robbed him and when Presley stuttered and giggled through his testimony, it sounded like the truth. The judge scolded him for being a thug and lacking remorse—like these were bad things—and sentenced him to a year in the Peninsula Youth Centre, out in the boondocks. Despite all the barbed wire and triple locks, the place was soft. Presley lifted weights, worked on the heavy bag, and ate like an athlete. He did the time standing on his head.

He had been out for two months and was having trouble adjusting to life on the outside. Inside there were rules, there was structure. Outside was a different story. There were rules, but structure was lacking. Outside, your biggest enemy sometimes was your very freedom. He was big for a fifteen-year-old, thick-wristed, and strong as a mule. He could throw a football fifty yards. The high school coach said if he wasn't such a hoodlum he could be an all-city quarterback. He liked fighting; it gave him a rush. And he could take a punch. A month ago he ran into these Fort Erie dudes at the Welland skateboard park who thought they were wizards, but they rolled like a clown posse. After he showed off some moves they called him over, and while one distracted him by asking stupid questions about his skateboard, another ran up and sucker-punched him in the temple. He saw stars but didn't go down. Then he knocked the motherfucker out with a straight right. His father had taught him to throw straight punches like that. The others watched bug-eyed, yaps gaping. No one said a word. Yeah. He could handle himself. He glanced at Bert. Even adults didn't intimidate him.

Ever since Presley's mom left two years ago and his dad hit the road again with the rigs, he had spent a lot of time alone. His probation orders forbade him from consorting with his old crew, and his friend Jasmine was so fucked up on crack these days he couldn't talk to her. He had known Jasmine since they were toddlers. Too bad he couldn't help her. That wasn't in the cards. Truth was, he had turned her onto crack. Best high in town, he convinced her. She was only thirteen then, already a little pothead, so she took to the pipe like a natural. Presley found it funny how fast she got hooked. She robbed people to support the habit, her neighbours, her mother, and her grandparents, to mention a few. Presley supplied her for the longest time, then when he got busted, she started buying from anyone who sold it. She even turned tricks for crack. Anyway, she had her own problems now, nothing he could help her with, that's the way it was. If you were flimsy enough to get flushed down the toilet like that there was no helping you, you were fucked, plain and simple.

Clair, a family friend from Newfoundland kept house and cooked meals for Presley and his father, but she drank all day and ran up crazy phone bills calling home. Presley didn't trust her. She came on to him once, last summer. He'd been playing hoops in the school-yard. He got home all sweaty and went upstairs to shower. Clair had just vacated it, a towel covering her breasts, her hair dripping wet. A few years younger than his mom, she wasn't as pretty—his friends thought his mother was hot, something he found disgusting, something he had biffed guys for sharing with him. Imagine them talking about his mother like that. Clair approached him, reeking of herbal shampoo and gin, and started saying stuff, like how she loved his blonde hair and his blonde eyelashes and his blue eyes and how tall he was and *strong*. She stressed that word. Then she dropped the towel.

Well, you'd think—it's not as if his father was boning her or anything. She was just a friend from back home. The old man paid her two hundred bucks a month to take care of the house and to cook Presley a few meals. That was it. Presley could have fucked her, maybe he should have. But she had these banana-shaped breasts and a horny horse-face he found more humorous than attractive. It's not that she was ugly, but she made him laugh. She would have been a funny comedienne, he figured, with that face and that smile. Anyway, when he refused her advances, she told his father that *he* had come on to her. His father lost it. He punched Presley in the forehead so hard he cracked his skull. He still suffered migraines from that. He split for a week after the incident, breaching his probation and risking another year in detention. He stayed with this eighteen-year-old skank he met in a crackhouse. She was useless but liked to fuck and always had money. She didn't hook so he didn't know where she got it from. He figured she had a sugar daddy or something else going on, he didn't care. He wound up taking a vicious beating from her toothless meth-head ex-boyfriend who showed up unannounced one day. The fucking guy tried to cut his throat with a straight-razor. Lucky he turned his attention to the girl. He used his fists on her, did a number. Presley just missed getting killed. It was funny how easily it could have happened. You just never knew when you were going to escape a bad situation with your life. You just never knew. One day a counsellor at the detention centre gave him a lecture on something called karma. He said Presley had bad karma. Presley scoffed at this when he understood what the guy was talking about. He felt there was no such thing as karma. Shit just happened. I could kill you right now

and all your karma would mean squat, he told the guy. But the counsellor wasn't amused and Presley wound up getting restrained by the
guards that day for uttering threats.

The pickup truck jerked to a stop, startling Presley from his
thoughts. They had come to a red light. Bert turned his head toward
him and for a moment looked like he wanted to say something; instead
his mouth fell open as a police car cruised by, manned by silhouettes.
These bikers always got weird when they saw cops. Presley heard a
grunt and then what could have been a laugh, but Bert assumed a rigid
posture and when the light turned green the pickup truck surged forward and stopped again, throwing Presley into the dash.

Put on your seatbelt, Bert told him. His voice sounded dry as an
ashtray. He gestured with his thick hand and Presley secured his
seatbelt with a snap. A hint of a smile edging Bert's profile irritated
Presley. Maybe this ex-biker thought he was heavy duty but he didn't
scare Presley a bit. The only things that frightened him were skunks,
and the dark. He still slept with a nightlight, this green plastic frog
his mom gave him. He glanced at the fat manilla envelope. His old
man never said how much weed Bert planned to score and Presley
didn't give a fuck, except that now he wondered how much money the
manilla envelope held. It looked like a lot. What the fuck are you
looking at? Bert said without turning to him.

The question, and the hostility underpinning it, took Presley by
surprise. He sat up and stared straight ahead. What a fucking joke.
These adults were so paranoid about everything. Like what did Bert
think, that he was going to jack him for the cash? Fucking moron. So
this guy, this so-called friend of his father, was a moron. He'd met
quite a few of them when he was locked up, inmates and guards alike.
People liked to jump to conclusions, they thought they knew what the
fucking score was when in fact they didn't have a clue.

Bert wiped his nose with the back of his fat hand. His ugly beard
could have used a trim. His ears looked like flaps, the lobes distended
from years of bearing earrings. What kind of man was he? Had he
ever done time? Had he ever killed anybody? Most bikers he had met
were scumbags. He didn't admire them. They had bullied his father

in the past—he had witnessed them roughing him up on more than one occasion—and had ripped him off a few times. His father said it was the price of doing business with them, but Presley found that lame. Bert turned into a drive-through donut shop. Presley looked at him. What a fucking goof, stopping right now. The Dacunhas would be pissed if they were late. Bert leaned to the metal box on a post and ordered a large hot chocolate. Who the fuck drinks a large hot chocolate? Presley thought with scorn. He didn't think Bert was going to order anything for him but at the last moment he asked him what he wanted. Presley requested a large triple-triple coffee, hoping to irritate him. But he didn't react. The sallow girl serving them looked familiar to Presley; he figured he had probably sold her weed or crack before.

The coffee was a good one. Presley drank it while it was nice and hot. Bert blew on his hot chocolate and sipped it carefully. He steered with one hand and gripped the paper cup with the other. Presley wished he would put on some music, but didn't want to ask in case the guy got touchy. He figured if Bert wanted to hear music he would have put it on already. What a fucking stiff not to put on some music. People were funny. They liked to demonstrate power any time they had a chance. They liked to control things whenever they could. This guy Bert struck Presley as a control freak. Look how clean the truck is, he thought, admiring the polished black dash and leather seats—a pristine interior, except for the ass smell. Presley noticed a gold coin ring on Bert's pinkie, a nice touch. He wanted a ring like that. It was cool.

They turned onto a country road near the canal and drove a good distance in pitch darkness, the headlights beaming into nothingness. Bert leaned forward and squinted. Fucking dark, he muttered. Presley nodded. He drained the rest of his coffee, rolled down the window and tossed out the cup. Bert jerked his head around and glared at him. What the fuck was that? he barked. Presley didn't know what to say. Well? Bert said, flexing his jaw muscles. I threw out the cup, Presley said. Bert slammed on the brakes and the truck fish-tailed to a screeching stop, its carriage creaking. Go get the fucking cup, Bert said. Presley thought he was joking for a second, but he looked serious. Go get the fucking cup, he repeated in a low voice. Presley climbed out of the truck, walked back in the darkness for a hundred metres and couldn't find the cup. He continued backtracking, swinging his head left and right. In the distance the pickup truck's brake lights glowed like a pair of red eyes.

After five minutes, Presley abandoned the search. It was too dark out there. He heard rustling in the surrounding brush, and prayed it wasn't a skunk, sniffing to make sure. Then he saw oncoming headlights and moved to the side of the road where his shoes crunched over glinting glass shards. As he bent down to inspect, a white van passed by, slowing as it approached the pickup truck, then swerving around it. The debris consisted of shattered cocktail glasses and two bottles, one in pieces, one intact and half-filled with an amber fluid. Someone had been partying. Presley glanced at the label, the letters indecipherable to him. He didn't know how to read. After going to school his whole life and sitting through countless classes with dozens of teachers and tutors, he could barely read his own name. He screwed off the cap and took a whiff; it smelled like whisky. He gulped from the bottle and fire filled his chest. He took another big gulp, and another. It was good stuff. Bert tooted his horn. Presley drank again. He saw something else among the glass shards: an icepick, the tip gleaming.

The handle looked to be fashioned from ivory; the pick itself shone like silver and came to a needle-like point. It was beautiful. All kinds of weird things got dumped on country roads. He returned to the pickup truck with his booty. When he climbed back in, Bert didn't look at him. He put the truck in gear and pushed ahead. After they had traveled a kilometre down the road, Presley uncapped the whisky bottle and drank. Bert eased up on the gas. What the fuck you got there? he asked. Whisky, Presley said. That's not whisky, Bert said. That's bourbon. Knob Creek. Where'd you find it? On the side of the road? Are you fucked up or something? He stopped the pickup truck and snatched the bottle from Presley. That's not whisky, okay, Bert said, flashing him the label. That's bourbon. Can't you read? Are you fucking stupid? Your old man didn't tell me you were stupid. He rolled down his window and chucked the bottle.

They drove in silence, the landscape a work in charcoals and flaked quartz. The effects of the whisky and the humming engine made Presley drowsy, his eyes half-shutting, his head lolling. Then a beast with yellow eyes sprang from the side of the road. Presley watched in horror as it lunged across the path of the oncoming pickup truck. He heard an ugly thunk and then nothing but the hum of the engine. Whatever it was got smoked on impact. Presley felt sick. Bert didn't so much as slow down. Presley wondered if it was maybe just a rabbit—but it sounded bigger, maybe a fawn or a raccoon. Aren't you going to stop? Presley asked. Bert didn't respond; he just kept driving. Hey, Presley said, sitting upright, I'm fucking talking to you. But Bert continued driving, a smile curling his lips.

A minute later Presley said, You just passed the farm. Bert glared at him and pulled over to the soft shoulder. You fucking goof, he said, but before he could say or do anything else Presley stuck the icepick into his right eye. Once it pricked the cornea it slid in so far his knuckle hit Bert's occipital bone. Bert's mouth opened wide and a strange sound came out of it. Then, with his eye gushing blood, he made a grab for Presley, who jabbed the icepick again, this time piercing his throat. That took the fight out of Bert.

Presley sat there listening to Bert gurgle and gasp. It went on for a minute, then he fell silent. His blood greased the manila envelope. One of his gold hoops had come off his ear and lay on the seat. Presley stroked his finger across the blood then jumped out of the pickup truck and started sprinting down the road. Man it was dark. He couldn't see his own hand in front of him. He felt fucked up. He started giggling. He couldn't help it. What the fuck did he just do? He stopped running. He was out of breath. He looked around him. He was standing nowhere.

Reckoning

He saw himself tented, with a little plastic window. Inside there, looking out. He saw the talking globe of the world and talked back to it under his breath. The skeleton hanging by the blackboard knew him, shook slightly when he stared at it. And the hamster Rafael knew him. He fed Rafael his pellets first thing. Then the little guy pooped or slept. It was his life. One day he would free him. One day. Then inside the tent and silence.

When the other students stomped into the classroom, Bradley was already there. They saw him and nudged each other. One of them said good morning but he said nothing. He was always that way. They could only bear so much. Daniel wanted to hang him—he crayoned pictures. Jesse said she would burn down his house. Ryan threatened to break his legs. He could do it. He was a giant. He wore red shirts to school because Jesse hated red. She once took a yardstick and jabbed it in Ryan's stomach. He collapsed on the floor screaming in pain, but no one moved a muscle to help him. Jesse struck Bradley between the eyes one time and it felt like walking into a wall in the dark. He saw sparks. Jesse, the only girl in the Section 20 class, hated everyone. Hatred oozed from her pores. She liked to pull things apart, lay them bare, make them as ugly and loathsome as she could.

Winter was Bradley's favourite season. He could sleep through most of it. He had wanted to sleep that morning, but his father wouldn't let him. He pulled him out of bed by his feet, threw him in the frozen red pick-up truck. When he dozed off in the truck his father cuffed him. Now he tried to sleep in the tent but the other students wouldn't let him.

"Hey, fuckhead, no manners?"

"He was born in a barn."

"He was born on a raft."

"Hey, Gypsy."

This was the song he heard every day and he didn't mind it. He'd been called worse things. They wanted him to come out of the tent and show his face but he wouldn't do it. They'd get too close to him. Jesse might touch him. He didn't want her touching him. She hurt. He would stay put for now. Nothing they could say or do would get him out of there. They continued taunting him for a time. Then their voices fell silent.

It was nice. A soft green inside the tent. He curled up tight, tried thinking of nothing. That was hard but he could do it now. Think of nothing. Then Daniel started braying like a donkey. He had silky blonde hair and flat blue eyes and often touched himself under the desk, turning pink, drooling ribbons. Mr. Chiasson let Daniel do his thing most of the time, but when he humped the desk or yanked his bob out of his trunks, he took him to another room to sit and write in a green notebook with a Happy Face sticker on it. This time Mr. Chiasson pulled Daniel out of class by the ear. Bradley wondered what Daniel wrote in that notebook. He was surprised he could write at all. Daniel's favourite thing was staring off into space. He saw something there. Sometimes he laughed at it.

Ryan talked too much, in his red tops. They said it was his sickness. He took powerful drugs for it. He scared Bradley sometimes, just from talking. That he was a giant didn't matter as much as the talking sickness. "My cousin . . ." and he always started with the cousin and some mischief they'd been up to. Then he talked about his life and his world. He talked about the cars he would buy when he was old enough to drive, and he talked about food, like what he had eaten for breakfast or what he had eaten for dinner the evening before, or what he would like to eat when he got home, or what he and his cousin had eaten at some wedding months ago. He talked about things he had done with girls and things he wanted to do, and he talked about songs. He knew the words to many and tried singing them, but his voice came out too high or too low, never right. Ryan's mother plugged his ears with cotton against infections and the noise factor. Noise made Ryan unfriendly unless he was making it. When it got too loud in the classroom his neck did this thing, then his head snapped to the left, and his mouth and eyes gaped. Daniel imitated it better than Jesse. He had the head part down.

Jesse neared Bradley. Blackheads peppered her nose. Her mouth fell open. She had eaten onions for breakfast. She said she'd cut off his lips if he didn't speak to her, but he didn't believe she would do that. He tried to imagine what no lips would be like. One time she offered him a tuna sandwich. He had no lunch that day but he liked being hungry. It made him strong. He liked eating, too. After he ate the sandwich she told him she had put a booger in it.

The teacher never talked to him; so they never talked. Bradley never complained. Mr. Chiasson gave him math quizzes and geometry exercises and books to read. Bradley enjoyed the math, it was easy, and he liked to spin out circles with the compass. But he never read the books. They were words. Pure words. He had to see the story. He couldn't read.

"Bradley," Jesse said. "Show us your weenie. Do you have one? He has no weenie, fellas. He's neutered. Bradley the kitty cat. Let's call him Bradley the kitty cat." She threw up her arms. "No! Nobody call him that! Ryan, are you eyeing me? If you're eyeing me I'll kill you and your mother."

"Don't talk about my mother. What did she do to you? You're a pig, Jesse."

Bradley stayed in his tent until lunchtime. Today he had a lunch. His mother had made him two salami sandwiches. His father ate one in the truck. Bradley ate his slowly in the cafeteria. The teacher made him eat in there with the others. He just made him. Whenever he refused, Mr. Chiasson called in this heavy guy Sam who would corner him and put him in a basket. That's what they called what he did. Putting someone in a basket. It hurt. But it felt okay, too. Bradley cried after the basket but only to get Mr. Chiasson going. Crying made him hop around like a kangaroo.

"Hey, Bradley," Jesse poked. She wore a creamy brown sweater and pants low on her hips, her puckered navel exposed. "When you went to bed last night did you say your prayers?"

He never prayed. He knew no church. The only one he'd ever visited made people kneel down. His father asked what good this was. Jesse reached over and slapped Daniel in the face. Daniel screeched like the parakeets at Pet Village, where they bought Rafael. Bradley glanced at the cage, wondering what the hamster thought of all this. Daniel continued screeching. Ryan covered his ears, shut his eyes and shouted obscenities. Jesse picked up a basketball on the floor and started bouncing. She bounced like she could do something. When she crossed the ball over from her right hand to her left, it struck the chess table and scattered the men. Everyone fell silent.

Mr. Chiasson returned. First he scolded Jesse, made her pick up the chessmen. Then he talked about the news. He said people were dying everywhere, there was war and famine, and other bad things, but that they should be happy, they were children. His teeth hurt you when he smiled. He always wore a dark green corduroy jacket with chalk on the back. It smelled like a house. He changed slacks and shoes but always wore the jacket. Jesse raised her ugly hand.

"What is it now?"

"I have to poop."

The boys howled.

"That's inappropriate, Jesse."

"Actually, it's a female problem."

Mr. Chiasson rolled his eyes and waved her out. Jesse exited holding herself. Daniel brayed and rocked back and forth in his seat. Mr. Chiasson yelled at him to stop. When he wouldn't, Mr. Chiasson seized his shoulder and shook it. Then he moved over to Ryan. Ryan's snoring head lay on his desk. Mr. Chiasson never tried to wake him when he fell asleep. One day a supply teacher covering for Mr. Chiasson woke Ryan up and he bashed a bowling trophy over her head. They had to get a new trophy, and a new supply teacher. The

trophy went to the best bowler at the end of the year. Bradley bowled
five-pin. Ten-pin balls weighed a ton. But he could handle the five-
pin balls. Ryan busted his arm bowling ten-pin one time. He threw
the ball funny and everyone heard a snapping sound. Ryan went
green and passed out. They removed his bowling shoes and called an
ambulance. Jesse bowled like a killer. Daniel like a chimpanzee. This
was every Wednesday afternoon. Today was Wednesday. Bradley came
out of the tent for bowling.

So that guy Sam drove them in a minivan to a place called Welland
Lanes. Old people came on Wednesdays too, and they were mean
bowlers. They didn't like too much noise, though, and stared at the
class. Mr. Chiasson tried to quiet the youth, but he had to make noise
to do it. People at the grill stopped eating their French fries and
watched Ryan when his turn came up. He swung the ball to his chest
and lurched forward. His way hurt everyone. Jesse mocked him until
he was twitching. Mr. Chiasson pulled her arm and said something in
her ear that made her stop. Bradley wondered what that could have
been. Daniel bowled nice in his little black cap and orange jacket. He
squealed when he knocked down pins. Fat people bowled too, balloon
men and women with small sweet feet. They tiptoed up with the ball
and let it flow. Bradley learned from them.

"Watch my form now, boys. Observe the follow-through." When
Mr. Chiasson hit a strike, he punched the air and sucked in his lips.
Bradley tiptoed up and let the ball flow. His strike was silent. Bowling
was good. He hit another strike, then another one. Mr. Chiasson had
to walk Jesse out when she started swearing at a senior in a red
pullover. Then Bradley got cold. His shots shook the lane. What happened? He lost his eye. When you lose your eye, the ball goes off,
runs away from the point. You had to see the point. Ryan slammed a
ball down the lane and it guttered. His face turned red. He swung his
long arms around and caught a short woman's shoulder. She spun
like a bulldog chasing its tail. The old woman beside her resembled a
sphinx. She blew dust at Ryan. Mr. Chiasson hurried in from the
cold, steaming and pale. Bradley felt like cement. He sat down.
Wearing a weasel face, Daniel walked up to a girl beside a broken man

in a wheelchair. The girl jumped. Her screams pierced every eardrum in the place. Then she caught a fistful of Daniel's pretty blonde hair and wrenched.

Mr. Chiasson rapped Ryan in the skull with his knuckles but this went wrong. Ryan kicked him in the groin and he dropped to all fours. All the problems then. People running, left, right. The porky owner in a black cowboy hat swung out from behind the cash register and legged his way to the action, pulling up his silver-buckled belt. He demanded to know what was going on. By now Mr. Chiasson had recovered his colour but pain still creased his face. Ryan stood staring at the teacher's feet.

"What the heck is wrong with you, Ryan?"

"I don't know."

"What does that mean, Ryan? Tell me what *I don't know* means."

Ryan's head twitched. "I don't know, Mr. C."

"Well," said the owner, a Mr. Stram, "I can call the po-lice, if you need 'em."

Mr. Chiasson's mouth opened, but by now Bradley had gone to the tent again. He left the window alone. He wanted to see nothing. Sounds still came, but the tent muffled them, and Bradley could hear his own heart beating. Life is nice, someone told him once, in a dark room. He wanted it to stop, back then. He said so. But he frightened himself and let it go on until he liked it. In the tent, blue light showed through the fabric; he liked it blue.

Coming back, Sam stopped the minivan on one of the icy canal bridges. Jesse had opened the door and said she wanted to jump into the frigid water. She said she wanted to die. Sam wouldn't tolerate her foolishness. He told her to die some other time. Daniel burst out laughing. Jesse walloped him in the crown. He whimpered but didn't start screeching. Sam said if she hit Daniel again he'd drive her straight to the cops and have her charged with assault. Sam spoke low and calm. Jesse listened.

The trip back to school continued. The landscape was snow. Honking Canada geese flew overhead in a giant V. They were early, or late. It made Bradley sad to think of them up there in the cold air. Did they know what they were doing? Jesse and Ryan had words. Jesse promised to burn down his house. Ryan swore his cousins would revenge it. Daniel tried to remove his thing from his pants before he got out of the van. His cheeks burned and drool dripped down his chin. He had seen Tammy the receptionist from afar. She looked like a blonde horse. She trotted up to her white car and waited for the boys to enter the building before she lit her cigarette. Mr. Chiasson dragged Daniel into the school by the arm. Jesse followed them, clapping. Ryan stumbled and fell over. Bradley tried not to laugh. Sam helped Ryan to his feet and said some words to him about being more mature, but judging from Ryan's expression he understood nothing.

Back in the classroom Bradley went tent again, but Mr. Chiasson came to the window and peered in. "Time, young man. Time." His face melted away. It was quiet for a moment. Then he could hear Ryan sobbing. Mr. Chiasson softly spoke to him. Jesse was quiet. Where was she? He peeked out the window and saw her standing a few feet away, expressionless. She stroked her finger across her throat and nodded. Bradley ducked down and curled up.

Jesse left before too long, with the others. Bradley came out of the tent. He approached the cage. The skeleton watched. The globe was quiet. Rafael's cheek pouches trembled. He was wise, Rafael. He understood. Bradley opened the cage. The rodent froze. Bradley had stroked the fur once before but not since then. He stroked now. Rafael tried so hard not to move. Bradley lifted him out of the cage. He held him to his chest and rocked from side to side. A loud clang behind him caused him to drop the hamster.

Bradley's father stood there in greasy blue jeans and a dark green jacket short on the sleeves. He didn't look too pleased.

Bradley was afraid to look down to see what had happened to Rafael. Was he hurt? Did he escape? His father glared at him with his hateful black eyes. Bradley wanted to say something, anything, but his mouth wouldn't open.

"What the fuck was that?" the father asked.

Bradley took a deep breath. "Rafael."

"Don't sass me, boy."

"He's a hamster."

"You've gotta be kidding me? Is that what I pay my taxes for?" He spat on the floor and pushed Bradley's shoulder. "Go on, get your ass moving."

"But I should . . ."

"You should what? Move it, you little prick."

The father said things all the way to the house. He said he was sick and tired of this nonsense, that Bradley had to come to a reckoning. That's right. A reckoning. He kept saying that word. It hit you. They drove past the house. They continued down to the park and climbed out of the truck. They walked to the monkey bars. He made Bradley get up there and hang. He told him if he let go he'd get no supper. Bradley lasted ten seconds. The father kicked the snow.

Love in Time

Give me a screech in the morning. Give me a bloody good screech in the morning, in my ear. Another mouse smeared on the Victory. The pockmarked walls receiving blunt yellow light. I'm on the floor. I fear the day ahead. My dreams did nothing special. Chased by grunting hogs again over their rutting grounds, slippery going. Yet I take no stock in dreams. Nothing more than little movies to help pass the long night, reminding one of nothing more than life itself, garbled, chaotic. What is this life inside my head? I shower and dress. Isn't life this? This getting dressed for it? My sandals stink. Adrienne came back from the coast but didn't call me last night. I told her never to call me again, and she didn't. I expected her to call one more time. I have to wash my sandals.

Cold coffee in the café next door and the morning paper and nothing better to do, though I'd swear that wasn't the case to a stranger. Tragedy, and politics left and right. And too much base-ball coverage, too much golf, for the swingers of the world. I have no beef. I am not bitter. I only ask for a place to rest my elbow when I'm flagging. Adrienne didn't call and today I cannot think of her. Head out in the sour morning rush and the violent universal mind of the world. I feel hopped up. I'm bouncing on my toes. I used to box a little. I can still go if I have to, but my hands hurt, my hands hurt like hell.

"Watch where you're going."

"What about you?"

"What about me, punk?"

The old guy refuses to relent, like some small rabid red-mouthed species of terrier. His cruel cane, too, I note. A right to the jaw would square him. But I'm not that way. I make progress. I know why the mail is slow: three posties at the corner talk about the soccer game. What soccer game? Meanwhile the people wait. I buy nuts from Bulk Foods. Munch them as I head down to the drugstore to fill a prescript for antidepressants. What month is it? It doesn't matter. Maybe June. June is good. The good light, the ease.

Crossing Montrose Avenue changes things. Grey sedan runs red, takes down man on bicycle. A spinning wheel annoys everyone watching. The driver jumps out, enraged. He shouts at the fallen cyclist. The wheel continues spinning. The cyclist springs to his feet, starts kicking the unscrupulous driver. We could all applaud him. But he doesn't stop for a while. Then the driver drops. The cyclist berates him, and what is this?

"Buddy," I say. "You made your point."

"Hey, you fucking squarehead," cries the cyclist, "you want some of this too?" He jabs his foot into the driver's spine.

The revolution begins. Flags flow over the landscape, horses. A trumpet blares. I bounce on my toes. He misses my knee on the first swipe and I catch him in the shoulder with a right hook. Hits my thigh with a second hoof, but his hands drop to his hips and my left followed by a right ends the story. Now another man takes offence.

In shorts with hairy legs and leather sandals, he charges from behind a parked car. Downs me with a shoulder blow. My pills dance across the asphalt. Now I'm the victim. Yet this isn't true, apparently. The sun in the sky, the falcon flying close to me, and the emptiness of everything surrounding these events: the universe feels hollow. A siren interjects. Two men in black leather clutch me. Something wrong down there, my hip numb. They rough me. They throw me into a black van. Then black inside. Then black inside my head.

Come winter they'll bring me back my shoes. They'll give me back my crucifix. Come winter I'll know where I stand in the system. I won't fool myself into thinking there's an easy way out. Cramps grip me now when the weather chills, when rain threatens. When the rain arrives at last, the cramps let up, but a constant pain persists. Hot baths help. Massages. My masseuse, Kaelin, lost her license last month for failing to pay registration dues. Came over to my place with her massage board and worked me over.

I'm too young to be so fucked up. Kaelin told me I was too young to be so fucked up. Hurt my feelings. I could think of more fucked up people. The guy next door with Tourette's, blathering all day and night. What about him? But Kaelin had a point. I'd let everything go to shit. What was wrong with me? I'm more sober today. I realize there's nothing I can do about the mayhem of the world. I'm better off keeping a distance. My last woman fled when I grew too engrossed with her. She told me she was afraid. I asked her what she was afraid of. She said she was afraid of making a terrible mistake.

I'm crippled then. Hobbling around like an old man. Kaelin suggested a cane. But I'll have none of that. A cane.

I met Adrienne at a poetry launch. She had no face at first. She talked. I watched her mouth. Another time she wore black-rimmed glasses and a red lycra top. I told her my story. Then we began a story.

The present holds more attraction. I want to wash my hands of everything preceding this moment. Not possible of course. But pleasant to think about. We'd been seeing each other for six months. Summer dragged on, then autumn. Life was killing me, but love lightened the load.

Then she was in Chicago. I waited for her return. And yet not happily. I visited George. George was a priest, but he gave up the cloth to write a play. On his eighth draft, something wasn't working. He hadn't bathed for days.

"Structurally," he said, "I find no fault. But perhaps I'm fooling myself."

"What do the boys say?"

"They say they like it. But can I trust them?"

"They mean well."

"Exactly."

George hooked up with a local amateur theatre troupe, amateur being the operative word. He wanted his play staged. We all make compromises. Sometimes there's no choice. He bared his nicotine-stained teeth. Lit another cigarette, rubbed his sparse beard. Foot smell, forgotten vegetable matter, baby-powder, and the smoke behind everything, the smoke in the atoms of that interior. He wore no socks.

"And you're in love," he said.

"Yes."

"That's nice. Ditty and I were in love once. I swear. After being a priest for so long I didn't think love was possible. She was a beautiful girl. When we got married I felt free."

"Where is Ditty these days?"

"Out west with a one hundred pound ass-less goof."

"You're still bitter."

"Sour's more like it. Sour."

George liked feeling that way. Fuel for the drama. Without malaise, without sourness, nothing clicked for him. I wanted to tell him more about Adrienne. I wanted to tell him everything but knew he might not want to hear my testimony, so I buttoned my lip. He had his own gorillas choking him out. I'd always admired George, though I never wanted to emulate him.

"So tell me about this girl," he said.

"I thought she understood me."

George smiled. "Let me tell you something, pally. Understanding brings responsibility."

"How do you mean?"

George lost interest in the conversation. He waved me off. I left in a tilted position. What was he getting at? When Adrienne returned from Chicago, I had no words for her. She kissed me but smelled different.

"What is it?" she asked.

"I don't know."

"You don't love me anymore?"

"It's not that. I still love you."

Adrienne's bloated face angled toward me. Her dark red lipstick daunting.

"I still love you, Adrienne. I've just had time to think."

"Thinking's dangerous."

"I know."

We went to her house in the Beaches. She refused my advances; then changed her mind. Then I changed mine. We did nothing. I made risotto. We ate, drank vino. She told me about Chicago. About the river, the food, the architecture, blues bars, Wrigley Field. I didn't want to hear anymore.

"What's the matter now?" she asked.

"We have to talk."

"Isn't that what we're doing?"

"No. You're talking."

Difficult man, making her life so tight. So tight she couldn't move, she couldn't breathe. She wanted to puncture me and watch me flop around the room until no gas remained. Then she wanted to float off.

"We have to talk," I insisted.

"Then talk, talk."

"You understand me, no?"

Adrienne frowned. Weary from the flight, weary from the parties, from the hotel debaucheries. And yet love beamed from her like so much warm light. I didn't understand what that was, why it blunted my dread, why it illuminated the darkest closets of my self. For a time, anyway. And then nothing helped, nothing brought laughter, nothing turned the clock back, nothing made music. We were stuck.

Only later, after the barricades come down, and the parade floats retire to the grand tent, and the clowns pull off their noses, only then do things come into focus. We pack up our peanuts, scrape the cotton candy from our heels. Then look out for elephants.

Adrienne sent me home.

"I'll talk to you in a couple of days, when your mood improves."

I walked home without self-loathing. Maybe a mistake after all. Maybe a little self-loathing goes a long way in the world. A legless man on a stool at the corner held out his hand. I wanted to ask him

who set him up like that. I wanted to ask him what if he had to go to
the bathroom. I gave him a few coins.

"God bless you."

"He didn't you," I said under my breath.

"Come again?" said the legless man.

"Never mind, it's not important."

"God works in mysterious ways."

Not so mysterious, my friend. I walked. And the sky pink all of a
sudden, the western sky pink, and they said this wasn't a good thing.
My legs felt longer than usual. The road dipped ahead. Trees sighed.
Raccoons climbed down. The sun died out. Then night, and the stars
above, a partial moon, and cooling air. Bats spit from silhouette
branches, silent dogs scuffed behind fences, a woman with a wide
white face passed me. Was she smiling? Her black hair massed over
her temples. I know this woman, I thought. I don't know this woman.
She disappeared under the viaduct.

What of the love one finds at the bottom of a barrel? What of
love in the naked morning, under the slime-tinged light? What of
love coming up from the drain wearing a fruity straw hat? I said my
prayers at night. I didn't know of any God. But said my prayers.
Home at last. There I pondered the day and its vicissitudes. Maybe
I was stubborn.

The neighbour knocked.

"What is it?"

"Look," he said, showing me the puncture wounds in his palms.

"What does it mean?" I asked.

"You don't know?"

I did know, but it bored me to tears. I feigned ignorance. On to
me, he recoiled with disgust. He could now return to his flat and bake
himself a cake.

I only did what I did. I couldn't help the others searching for fellow
disciples. I couldn't bring anything to their tables. They made me
regret life.

I was looking forward to winter already, if it wasn't winter already.
A look out the window confirmed that a few rusty leaves still clung to

the branches, autumn hanging on by a hair. The plump annoying squirrels overdue for a winter fast. The air like steel. My teeth ached. I shut my mouth. I retired to my bedroom. I wanted to call Adrienne but I was afraid. I'd give her time.

Time passed.

I was absolved of wrongdoing in the bicycle trial. Adrienne returned from California. But no word from her yet. Nor have I called. I've decided not to go that way. It's up to her.

And still, spontaneity invades the dead street: a man with a bad voice attempts to sing a song in a register too high for him. His effort splutters. It's not that I take issue with him or with the toneless banality of the street, but I imagined better music at least, better songs. I cannot call Adrienne. She wouldn't be friendly now if I did.

On the subway a man elbows me in the ribs. Dark blue business suit, brown tasseled shoes, briefcase. He doesn't apologize. I dare say it was deliberate. But I give him the benefit of the doubt. We have to coexist somehow. And then another elbow in the ribs, same exact spot.

"Hey man," I say. "What's up with the elbows?"

"Are you talking to me?"

"I should kill you."

But the conversation has already gone on too long. Let me not talk of murder here. Let me talk of brotherly and sisterly love, the kind you're not finding around town these days. Small acts of mercy. Charity. A clap on everyone's back. Everyone feel good? Good. My plate is full already. My appetite dulled by noxious traffic fumes and nauseating opinions; I mean, opinions period. My hands ache. I have a tumour in my left calf muscle. The doctor tells me it must go. Adrienne never does call me back. Let's jump ahead a bit. Adrienne marries a real-estate guy from Scarborough, Eamon. Last I heard, they bought a house in the Beaches with a tilted kitchen floor. Eamon has a very low sperm count. It took me a long time to get over Adrienne.

George finishes the play at last. The boys perform it to mixed reviews. One critic points out the lack of structure, the deliberate breaking down of a classic dramatic arc; but to what end? he wants to know. To what end. I wouldn't dare broach the subject with George. He's grown more sensitive over time. I lost my leg after the operation, but the prosthetic leg works fine. In a year they intend to replace it with an even more efficient one. My doctor promises I'll be able to run if I want. Like I ran when I had both legs.

One day on the strip I bump into Adrienne. She's ballooned.

"You haven't changed a bit," she says.

"Neither have you. How's life?"

"Golden right now. Golden."

"I'm glad for you."

And we continue our separate ways. It's nice like this. But then life can be nice if you let it. Things come into being for a reason. We're unsure what that reason is, but maybe if we just let it all play itself out without thinking about it too much—I don't know. George would have structured it once upon a time. Then he abandoned structure. And we do that. We abandon structures. And we are proud of our efforts, but no one else is.

The Skunk

Inside, the wife berates me from the bathroom about something I failed
to do several days ago. The matter, small then, has become microscopic
to me, so I bring no heat to the battle. And so it happens. Helen wins in
a rout. I was wrong, I was wrong, I am evil, I am Beelzebub. But not content with mere victory, she now wants to rip my heart out and eat it; she
wants to eviscerate me and fill my body cavity with hot stones; she wants
to jab her toothbrush in my eye, and I'm convinced she'd do it if she
could get away with it. Then again, there's no telling what I would do
given impunity. This is how things stand right now. I raise my hands in
surrender, tell her I need air. The bathroom door slams shut.

Outside it smells like a tire fire. I stand in the driveway with my
hands on my hips and the high August sun scorching my head. As I
stagger to the back, a blue jay whirs by me and I eye it to the bough of
the oak tree where it harries a cardinal, of all things. Feathers fly. An
orange tabby under the tree watches the tussle with sinister absorp-
tion. And not to be outdone, the squirrels square off, black versus
gray, screeching and tearing at each others eyes. The world is a bat-
tlefield, make no mistake.

I glance next door. The neighbour, a stocky man with salt-and-
pepper hair and a tightly trimmed moustache, stands on his deck
taking in the action. He and his wife and two boys moved in a few
months ago and even though we've bandied nods I don't know his
name. What does that say about me, about him, about the way things
are right now? I find it hard to be objective these days.

Poking his head over the privacy fence, the neighbour declares that a skunk has taken refuge under his shed. This explains everything. No wonder Larry Holmes, our lab-husky mix, wouldn't venture out. Last summer in the park down the street he ran into his first skunk. It wasn't pleasant. Wildlife abounds in this neck of the woods: coyote, fox, raccoon, and deer. Just the other day a doe and fawn clattered up the driveway, giving me a good fright. No bears have been sighted, but it wouldn't surprise me. A bear in the driveway would get the old ticker clapping, yes it would. The neighbour has more to say.

"Last guy who owned the house didn't concrete the space under the shed."

"He didn't?"

"He did not. What kind of man doesn't concrete the space under his shed?"

✢   ✢   ✢

When I tell Helen about the skunk, first she rebukes me for not telling her sooner, then she trumpets fears about the dog's safety.

"He's not stupid enough to mess with another skunk, honey."

"Just keep your eyes open, Ralph. Especially at night. Skunks are nocturnal."

I don't know much about skunks, except for the obvious. I mean what's there to know? It wouldn't be hard to find out more about them, but the idea of it bores me. Lately everything bores me. I've stopped watching television and movies. I can't read anything, not even magazines. I don't sleep well at night.

✢   ✢   ✢

Helen hates her job at the hotel. She claims the other girls gang up on her, whisper behind her back, sabotage her work. Just the other day she heard them laughing it up in the washroom—they never laugh when she's around, this is the thing. Every workplace has its problems, I tell her. Stand up for yourself, do a good job and no one can touch you. She tells me I'm full of hot air then starts crying. My efforts to comfort her produce a shoulder shift. I understand. She begrudges my position—I'm a youth counsellor, well paid with full benefits. But it's heartbreaking work and takes its toll on you. I've lost my sense of humour, my spark. But this is not about me. Despite having many marketable talents and a supple intellect, Helen has resigned herself. Get another job, I encourage her, but she can't bring herself to do it, to search, to go through the rigmarole of the interviews and so on. I've stopped listening to her complaints about work, though I let her vent. I do that with the kids I counsel—let them vent, without getting too involved.

‡   ‡   ‡

One morning I'm taking out the garbage. Viola, the blue-haired widow from across the street with hips like a chesterfield, waves to me and shouts something I don't catch. I gesture.

"There's a skunk loose, Ralph."

"Yes, there is. He's under my next-door neighbour's shed."

"It's a female."

She finds this amusing. She has no children, no grandchildren, no pets. I often get the feeling she's making sport of me. Helen says I remind Viola of her dead husband, something disconcerting on many levels.

"They're hard to kill," she cackles.

"It's not funny, Viola."

"But it is, Ralph. It is."

Back inside I describe the above encounter to Helen. She's getting ready for work, darting back and forth between the bedroom and the bathroom, whipping clothes and shoes about, spilling powders and creams, convulsing with hysterical energy. She abruptly stops what she's doing and glares at me, her chest heaving. Then she whips a hairbrush down the hall, bouncing it off the pantry door.

"Viola's fucking batty, now out of my way, I'm late."

"But I resent people mocking me."

"Tell it to the marines."

✢ ✢ ✢

I see the neighbour poking around his tomatoes with a long wooden pole. They look ill, the tomatoes, pale, mealy. I wouldn't eat one if you paid me. The sky is a pretty blue today, angelic clouds frame the jet streaks chalking it. And birds flit from branch to branch, finches spiked among the sparrows and the grackles, but are they finches? And where is yesterday's blue jay? So nervy, so bold. A chirp like a bark. A dog of a bird, dogging the others. I know little about nature, only what I've seen on the television and most of that I have forgotten. The neighbour detects my presence and approaches the fence, breathing heavily. I can see him through the slats, in a canary yellow shirt, the armpits soaked.

"Thought I had the bugger."

"Don't you fear being sprayed?"

"That's why I've got the pole."

But surely a skunk has more range than that, I surmise, though I'm not in the mood to debate it.

✢ ✢ ✢

Helen and I sip nightcaps on the front porch. She makes a beautiful martini. I suck the pimento out of the second olive, take a tasty gulp. That's what I'm talking about. Larry Holmes snores at our feet. A candle Helen lit flickers on the little table between us; Orion glitters above us. Except for the clicking of bats, a hushed tranquility envelopes the street. Helen sighs.

"It's lovely out."

"It is," I say with feeling.

"What's that?" She points to the dim corner.

For a moment I see nothing; then, through a pale shaft of streetlight, a white stripe slashes into view.

"Oh my God," Helen says.

I lean forward in my chair. The skunk. She has stopped at a mail-box. I wonder for what reason. She probes with fascination, fearless, omnipotent, an enigma. But this won't last. She will cross the street and come right for us, I conjecture, because things often happen that way. So when she crosses the street and comes right for us I am not surprised.

Larry Holmes jumps up but freezes in mid-frame like a bronze relief. Helen looks at me, eyes moist with fear, hands bunched to her chin. I don't know what to do. Screaming seems wrong; running wronger still. The skunk bears down on us, primeval, cartoonish, horrific, but at the last moment makes a sudden turn and shuffles to the neighbour's driveway where she dives into the shadows.

Later, in bed, when I rest my hand on Helen's hip, she pretends to sleep, even feigning a delicate snore. The hip feels cold, all bone. I listen to her snoring. I know the difference. I keep my hand on her hip for a long time. It doesn't warm up. At one point she pretends to dream, mutters something, and shifts away from me on the bed, clinging to the airy precipice of her side.

☩　☩　☩.

Next morning in the kitchen, Helen smashes an orange majolica rooster into smithereens. Shards fly across the floor tiles. Larry Holmes cowers under the table. I let her vent. It is nothing I have done, or so I believe.

"What's the matter now?"

"I'm not happy."

"Tell me something I don't know." I think she's going to take a swing at me, but she goes quiet, stills her body. Then I think she's going to cry but she doesn't; she walks out of the kitchen and locks herself in the bathroom.

☩　☩　☩

At twilight Larry Holmes steps out. After his evening piss he likes to do a perimeter check around the backyard. It's all bullshit if you ask me, but it makes him feel powerful I suppose, master of his domain. I expect him to come scratching at the side door any second. Then I hear the yelp. My knees buckle. I know what that yelp means. I know. It's one of those moments again. Any second I expect Helen to come running out of the bathroom, and she does, though plastered with a luminous green face cream. We stare at each other, then bolt for the door.

✝   ✝   ✝

It takes five or six hosings and the application of special shampoo to clean the dog's fur, and even then his face exudes the smell, poor bastard. You've never beheld a more miserable animal. Helen vetoed the use of tomato juice, citing several studies questioning its efficacy to neutralize skunk excretions. Who would argue with that?

What a scene. The skunk got Larry Holmes square in the chops, blinding him and causing him to vomit and convulse in a seizure of revulsion and wretchedness. The dog can be dramatic yes, but an objective evaluation would grant him good cause for the show on this occasion. His pain is real; I feel for him. The only one more miserable than Larry Holmes is Helen.

"We should have been more vigilant," she intones.

"The dog needs his space."

"He's shattered."

"He'll get over it."

Helen dips her head and bursts into tears. Jesus Christ. "Helen," I say, touching her shoulder, expecting another rebuff. But rather than retreating she lets me embrace her and then wraps her arms around my neck, burying her face in my chest, shaking with sobs, clinging to me long after the weeping stops.

✝   ✝   ✝

The neighbour told me that bright lights keep skunks away, so I retrieve the stepladder, intent on replacing the burnt-out bulb above the side door. I'm the first to admit I'm useless as a handyman. I have no feel for it. The slightest task makes me cringe with anxiety. I look at a hammer or a wrench and I want to run for the hills. Perhaps if I took the time to learn a few basics I would save myself a lot of trouble, but I can't see that happening in this lifetime.

I'm not up on the ladder for more than a minute when I detect movement at the end of the driveway. Nothing. Maybe just a cat or the wind, though there's no wind. I continue with my task. The fucking thing is jammed or something, the bulb, and I'm afraid to break the fragile glass by forcing it. That happened to me when we first moved into the house. While unscrewing a dead light bulb above the stove it broke in my hand. I sustained a wound on my palm and when I tried to get out the rest of the light bulb I received a nasty shock. Helen laughed her head off, though I failed to see the humour in it. My arm ached for days. She chided me for whining. Maybe I milked it some, taking the week off work and loafing around the house.

I unscrew the present dead light bulb without issue and I'm about to replace it when I see a white stripe moving toward me like a banner. I hear myself scream. That I could make such a sound is scary. Larry Holmes starts freaking out inside. I freeze like a sloth on the ladder as the skunk moves in. I hear Helen calling me. Not now, I say in my head, not now. I'm afraid to look, but I must look. I take a deep breath. I look.

The skunk is not alone. Three little ones surround her, chirping, tails raised.

✝   ✝   ✝

"Skunks are nearly blind," the neighbour explains, working on a wedge of rich red watermelon. "But they're fearless, for obvious reasons. They shoot the offensive pungence from anal glands. They say even skunks can't stand their own smell. Cats keep their distance and only dogs that haven't been sprayed bother them."

"I saw her last night with little ones."

"They're called kits." He spits some pits and bears down again.

"I don't scare easy but I almost shit my pants."

The neighbour grins. "No doubt. I concreted the space under my shed. She must be staying someplace else." He wipes his lips with the back of his hand and tosses the watermelon rind among his sick tomatoes.

☩　☩　☩

Helen's been in the bathroom for over an hour when I decide to knock. She doesn't answer at first. I try the doorknob: locked.

"Helen?"

"Yeah?"

"I have to go."

The door opens. I start. Helen has dyed her hair jet black. She asks me what I think about it and I tell her it looks very Goth, is that what she wants? She brushes by me, pumping her elbows. I follow her into the kitchen. She looks like another person with the black hair. I find it alarming. She stands at the sink and stares out the window.

"Helen, what's going on?"

"I hate you, Ralph."

"Well, I'm glad we got that out of the way."

"No, I mean I really hate you."

"Yes."

"You're not listening, Ralph. You're not listening to me."

☩　☩　☩

When I get home from a bike ride one afternoon, Larry Holmes greets me howling at the door and does a tap-dance, so I know he has knocked down the baby gate that kept him confined to the kitchen. But Helen left the bedroom door open and Larry Holmes took a nap on the bed and, perhaps in his guilty excitement upon my arriving, peed on it. I strip down the mattress and launder the soiled bedding.

Stain-repellant saved the mattress, and it's nice to know that some things in life work and are worth the extra money. I banish Larry Holmes to the backyard for the rest of the day where he sulks under the oak tree. When Helen comes home she refuses to believe he peed on the bed.

"I demand proof."

"But I laundered everything."

"You're a terrible person."

✝   ✝   ✝

An argument erupts next door, shattering a peaceful, violet evening. Larry Holmes stirs in his sleep. Helen looks up from her *Vanity Fair*, sniffs, and despite the poor light returns to reading, though a quiver in her upper lip puts me on alert. Something has gone off in her head, has irked her, something she read, the drama next door, maybe something in the back of her mind, but it will fall on me like stones, it will bury me alive. I can feel it coming.

Meanwhile the fight next door continues until I hear what sounds like a clap or a slap; then a screen door opens and shuts. My neighbour remains on his deck, attacking a wire coat hanger with needle-nosed pliers. Helen seethes in the dying light. Larry Holmes goes back to sleep. Stomach cramps force me inside.

✝   ✝   ✝

A few days later an ambulance pulls up to Viola's house. Two burly paramedics push a gurney up the driveway. Moments later they roll a body out of the house. Even though they've covered her up, an arm dangles loose and I can tell by the porky fingers and the chintzy rings that it is Viola.

When I break the news to Helen she buries her face in her hands and sobs. She liked the old woman. They shared something precious, something human. Tears pour through her fingers and she rocks to and fro, inconsolable. I don't know what to say or do to comfort her.

When I venture too close she makes a hissing sound. That's a new thing, the hissing.

✢   ✢   ✢

Next morning, under cloudy skies, the neighbour descends the porch steps with a crimson cap pulled low on his head. Spotting Larry Holmes he slows down, though he sees the leash. Larry Holmes can do this to people, but then I notice the man's black eye and his slumping shoulders, and I reckon that this victim of violence needs comfort, reassurance.

"Hey, neighbour," I say in my most natural voice.

He stares at me, pained, tense, fragile, and looks as if he is about to say something when, without warning, he bursts into tears. It's amazing. I don't know how to treat it. Empathy is my forte but I reckon mere words will not assuage him. I am not beyond strong measures when the situation calls for them and so I do not hesitate to stretch out my arm and with my hand grip his neck, massaging him through his pain, though he snaps out of it and hurries down the street, glancing once over his shoulder.

✢   ✢   ✢

But the following morning the neighbour greets me from his deck with jubilation. What could it be? I wonder. Has he knocked up the wife again? Has he won the lottery? And yes, it's a beautiful day, the sky so blue it makes me want to scream. Everything is fabulous. Blue jays flock with cardinals. Black squirrels marry gray. Rose of Sharon blooms gaily in my garden and its saucy pinks merit praise. I feel light as a balloon, helium-filled, colourful. Not a cloud on my horizon, save for the wife in bed with a rubber hot-water bottle, warming her back spasms. But what, there is more? Larry Holmes circles around the yard sniffing the earth, his tail like a pole. What's going on here, eh? What's afoot?

The happy neighbour says, "The skunk is dead."

"The skunk is dead?"

"My youngest pinged her in the skull with a slingshot ball bearing."

"You're kidding me."

"I'm not kidding you. That boy has talent."

"It was the mamma skunk?"

"It was the mamma skunk, that's right."

☩   ☩   ☩

I don't know how I feel about it. On the one hand I'm gripped by a weird nostalgia for the events that have just passed, though few of them were pleasant. I admit I miss the skunk, and wonder what will become of the little ones. Will they stink up some other neighbourhood? On the other hand, my sentiment for the skunks falls short of true sadness. I mean, they were skunks.

Helen packed her bags in the night. She's going up north for a while to visit her mother and to think about things. I've got things to think about myself, but this is irrelevant right now.

After Helen loads up the rental car and gets behind the wheel, Larry Holmes starts howling. Brushing a strand of black hair from her face, she smiles, and with a little wave departs. It's the last time we'll ever see her, I imagine. It happens.

I take Larry Holmes for a walk to the park. We spot a coyote by a stand of birches and it puzzles the dog. He doesn't know what to do. He looks at me and whines but I have nothing for him. It is what it is. Later, he dozes at my feet as I sip a gin and tonic on the front porch, sniffing the dark air, wondering where the summer went.

Lion Days

People came up the stairs. Lion glanced at the eight-foot partition, then at the door. He jumped off his pedestal.

"You mean to tell me . . ."

"It's not about the . . ."

"Bonnie, he doesn't even . . ."

The voices faded in and out. They whispered a lot, spoke low. He could hear them when he had to hear them, when they wanted him to hear. They were planning. What were they planning? It didn't matter. He opened the window to air out the room. It smelled rooty. The air coming in smelled of water. Then he threw himself onto his straw bed and imagined it was an enormous water buffalo, eviscerated and spread out. He stretched across the ribs and spine.

"Lion!"

The mother called. She always called for something. Her voice had long arms. His body roared at him not to lie across the ribs. It wanted water. He took the carcass out, paddling with his paws. The water looked like petroleum. Bodies floated in it. Charlie the neighbour skimmed across the surface in his blue postman's uniform. They had fought before over property. Charlie always crossed the line, and when he crossed the line Lion wanted to shred him. Now he floated, dead. Lion reached into the water but could not touch him.

Lion's green eyes blazed when the mother opened his door so she left him alone. He came to a shore. The water buffalo slid into the sand. Lion dug with his claws. Water oozed around his limbs. His claws curled around something hard: a skull. The treasure had a cracked crown. He rolled it. He took it in his jaws. He returned home.

The mother entered and stood beside the partition. "You can't do that all day."

Lion pretended to be sleeping on his straw bed. He stirred his legs as if running in a dream. He was chasing a fat zebra, about to clamp down on a hind. The mother sighed and went out again. He heard her murmuring in the hall. Then the door closed.

Lion felt playful. He looked at the twin dolls in the toy basket. The little moustaches twitched. He touched their tweed caps, licked their shooting coats, and scratched their check stockings. Then he watched them smoke their pipes. Purple smoke went up in the air. It smelled pleasant, of plums. He climbed into his crate and lowered the lid down over himself. Then he burst through it like a jack-in-the-box, leaping out of the crate and tearing the dolls to pieces.

They put him in the garage once. He made so much noise the neighbours threatened to call the police. Then Dad fed him horse-meat and he stopped tearing about. He let him play on the wet lawn in the back yard. Lion shook his paws; he didn't like the damp, but Dad wanted to try the head-in-mouth trick. When he pulled Lion's mouth open, lifting his face and nose to the sky, he noticed a muscular tension in his jaws. Lion tensed all over. Dad's head went in anyway. He counted to ten slowly and then gave the usual tap-on-jaw cue to release. No response. He tapped the jaw again. But Lion gazed at the clouds, wondering if rain would fall.

Men in white coats came and put an oxygen mask over Dad's face. The throb of a resuscitator in Lion's ears enraged him. He paced back and forth. Someone felt Dad's pulse and a stethoscope went down on his heart. It was a terrible moment. Sticks hit Lion. Someone from a distance darted him. He went to sleep.

The mother reached over the partition and touched his whiskers. It was a cold hand, ugly. It smelled like fish. He bit it. It tasted sour. It recoiled. He turned the skull in his hands and held it under the green lamp on the night table. Green light bathed the flaw in it, the crack. Lion's body was thin and green. Yesterday he was tan and thick out back playing with Toby the white bull terrier. Toby jumped on Lion. Lion held him against his body. Toby didn't like that. It pleased Lion to think about the dog but not to be with him all the time. Dad said to play with him for the peace and the fresh air. But it puzzled Lion when Toby pinned back his ears and growled. It puzzled him when he didn't listen to him or when he peed without asking. It puzzled him when the dog ate his own poop.

Parrot visited that afternoon. The colouring of the bird was blue but overlaid with green stripes and yellow spots. Streaks of crimson in the deep blue head gave it richness. They sat in the living room for a time, neither with much to say. Parrot noted the figurine on the mantelpiece: a pink majolica cockatoo. He laughed at it. Lion laughed too though he thought it not funny. Then they ate little sandwiches and drank tea. The afternoon receded. A freakish winking of Parrot's eyes, like stars, gave Lion cause for speculation. Was it a deliberate difference of design? Then Parrot admitted he had painted on the spots. Everyone has to be themselves, he argued. Lion couldn't judge his friend, but he felt he had grown vain over the years.

After one more tea, Parrot made apologies and left. He was usually good for a couple of pots. But things change even with the best of friends. They get full of themselves, or they run out of things to say. Lion had run out of things to say a long time ago. It happens. You talk and talk and your mouth gets dry, then your mind gets dry. All we can do is go with it. Fighting the inevitable just makes it harder to accept.

Lion returned to his room to improvise with string. The mother thought it would help him pass the time. She provided a big ball of string for him. He nervously tapped at it. Then it began to unravel. He pulled string over his bed and over his dresser.

It was so hard to concentrate; the punch in the eye didn't help. Dad punched again: the other eye. They said they would put Lion in the crate if he roared. He tried to be quiet. It wasn't easy. Dad pointed at him, then rubbed his head. Lion didn't care for it. Later the mother and Dad ate cucumber sandwiches side by side on the couch and when they finished they shook themselves of crumbs and kissed on the lips. Lion took his bowl of milk and looked at it in silence.

Dad filled his pipe and smoked. His eyes glazed over. Lion licked his milk. It tasted sour. He knocked the bowl with his paw and milk spilled onto the floor in a white blob. Then he lapped up the milk left in the bowl.

Dad stroked Lion's mane. "To return to what I was saying . . ."

"Be careful around him," the mother said. She wiped her hands with her apron and slapped her thighs. "Come here, big guy."

Lion went to approach her but Dad jumped out of his chair and crawled to her on all fours. She patted his head and slipped him a cracker. Lion wandered into the nursery. He touched the hideous bride-doll on the mantelpiece. He could sense its power coursing through the house. He wanted to shred it but feared punishment. He had been punished for less. Its eyes locked with his and would not look away. How horrible! And its flesh was like glass! He returned to the kitchen. At the table Dad wore a shiny visor and bifocals and sorted through a pile of bills and letters. The mother stood behind him looking on. She glanced at Lion, then spoke under her breath.

"His mind is thinking of something else," she said.

"He blends so profoundly the stuff of thought."

"He's one with himself."

"I think our plan is working."

"What would you like for dinner, dear? Pork roast?"

"I love your pork roast."

One day when Dad was angry he took out the lasso, slipped the noose through the slats and over Lion's head. Lion let out a screech that sent the mother running. Another time Dad took a broomstick and poked the rounded end into Lion's mouth. He pushed the broomstick through his mouth until his wrist rested between his fangs. Then Dad stuffed a cardboard funnel with chloroformed rags and strapped it to Lion's face. Dad said he needed a stronger cage. This one he had bought at an auction, part of a collection of circus mementos, but flimsy.

Lion fell asleep. He dreamed of zebras. They ran slowly, their plump flanks flexing in the sunlight. He could feel their heat as he closed the distance, hear their hearts beating, taste their fear. His powerful muscles moved under his bristly coat and his jaws snapped, catching nothing but dust. They were so close! He started up again, bounding.

Dad hooked a chain to Lion's collar and clipped two ropes to it. Then he double-locked the cage. While Lion slept he heard voices.

"How do you train him?"

"I wish I could tell you."

"A blank-cartridge revolver? A whip and a stick?"

Laughter ensued. Then Lion heard the clatter of cutlery and glasses. They were feasting? Was it someone's birthday? Lion's fell in August. He didn't know what month it was but it wasn't August. The air had a cool edge. August was never that cool. Perhaps it was March or April. And yet he had no memory of winter. He tried to move but could not. He bit at the chain but it hurt his teeth. He could see figures dancing about his room.

"I've used a chair for training purposes."

"And I notice you always wear the thickest horsehide jacket."

"Indeed."

Lion burned like a flame in the black room. He had a fever. The mother applied a cold compress. She gave him bitter liquids to drink. He vomited into a can. The room smelled rank. He wanted to run but they kept him penned in. He growled in misery and the mother stroked his head. Dad came and went with a worried look on his face. What was he up to?

Lion slept for three days and awoke in the living room. Strange. What happened? How long was he out? He looked at the pink cockatoo on the mantelpiece and roared. Its presence reassured him. A near empty glass sat on the coffee table. The Tiffany lamp flickered. Someone had just been there. He went up and waited on the staircase, peeking through the wooden railings.

"I have a queer sense that old carpetbags is hanging around."

"I can smell him."

"The appearance of his room depressed me this afternoon."

"What can we do about it?"

"Redecorate."

Lion imagined crimson and gold lacquer cabinets adorned with mother-of-pearl flamingos, or silvery peacocks, and rose petals falling from baskets, and fragrant firelight. Or a marble-topped table beside a looking-glass with Parrot fluttering about, something fixed and fluid at the same time.

Dad came in, took a chair by the window and watched. He was wearing white gloves. He watched him all the time now. He hadn't seen the mother in days. He feared he may have eaten her. He tried to ask Dad about it, but as if stuffed with straw, he didn't move or say anything. He just sat there. His eyes looked patched. Lion gave a startled snarl and sprang to his pedestal.

What just happened? Through rips in Dad's trousers he saw bloody gashes. Lion licked blood from his paws. Beyond the hot lights a multitude of faces watched him.

He sat in a mental arena of chicken wire with battle-scarred alley cats shaved to look strange and marched before him for gladiatorial combat. No room for bashful creatures here. He fought them all, devoured them all, left nothing but bloodstains and gore for the vultures to pick through. What were they thinking, these entrepreneurs, these impresarios?

Lion stood by the window. He stood perfectly still. Sunlight bathed him gold. Small golden animals scampered in. When Dad had them seated he walked to a lacquered black chest and exchanged his bloodied white gloves for a gun and a whip. Lion wasn't game for this. He leapt from the pedestal and landed near the chest. Then he jumped the partition and slipped out the door.

The Venetian

Giuseppe, the barista at Bar Italia in Toronto's Little Italy, introduced me to the Venetian one summer evening. His name was Antonio Gallo, thin, balding, bearded, with a great beak of a nose and horn-rimmed glasses. He looked like an intellectual, if one can look so, or at the very least like a species of professor. Giuseppe informed me that the man had only recently come to Canada and spoke no English. Indulge him, he told me, since he knew I spoke passable Italian. I introduced myself; Antonio shook my hand and said he was pleased to make my acquaintance. He had a raspy voice and spoke with a sharp Venetian cadence. I felt awkward at first but when he detected Sicilian in my accent he put me at ease by telling me he had spent time in Sicily as a young man, and loved the island and its people. He inquired about my family and listened to what I had to say with inter-est. I told him how my parents had married by proxy. My father had immigrated to Canada in 1955 and after a couple of years here wasn't having the best go of it; alone, homesick, and miserable, he seriously contemplated returning to Sicily. One day while getting a trim, he explained his dilemma to his barber. It's too hard, he admitted. The weather, the language . . . I don't think I can do it. What you need is a wife, the barber told him. You'll get nowhere without a good woman. The barber then presented him with a photograph of his niece, a beautiful blue-eyed girl from Palermo, Sicily. My father was impressed. Carmela will make a good wife, the barber assured him, and my father took him at his word. After an exchange of letters, a written proposal and acceptance, a dual ceremony followed, one in Canada, one in Sicily, and that girl embarked to North America as my father's new wife. A few years later she became my mother. And they loved each other, Antonio said almost to himself. Yes, they did, I told him, recalling how my mother had mourned my father's death. I think they loved each other very much.

✝ ✝ ✝

After two intense years together, Melissa and I were on the decline. Things had started going sour around Christmas. I didn't feel it anymore, and I don't think she did either. I had tried to break up with her as early as February—guilt and sexual jealousy had sent me scurrying back. But she had changed since the aborted break-up, had become more secretive, less generous, less humorous. The woman had a right to protect herself, given what had happened—she no longer trusted my intentions, or my commitment to her. But I sensed that something else was going on. I had never been unfaithful to Melissa, and had assumed the same for her. Early on we had agreed to be honest with each other if we strayed, but that's difficult to do when the time comes. You clam up, feel guilty, afraid, protective, angry—in the end you say nothing and let the thing play out as it will.

✝ ✝ ✝

Bar Italia's proprietor, Michael Conte, had a hard head and a sharp tongue, and I didn't particularly care for his brand of ball-breaking. He had a way of getting under my skin. But Giuseppe didn't start work until noon, and my need for a morning espresso superseded any disquiet Michael caused me. Tell me something, he said confidentially, is my coffee nice? I looked into his deep-set black eyes and wondered if he was joking. Is it? he asked. It's nice, I said. That's all I want to hear, he said, that my coffee's nice. It's music to me. Antonio entered the bar wearing a belted brown wool cardigan. Michael rolled his eyes. Antonio said he had a summer cold, awful business. *Porca miseria*, he complained as he blew his nose into a sodden handkerchief. *Ho bisogno un lenzuolo.* Speak English, Michael said, slapping his hands on the counter. Antonio shrugged and glanced at me. What's the problem? I asked Michael. Tell your friend here to speak English in my joint, he said. But he's Italian, I said, from Venice. I know where he's from, Michael nodded, I know.

✦   ✦   ✦

I loved Bar Italia in the late afternoon. It was cool and quiet, far less trafficked than at lunch and early evening when it thronged with yuppies and artiste-types. I rested my arms on the cool marble counter, enjoying a delicious iced latte. A few regulars sat around sipping espresso, reading, lost in their thoughts. I ordered another iced latte from Giuseppe. He had shaved his head that morning and had applied a skin lotion that caused it to shine under the bar lights. I paid a fortune for the shit, he confessed, rubbing a paper serviette over his head. By the way, he said, what do you make of Antonio? He seems harmless enough, I said, a little opinionated maybe. He loves Toronto, can't say enough about it. And he did love the city—though he somewhat overstated the case at times, going on about air-conditioned subways, multilingual street signs and such. This was a man who had lived in Venice. How could he be so impressed by Toronto, given that? On the other hand, Toronto was a very livable city. Unlike the museum of Venice, it was a city of the future, still evolving and growing. I had been to Venice twice and for all of its beauty and moody splendour, I couldn't escape the impression it was a relic, a thing of the past, with nothing for it to anticipate except the encroaching sea. Giuseppe served me a glass of ice water and asked where Melissa was; she often accompanied me for a late afternoon drink. She's working, I told him. She had a gig researching a music documentary and was meeting with her producer Gary and then going to a business dinner with some investors. What is she again? Giuseppe asked. A researcher, I said, but he had wandered off to the end of the bar.

✝   ✝   ✝

That evening he launched into a discourse on Doges after I confessed I knew nothing about them. Doges held no interest for me, but I loved listening to Antonio; the more passionate he felt about a subject, the more lovely and expressive his Italian became. He told me that Venice wouldn't survive the twenty-first century. All the technology and engineering in the world couldn't save it. Venice was doomed to be submerged. *Venezia e quasi finita, caro mio*, he lamented. *Ho venuto qui in tempo.* I asked him why he had come to Toronto and he told me it was a long story—he had a bachelor uncle here, his last living relative, sad really, no one left to continue the line. I assumed that Antonio also was a bachelor, though I gathered from the way he ogled pretty girls in the café that he liked the opposite sex. He inquired about my relationship with Melissa. I told him I had been seeing her for a couple of years but maybe not for much longer. I'm sorry to hear that, he said. You looked happy.

✝   ✝   ✝

She had finished off one bottle of wine and uncorked a second, her teeth dark, her movements languid, hazy. She took a seat on a chair against the wall. I heard her sigh. I switched on the lamp in the corner and sat on the sofa across from her. I removed my shoes and socks. You're not planning to stay, are you? she asked. I didn't answer. I glanced at my bare feet, then looked at her. She stared straight ahead. Wine often made her sentimental, but not this time.

✝   ✝   ✝

Giuseppe had been studying aikido for years and liked to talk about his instructor, a fellow called Mo. Just Mo. From the sounds of it he was a strange cat, maybe a bit too serious for his own good. He can kill a man with his bare hands in ten seconds, Giuseppe told me. That long? I said. Seriously, Giuseppe said, Mo is extraordinary. Yes, I thought, a man I want to hang out with, learn from. Giuseppe was growing a goatee. I asked him about it. I'm bored with my face, he said. Ever get bored with your own face? I didn't know how to answer. Bored wasn't the right word for how I felt about it. We came to a wall in the conversation; Giuseppe moved on to grind coffee beans. I sat there for a long time resting my elbows on the marble counter, my face in my hands.

✝   ✝   ✝

They were lunching at Soto Voce, this tony little place across the street from Bar Italia. I happened to be walking by and saw them at a table near the window, engaged in an intense tête à tête. Sparsely bearded, pencil-necked, insipid, Gary had nothing going for him except his producer status. On any other plain, physical, intellectual, artistic, he would have been what he was, untalented and weak. Nevertheless, he commanded respect—women in the business probably thought he was hot. His confidence, and his power, gave him sex appeal among other things. It was simple. I understood the situation. I didn't stop and make a scene.

✝   ✝   ✝

I spent two days in my bedroom. My roommate Pat was visiting his sister in Saskatchewan. I welcomed the solitude. I cried a lot. I felt foolish for that, but more foolish that I'd let a beautiful girl like Melissa get away from me. The thought of her with someone else made my heart ache. On the other hand, she wasn't perfect. She drank a lot, and I detested her drunken personality, though others found it comical, charming. Still, I convinced myself I wanted her back, and during those two days an ember of hope still glowing in my heart gathered light and warmth. I entertained the possibility of rec-onciling with her—doing what I needed to repair the breach—and then moving on to the next phase of our relationship. I wasn't ready to give up yet, and if it had become some kind of contest between

Gary and me, then I was game: I'd show him. But my bravado felt forced. A deeper part of me knew I was going through the motions, maybe for the sake of pride, or to finish off that chapter of my life with a flourish.

✝   ✝   ✝

Domenic Buonanote, a Bar Italia regular, pulled up that afternoon in a crimson tank top, his bunchy muscles contracting. I just finished working out, he announced. Despite his impressive musculature, Domenic stood an inch short of five feet. Giuseppe, hook me up with an iced espresso and a bucket of cold water. Giuseppe stared at him for a moment before he got to the espresso. You don't work out enough, Domenic said, looking me up and down. Your body—you used to be an athlete, no? That's right, I said. Played some football in university. Middle linebacker. Domenic nodded. Yeah-yeah, he said. Me, I was always too small, too small. I wrestled. Won the Ontario's my senior year. I could probably kick your ass. I don't think so, I said. No? Domenic said. No, I said. Hey, Giuseppe, do you think I can kick his ass? Giuseppe stopped what he was doing and squinted. You wanna kiss his ass? he said. Not *kiss*, Domenic said. Kick, *kick*. Giuseppe burst out laughing while I debated whether to settle the issue with Domenic right there and then.

✝   ✝   ✝

We had dinner at Senior's on Yonge Street, an old-school steakhouse I used to frequent in the late eighties. Still going strong, it hadn't changed a bit. Even the black-haired waiters looked original in their loose white shirts and bowties. Melissa wore a green silk dress with black playing card symbols: clubs, diamonds, hearts, and spades. Her green eyes sparkled. She looked happy. She drank two martinis before the steaks arrived. She shaved her words. I probed, trying to uncover the state of her heart but she proved to be elusive. Let's just have fun tonight, she said. Let's pretend this is a first date. Sounded fine by me. I tried to recall our first date. Actually, it occurred in her bedroom one steamy August evening. Later we agreed it was the closest thing to insanity we had ever experienced. But we never repeated that performance. It was a hard act to follow.

✝   ✝   ✝

Again you, Michael said. His hair had been trimmed too short on the sideburns and his ears yawned. I stared at them until his nose started twitching self-consciously. He leaned to me. What if I barred you from here, he said, what would you do? I thought about it for a moment. I would lose my mind, Mike, I replied. I could not live for more than a day or two without your coffee. That's the truth. He squinted and scrutinized my face. I couldn't help but laugh. It's funny? he said. It's funny, I said. Here comes your soul-mate, Michael nodded. What is it with him? I don't know, I said. Antonio marched into the bar. He was angry or put off about something, muttering and clenching his jaws. Antonio, I said, *cosa mi dicci*? *Mah*, he said, *sopratutto uno cornuto ma datto il ditto cosi*—he gestured. I told him someone gave me the finger every day. No big deal. *E pure*, he said, *mi fa male la gamba—madonna com'e dolorosa*. His leg ached. He turned it gently this way and that. *Il ginocchio*, he stated, pointing at the knee. His twisted face convinced me of his pain. Michael stood by the espresso machine, unconvinced.

✝   ✝   ✝

Melissa walked away from me. The sun had set, the warm evening smelled of barbecue, exhaust fumes, and garbage. She wanted a good night's sleep—she was meeting Gary tomorrow and needed a clear head. Gary's a married man, she added, he has two teenaged daughters and loves his wife. This was supposed to quiet my concerns, but I wasn't so easily thrown off the trail. Anyway, she said, he doesn't find me attractive. That meant what exactly? I didn't know. The thing was dead, I should have just buried it. I was holding back out of vanity perhaps. I walked home, passing pubs and cafés full of young nubile bodies and optimistic, sensuous faces. Look at them, I thought, living. I wanted to join in the exuberance, take off my shirt and throw myself in there, but I knew I would have only drawn blank stares or gasps of horror.

✝   ✝   ✝

Show me a few moves, I said to Giuseppe one overcast afternoon. Hey, he said, you and Melissa are finished? Well, I don't know, I said, why? Nothing, he said, I never see her with you anymore. Perhaps implying he had seen her with someone other than me. That was okay, he didn't have to spell it out. Take a swing, he said. I threw a wide right at his head. He redirected my arm with his just enough for my fist to miss his jaw. Then he used my momentum to pull me toward him in a circular motion, around and around, until I corkscrewed to the floor, my arm wrenched behind me and Giuseppe's knee in the small of my back. That was pretty cool, I told him as I jumped up, brushed myself off and stretched out a kink in my shoulder blade. I resented him for putting me on the ground. Let me show you something, I said. I had studied jujitsu as a teenager and still knew a few moves. Without too much difficulty I locked Giuseppe's left arm and forced him to his knees. His bald head turned red and he yelped in pain. I held on for a second or two longer than necessary before I released him.

✝   ✝   ✝

I think I might settle here, Antonio mused one evening. A friend at the Italian Consulate has promised to help me land a position. I have found a good rhythm in this city—his English still betrayed him, he admitted, so he preferred conversing with me in Italian. My Italian had improved a lot since I had met him. He corrected my more egregious errors and praised any progress I made. I must say that I'd grown addicted to our conversations; there's a music to Italian and an emotional register that English simply didn't have. I asked him how his love life was going. He removed his glasses and rubbed them with tissue paper. His brown eyes looked liquid and sad. My problem, he said, is that I like young women—in their twenties. Women in their thirties are bitter and I am not attracted to women in their forties. I'd like to have kids one day, perhaps sooner rather than later. I am fifty years old. I am not rich, nor am I handsome. All I have is my personality, my experience, my story.

✝   ✝   ✝

Somehow we wound up in the Beaches on our bicycles. Melissa insisted on stopping at Gary's house. He and his family lived near the water. I don't know why I agreed to go along. The sun must have burned my brain. He lived in a beautiful brick and glass home facing Lake Ontario. He was expecting us. Pleasant surprise, he lied. He had on shorts and sandals. His knees looked like ostrich eggs. His toes were broad and hairy. His wife and kids were out of town for a week. Can I get you guys a beer? he asked. I wanted water; Melissa nodded to the beer. I hated being there. I wanted to get on my bicycle and split. Gary led us into the back yard and showed us his garden. It was impressive as gardens go, but I didn't give a damn. I had to pee. Gary told me to go in through the sliding glass doors and turn left off the kitchen, last door. The bathroom colour scheme disturbed me: black and pink tiles, black and pink wallpaper, black toilet bowl and sink, black and pink soaps, pink toilet paper, and so on. I glanced out the window, which overlooked the garden, for relief. Melissa and Gary sat on a bench with their backs to me, very close together. Gary put his arm around her shoulder and said something in her ear that made her laugh. Then he kissed her neck and looked up at me.

✝   ✝   ✝

My head ached one morning over coffee. Sensing my pain, Michael spared me his jibes. I had to find a job; my funds were running low. I didn't know how I'd pay my August rent. Antonio came in for his morning espresso sporting an azure neck kerchief. The Italians were playing a World Cup qualifier. The bar crackled with nervous energy, the conversations loud, overly animated, a spastic restlessness afflicting everyone. Even Michael admitted suffering from pre-game apprehension. I asked who the Italians were playing but no one supplied an answer. Antonio said something to a man ordering espresso that sounded like normal, unaccented English—but I found such a thing so improbable I dismissed it and blamed the noise level for distorting what I'd heard. Antonio then turned and looked at me with such a strange expression; for a moment I felt I didn't know the man at all.

✝   ✝   ✝

Later that day I ran into him again and in contrast to his morning performance, he was effusive and chatty, grabbing my hands as he told me the Italians had won 2-0, Vieri and DelPiero providing the markers. What a strike force the *azzuri* had! I asked Antonio if he missed Italy at times like this and for a moment he looked mystified—then I realized I had asked him the question in English and restated it in Italian. He smiled and said yes, at times like this it would have been a joy to be in a proper piazza celebrating the great victory with his people. His chief criticism of Toronto was its lack of piazzas. Antonio ordered a beer from Giuseppe, who stood behind the bar, his head bandaged up with gauze and tape. He had said nothing about his injury but I felt obliged to ask. Mo, he said, lost his mind this morning. I don't know what I did to tick him off but I've never seen him so angry. Thought he was going to kill me. Maybe you should find another master, I suggested. That's what Mo said, Giuseppe muttered. Antonio joined two young ladies sitting in a booth. He appeared convivial, summoning every trick in his arsenal to charm them. They laughed at his audacity, his zest.

✝   ✝   ✝

Then one day on College Street little Domenic almost ran me over with his stupid mountain bike. Outfitted in a full riding kit, complete with cap and goggles, gloves, spandex trunks, and so forth, he hopped off his bike and grabbed my arm. Guess what Michael told me this morning, he wheezed. What? I asked. Turns out, Domenic said, that Antonio isn't so Venetian after all. He just taught English there for a couple of years, *English*. He was born right here in the hood. Moved to North York as a teen. Michael always thought he looked familiar—then his Uncle Alphonse spots the guy in the bar and swears they went to school together. Do you believe this shit? Wow, I said, not surprised but disappointed. I had a feeling Antonio knew more English than he ever admitted, but for him to carry on that subterfuge for so long was ridiculous, perhaps even pathological. I would have been pissed off if we were more than just acquaintances, but that's all we were, I couldn't call him a friend. If the guy wanted or needed to play the Venetian, power to him, but it had probably taken more effort than it was worth.

✝   ✝   ✝

Misery loves company—but I preferred solitude. My roommate Pat was off on another adventure—this time to Prince Edward Island for a cycling trip. I had the apartment to myself again and spent much of the time on my futon thinking about everything, often about nothing. I was too restless to read or watch television. I tried smoking pot but it made me paranoid. I was fucked. Though I fought the urge, I called Melissa. She never picked up. I left a few ludicrous messages, insulting her, accusing her of dishonesty, infidelity and so on, hoping to provoke a return call, even if to tell me to cease and desist, but she didn't call back. I rode my bicycle down to her house one night. The lights were on. I tried to get a glimpse inside through the curtained front window but I could see nothing. I heard music, however, and laughter, and I had half a mind to pound on the door and make a scene. I had been good for them in the past. But it was too late for scenes. I mounted my bicycle and rode home.

✝   ✝   ✝

My deepest apologies, Antonio said in perfect Toronto English, bowing his head a little and taking my hands in his. You of all people, he said, you who never presumed, never judged, and yet I've seen you suffering and you've never spared a smile or a good word. I beg your forgiveness. I've offended you and . . . He went on at some length. I told him to forget about it. I wasn't going to hold a grudge. We all have our reasons for hiding behind masks. Don't sweat it, I told him, all's forgiven. Today is a new day. He happily ordered two grappas from Giuseppe. Pour one for yourself as well, Antonio said. We clinked glasses and drank. It burned nicely going down, the aftertaste pinching my tongue. Several young women entered the bar in a swirl of perfume, hair, and sunlight. No reason to despair, I thought. There was a lot of summer left, and I intended to make the best of it. Just one more thing, I said to Antonio, still batting his eyes with regret and solicitation. Shall we continue speaking in Italian?

Ham and Eggs

Two men were beating another man senseless in front of a darkened
tavern. It was late, well past closing time. I watched in silence as the
two kicked the other into unconsciousness. His body and head
shook from the blows; his assailants didn't look like they intended
to stop. Under the gloomy street lamps their eyes flashed and their
leering faces shone. Except for them, and the unconscious man, the
street was deserted. They hadn't noticed me yet. I stood there calmly
watching as they continued to kick away, grunting with effort. Takes
some work to kick a man to death. A gun or a knife would have been
quicker but surely not as satisfying, and not as earned. Finally, I
stepped forward.

"Hey," I said.

My presence startled them.

"Who the fuck are you?" said one, taller and uglier than the other,
who was short and ugly.

"Don't you think he's had enough?"

"What business is it of yours, motherfucker?" barked the short
one.

"It's not any of my business. I'm sure he deserved the beating, but
unless this is a contract thing—I mean, what are we, animals here?"

The two looked at each other. The short one kicked the limp body
one more time and then approached me with his partner on his
heels.

The little man opened his yap as if to bark out something else, but

before he could I kicked him squarely in the chest and dropped him
cold. The tall one, surprised by the suddenness of the action, backed
off, turned around, and started running with a flat-footed gait.

Didn't take long to catch up to him. I tripped him and stomped
his face until it was unrecognizable. Then I dislocated both of his
shoulders.

Went back to the other short one. He hadn't gotten up, but he was
conscious, though his breathing faltered.

"Fuck . . . fucking . . . bastard . . ."

Sat on his chest and with my thumbs, pressed his eyes until blood
began to spurt. He couldn't scream; most likely the kick had cracked
his sternum, a horrible thing to suffer, but I'm sure he wanted to
scream, I'm sure in his way he was screaming. I slapped him a few
times, more for myself than anything. The slaps were the least of his
worries, the slaps. I had an idea. I dragged him to the side of the
road. Straightened his legs, positioned his feet on the edge of the
curb. Then I jumped on his knees.

The dude beaten up by the pair stood there.

"You . . ." His mouth gurgled blood.

"What is it?" I said.

He staggered toward me, clawing at the air with his bloody hands.
He was all broken, his intentions unclear. I stepped up to him and
cracked him one across the chin. He went down in a heap.

My hands ached as I walked home. What was wrong with people? I
hated all of them, all of them. They made me hate myself. They made
me hate myself and that was unforgivable. But I didn't know myself
back then. Things had gotten savage. I had to survive. The only thing
I had left was self-preservation.

The cockroaches rustled when I switched on the bedroom light.
Most of them scattered under the litter, but the bolder ones knew I
posed no threat. They never touched me and I respected them for
that, small hardy bastards. I saw genius in their form. What else
would you call it?

And just as I saw genius in all things, in all the myriad forms and
constructs, all the movements and machinations, I saw how even my

existence had genius guiding it, the genius of all things. But I needed to sleep. I needed to shut my eyes and clear my mind, for there was chatter filling it up. I touched myself. But no, I couldn't under the circumstance.

Unable to sleep, I got up and dressed. It was almost dawn. I stepped out. A fine drizzle fell, disturbing my eyes.

A large black dog came trotting toward me but he stopped abruptly and veered across the street. He knew better. Walking, walking. Pum, pum. And then it was morning. I found myself sitting on a bench near the harbourfront. Gulls, ugly gulls, filled the low grey sky. The lake looked like iron. My knuckles throbbed. I shook out my hands. A man on an orange bicycle pulled up.

"Yo," he said.

"What?"

"Whatta ya mean, what?"

The small pale globe of his face bobbed as he sized me up. His eyes looked like ink spots.

"What the fuck do you want?" I asked.

"Easy, big guy. I'm just seeing if you wanna buy some primo herb, see. I'm the man around here. If you want, I got, 'cause I am the man. Word."

"Get the fuck out of my face."

"Are you a cop?"

I stood up and pushed the bicycle over with him straddled on it.

"You fucker!" he cried. "You shitty fucker!"

Kicked him hard in the stomach and this brought quiet for a time. I pulled the bicycle away from his twisted legs. It was surprisingly light. I hoisted it over my shoulder and walked down to the concrete lake barrier. I heaved the bicycle into the water. It sank without a ripple.

The guy stood up now and ran toward me spitting and cursing, his arms akimbo. What did he expect to do? What did any of them expect to do? I flipped the dude and he went head over heels into the lake and sank like his fucking bicycle.

I walked away from the lake and found a decrepit diner up on

Parliament full of losers and drunkards. I wasn't hungry at all but thought I should eat something. I was feeling light-headed and perhaps even vulnerable. Little black asterisks floated before my eyes. They weren't unpleasant, distinguished by lovely movements and patterns. But they interfered with everything.

I ordered ham and eggs from the wall-eyed, grimacing waiter. He asked if I wanted a beer.

"For breakfast?"

"It's normal around here. No offence. How 'bout a hot cup of joe?"

"Okay."

Okay it was. The waiter walked with an ugly limp, his hand sprawling behind his hip, his shoulders jerking. Other patrons sat around sucking on their beers and smoking foul cigarettes, lost in their thoughts. The waiter returned with a plate of glistening ham and eggs. He refilled my coffee cup.

"Thanks."

"No problem. You're not from around here."

"No. So what?"

The waiter smiled with yellow cement teeth.

"What's so funny?" I asked.

"Truth is, no one's from around here. Everyone's from somewhere else. I'm from Wisconsin. Can you believe that?"

"Wisconsin?"

"Yup, that's right. Enjoy the grub."

He loped away. The food tasted bland, forgettable. I expected no better. I ate quickly, paid, and left.

The asterisks had all but dissipated, except for a stray or two which held on fluidly at the edges of my field of vision, and I accepted them for they garnished my reality, and I can't say enough about that kind of thing.

Where then? Nowhere, of course. I didn't want to go home but I had nowhere else to go. That didn't stop me, it never had. Step one, step two, step three, and so on. Well-fueled, I could go for hours.

I headed out to the west end. I knew no one out there. Everyone walked in twos or threes. Was it Sunday? I wasn't sure. I heard bells ringing. But they rang on Saturday also. In twos and threes, well dressed. I could not distinguish a single face among them, though I felt them studying me with aplomb.

I came to a green park. Some children played by the swings. A few adults stood aside, chatting, or taking in the cool damp air. The children wore crayon colours, slightly smudged. The adults looked like grey silhouettes, sombre, too serious for their own good. I glanced at my legs. Grey. I was one of the adults. But I was alone, childless, an intruder.

Quite possibly I was a threat. Imagine that, me a threat to children. They didn't know me. But they must have known I had a mother too once, that I was a child once. That indeed, I understood.

They didn't know I sought only justice. No, that's not it. I didn't know what I was doing. I've never known what I'm doing.

I'd be astonished quite frankly to find someone out there who really knows what they're doing. Those stepping forward claiming knowledge would be liars for the most part, bald-faced liars. Who can say with absolute certainty that they know what they're doing? I stood up straight, tilted my chin and thinned my eyes. Two women with pointed faces approached me.

"What do you think you're doing?" said one.

"Yeah," said the other, standing a yard or so behind.

"Is it a crime to take in some air?" I asked.

They looked at each other.

Was the truth too much for them? Or not enough? Didn't matter. They didn't bite.

"Leave."

"Leave or we'll call the cops."

"We know what you're up to."

"That's right. So leave."

I clapped my hands to my pounding temples and shut my eyes, hoping the ladies would just vanish. But when I opened my eyes they still stood there in all their righteousness, for they were righteous if nothing else, and had I been in their shoes, I would have been too.

"Okay, okay," I said. "But I have nowhere to go."

"Not here."

"No, not here."

I reached over and hugged the closer woman, taking her by surprise. Her friend yelped, mistaking my intentions, which I can assure you were pure and good. I hugged her warmly, but perhaps I did not know my own strength, perhaps I did, but I did not know how it applied to human beings. I felt her ribs crack beneath my arms. But surely she was too fragile. Surely I could not be faulted for her fragility. She passed out at my feet. Her friend shouted abominations and the children screamed as the other adults herded them together. Sirens wailed in the distance.

So I ambled away, with no bitterness, though confused, perhaps, by what had gone on, confused and perhaps a little sad.

I kept walking until my feet were sore. I had to sit down. I also needed a refreshing beverage.

A small café near an abandoned warehouse appeared. A rough place populated by grizzled bohemians and a sullen group with tattooed arms and metal things sticking out of their heads. I felt nothing. I ordered an iced tea from the bald barkeep. He had a nose-ring and a rod jutting out of an ear. His flat grey eyes studied me as he popped open a tin of iced tea and poured it into a glass.

"What?" I said.

"Do I know you?"

"I don't think so."

"No, man. I'm sure I know you."

"I think you're mistaken. I think I would remember a mug like yours."

"How's that?"

"I'm thirsty, dude. Give me my iced tea."

He flipped the empty tin in the trash and slid the glass over but continued staring at me even while I drank it down. I finished and rested the glass on the counter. He continued.

"Quit fucking staring," I said.

"You're a ballsy fuck, aren't you?"

"Hey, pal, what did I do to deserve this?"

"It's just your face. I don't like it."

"Just my face?"

"Yah, your fucking face. I hate it."

"Is that it? Is that how simple it is?"

He said nothing.

Why was I engaging? It could only lead to bad, it could only lead to harm. And what was he doing? Was he conscious at all? Did he have any idea at all? I paid him and even left a tip.

"I don't need your chump change!" he screamed, flinging the coins at me.

What then? What does one do then? I grabbed one of the wooden chairs and whipped it at the barkeep. Slow to react, he caught the brunt of the impact with his face. Then I picked up a table and threw it at him. The bohemians scattered. The tattooed people watched expressionless, impressed. I climbed over the counter and pushed the table off the bartender. Then I grabbed him by the jaw and lifted him to his feet. I head-butted him in the nose and he crumpled up, shooting blood.

I climbed on top of the counter and jumped down on him. I repeated this three times. Each time he grew softer. The tattooed people continued watching with blank expressions. What more did they want? What did any of them want? Then I walked home. I needed to sleep. I needed nothing more than to shut my eyes and sleep for one long blissful stretch, and maybe even dream a little. Dream about my childhood and my mother who loved me. Dream about the happy life that perhaps lay before me, glittering, full of flowers and music.

But I would not sleep that night nor dream of my sunny childhood, nor of my loving mother, nor of my merry future.

Denied even this. Denied.

I had to go back to the beginning, that was my sentence after all. To be caught forever in the loop. For where does one go when all is said and done? Where does someone like me go, except to where he started?

And at some point in my return, I revisited the dingy diner with the limping wall-eyed waiter.

"You again?" he said.

"Looks like it."

"Ham and eggs, right?"

"You're good."

"I know."

"And a beer, sir."

"Right on."

He lurched away. And I wondered how long he'd been doing this stinking job in this hole. There had to be something better out there, but what did I know? What did I know? I who kept moving around without purpose, yet purposeful, no? My hands ached.

At the tavern two men were beating a third, really pulping him. They grunted with effort. It made no sense for me to interrupt. They were doing something important. It wasn't my place to upset the natural balance of things, to impose myself gratuitously onto the polished act. It took practice to get those chops, and cunning to maintain the conceit. I was best off as a silent observer, taking mental notes, passing no judgement on the participants. They were like athletes, after all. As for the guy getting the beating, everyone gets a beating in the end.

Maid of the Mist

A group of deaf children came to the wicket with a tall man in a red blazer. A warm June day, not a cloud marred the sky, but thunderstorms had been forecast. Irene McBride counted out seven tickets for the children and a ticket for their escort. Had he presented a voucher from a tour company or a legitimate social agency, she would have given him a complimentary ticket, but the man paid in cash and didn't smile. He looked about forty, dark-haired, square-jawed, on the gaunt side. He reminded Irene of Jacob Tate, a man who had worked for her father back on the farm. Jacob was tall, had the same way about him and a similar face.

The man took the tickets from her. He wasn't wearing a wedding band. The gold pinky ring on his right hand featured a red stone, maybe a ruby. Men who wore pinky rings tended to be vain. The children signed furiously to each other and made guttural sounds as they waited for the boat. The man could not have looked less interested in boarding the Maid of the Mist, in viewing the Falls up close. Irene couldn't see a nametag or tour guide identifier on his jacket. The fine red cloth reminded her of an equestrian's coat, though its wearer looked too tall to be comfortable on horses.

As a child, Irene had ridden horses at the family farm on Garner Road. That was before the Falls became a mini-Vegas. They sold the farm when Daddy died, like others around them had sold, the land parceled off and turned into housing surveys or golf courses that stretched all the way to Thorold. What with the wineries and casinos,

and the Falls still drawing fourteen million people a year, the
Peninsula was booming. New attractions like the Great Wolf Lodge
kept the tourists in town for longer stays than ever. None of that
mattered to Irene; she preferred Niagara Falls when it was a hick
town and most of her family was alive. The man in the red blazer led the deaf children to the gates. He
surprised Irene when he stopped to light a cigarette. The children
paid no notice and smoking wasn't prohibited in the outdoor areas,
but the way he held the cigarette to his lips and drew on it with his
eyes half-closed and his head tipped back troubled Irene. Jacob used
to smoke like that. Before he skipped town he robbed her father of
some cash—she never found out how much, but her father cursed him
until his dying day. What became of Jacob Tate was anyone's guess.
Irene suspected that wasn't even his real name. In retrospect it
sounded made up. The man in the red blazer could not have been
Jacob. The resemblance was superficial, she concluded; Jacob would
have been almost fifty now, if not older.

The man turned around and looked in her direction. She doubted
that he detected her spying on him; the wicket's tinted glass obscured
the ticket vendors even up close. But maybe he had sensed her scrutiny.
Certain folks have a radar for that, especially those with something to
hide. He finished his cigarette and crushed the butt under the heel of
his big black shoe before rejoining the children. Irene wondered what
his story was. He didn't fit the profile of someone who cared for the
challenged. He didn't appear that interested in what he was doing,
scarcely looking at the kids, and making no effort to communicate
with them. She doubted he knew how to sign.

She watched him pass through the gates. She'd always liked tall
men. Even if their faces weren't perfect, they seemed more handsome than shorter men. She had dated a tall boy in high school.
Marty Banfield played on the basketball team and though he lacked
coordination and shooting touch his height made him indispensable.
But Marty was only interested in one thing and when she refused his
apish advances he stopped calling her. Back then Irene had a figure.
She had gained one hundred pounds since high school. One hundred

pounds. It seemed absurd to her. How had it happened in just ten years? Not a huge eater, a Pepsi addiction played a part. She drank it by the gallons and hated the sugar-free stuff. She'd tried switching to coffee, then tea, even fruit juices, but always returned to Pepsi.

A customer with a turban came to the wicket and asked if he could get a group rate for his party of twelve. When Irene quoted him the discounted price he balked.

"Only ten per cent?"

"I don't set the rates, sir." But she felt soft that day and after a moment's consideration offered to give him one ticket on the house. The man beamed upon hearing this and summoned his gang. He paid in American dollars with a favourable exchange rate.

"You are very honest people," he said.

"Excuse me?"

"People in Niagara Falls are very honest."

She almost warned him not to be too trusting of the locals, but maybe he was right after all. Most people she knew were decent. Maybe no saints and angels among them, but she hadn't met many compulsive liars or evil people in the Falls. A few rotten apples, of course. One day while she was visiting her mother in the cancer ward, a group of neighbourhood boys broke into her house. They stole her television, some jewelry, and ripped up the place. When she found out they lived around the corner—one of the sisters ratted them out— she felt sad, sad that these kids she thought she knew could be so malicious, so destructive. What if she or her mother had been home?

It smelled stale inside the booth. Irene opened a drawer and removed an aerosol can of air freshener. She pressed the nozzle and filled the space with a sickening reek of lavender. Now the booth smelled like a funeral home. As it was, dark clouds mounted in the western sky and the forecasted thunderstorm started banging its war drums. She hoped it would hold off until the deaf children completed their trip. She wondered if the man in the red blazer would stand near the rails and get soaked. Would the red of his jacket run? How awful that would be. The flimsy raincoats provided by the operators barely kept out the mist, let alone a real downpour.

A crack of lightning branching blue and electric from the sky sent a bunch of Italian tourists scurrying from the wicket back to their bus. The ensuing clap of thunder gave Irene such a start she almost fainted. She took a few deep breaths and unclenched her tight white hands. She suffered from high blood pressure, among other things, but refused to take medication for it. Another clap of thunder shook the booth. No one had been zapped on the Maid of the Mist, or so the operators claimed, citing a perfect safety record. The locals knew better. But why wreck the myth? It kept everyone eating and that was more important than getting a few facts straight. Lightning, not water, had been the culprit on more than one occasion, and those who knew that kept it to themselves.

The sky darkened. Raindrops spat down. Irene emptied the cash register and locked the money in a canvas security bag. She raised the CLOSED sign and exited the booth as the rain started pouring. Last time she tried to run she almost broke her hip. When she got to the staff room she was so drenched even her shoes squelched. Everyone had a little giggle about it, but they never went too far mocking Irene. They had seen her in pain over the years and would do nothing to hurt her. She laughed along with them, admitting that she moved like a turtle. No one there had anything to say about her weight; most of the gals were hefty, Irene not the biggest among them. Blame salt and sugar, twin balms for tedium: pizza, fried chicken, submarine sandwiches, burgers, fries, donuts, and chocolates someone was always selling for their kids. Right now they worked over bags of potato chips, crushing them with gusto. Fat Louie held a bag under Irene's nose but she craved a sweet. Fat Louie was the skinniest staff member. He loved the nickname. Joanna had given it to him. Joanna watched Irene dry her hair with paper towels.

"I've got a proper towel in my locker if you want to use it," Joanna offered.

"That's okay, I'm almost dry."

"You look like a drowned rat. Let me get the towel."

"Okay, Joanna. Sure."

Joanna had stolen her lunch from the staff refrigerator a couple of times. At least, Irene suspected her. All she had to do was ask and she could have probably had what she wanted. But it wasn't about asking or not asking; it thrilled Joanna to get away with stuff like that, small potatoes, nothings. Now with the towel, she must have been up to something. Irene wondered if Joanna was going to ask a favour, maybe a shift switch. When Joanna returned she tossed Irene a hunter green towel that smelled of the dryer. Irene rubbed her hair with it and dried her face and hands. The towel felt lovely, its smell, its softness.

A clap of thunder provoked a few yelps.

"You think the boat's back yet?" Fat Louie asked.

"Will be soon."

"It's really coming down."

"Where's Connie?"

Connie, the shift supervisor, was probably scolding the kids in the supply shed for something or other. Irene didn't know why they kept hiring summer students. They saved on their wages but what a pain in the ass they could be. Connie, a decent person, had been pushed to the breaking point and the season was just hitting stride. Everyone wondered if she'd make it through the summer.

"So, Irene," Joanna said, "anything exciting at the wicket today?"

Irene caught herself thinking about the man in the red blazer— was he wet now?—and Joanna sensed that something had happened.

"Come on, Irene, spill the beans."

The others paused what they were doing and listened.

"Well," Irene said, "just before the storm—and they're on the boat now—this man came in with some deaf kids. He was wearing a red blazer, really nice. Handsome, you know, tall."

"He's with Toronto Tours?"

They were known for crimson gear and the company logo of *TT*. Irene shook her head. "He wasn't wearing a uniform. Just the jacket and regular black slacks. He didn't have a crest or a logo, or even a tour guide pass. Nothing. Just this tall guy and seven deaf children."

"How do you know they were deaf?" Fat Louie asked.

"I saw them signing, dimwit. Anyway, just before the gates, the guy lights up a smoke."

Joanna furled her dark brow and turned her lower lip out. Irene's story dissatisfied her, bent as she was on gorier details. But Irene could not summon words to express the discomfort she had felt, the disquiet, as she observed the man. The others were patient. Irene often took time to spit something out, but she was no trifler.

"I mean, it was strange, him smoking around those kids, that's all. And he didn't seem that interested in them. I didn't see him signing. He reminded me of this crooked man who used to work for my father."

"How old were you back then?" Joanna asked Irene.

"He started for Daddy when I was twelve, and he stayed on for three years." Irene blushed and covered her mouth.

"Did you have a crush on that crooked man?" Joanna asked.

"What are you talking about? I was a young girl."

"You weren't that young, sister." Joanna leaned closer. "So you didn't have a crush on him?"

Irene stared at Joanna for a moment, then burst out laughing. Smiling like a giant Cheshire cat, Joanna slowly turned to the other women and they all started laughing.

✝   ✝   ✝

An hour later the rain abated. Irene finished off the shift feeling strange. Memories of Jacob Tate flooded back. Maybe she was too young for him at fourteen. But her body insisted otherwise and she listened to it. Back then sexual relations with a person under the age of sixteen constituted statutory rape, a charge Jacob dreaded. That's why he swore her to secrecy. Some nights he'd creep into her room or they'd sneak off to the barn or the stables for quickies. Irene's mother never suspected, but she was too boozed up on gin to notice anything. Her father had an inkling, but jealous and paranoid by nature, he would have been suspicious even if nothing was going on.

Before she met Jacob, Irene had never done anything remotely sexual. And he had not instigated the relationship. She had targeted him the minute she saw his broad shoulders. Indeed he expressed surprise and, initially, reluctance to go ahead. But in the end, she won out. That was the way she saw it then. Maybe his reluctance had been a ruse and he had duped her, like he later duped her father. But what did that matter? She loved him and she loved it. She loved the sex and felt no shame about it then or now. He taught her things, how to touch him, how to touch herself, how to move in rhythm and breathe and open herself to the experience. More than anything she remembered his smell. She recalled the tobacco on his breath and his fingers, and how he stank of sweat sometimes—she never minded that. She cried for days when he departed without saying goodbye. She cried so much her father caught on and then he wanted to hunt Jacob down and kill him. But all that passed, the sadness, the fury. Memories of Jacob receded, her father died, life continued. Yet here she was reliving them again. She let herself drift into daydream. It was him. It was Jacob. He had returned for her . . .

But no. He would have laughed at her, if it was him. My God, Irene, you're a fat horse! And look how handsome I've remained after all these years! But what if it *had* been him with those children? She would have said, Nice to see you, Jacob. At least time has been kind to one of us. The booth smelled musky. She looked forward to getting home and soaking in a hot bath with a Pepsi and a magazine. She locked up and carried her money bag to the staff room where Connie took it.

"Slow day, eh?" Connie said. Darkness circled her eyes and her hair cried for fresh bleach.

"The storm scared everybody off."

"Fired two of those brats today, Jody and that little creep Kyle. Caught them stealing candy from the snack bar. Hey, Joanna told me about some weirdo in a red blazer."

"Joanna should mind her own business."

"Well, at least let me in on it."

Irene blushed. "Oh, it's nothing, Connie. That guy reminded me of someone."

"The guy in the red blazer."

"The guy in the red blazer. He was with a group of deaf children. It seemed, I don't know, odd. He reminded me of this guy I used to know, but also something about him being with those kids didn't feel right."

"Did you think of calling security?"

"No. I had no grounds for that. It was just . . . Connie, it's a long story, and I'll tell it to you tomorrow, promise. But right now I'm dead tired and I'm going home."

Connie didn't press the issue. She squeezed Irene's shoulder and moved on to other business. Irene punched out and departed. When she got to her car in the staff lot by the old powerhouse her legs ached so badly she didn't think she could drive. She sat in the car for a few minutes until the pain subsided. She drove home, pit-stopping at a KFC for take-out.

Irene ate the chicken while she ran a bath. She couldn't believe how good it tasted, this food that was so bad for her. Then she eased into the tub with a bottle of Pepsi and a *Soap Opera Digest*. In the water her legs looked like the trunks of soft white trees. Her breasts ballooned above her thick waist and pushed out on her arms. Her nipples appeared darker than usual, almost purple. She had been with a man the week before, something she had put in a back drawer of her mind. She wasn't exactly proud of herself but didn't feel terrible either. The man, Tony, worked as a gardener for Niagara Parks. He was married with three children, a loser in every way, except that Irene turned him on. Flattered by his lust, she invited him over one day after work and they hit the sheets. She smiled as she recalled his wiry body, his horniness. She flipped through the magazine, unable to focus. The warm water eased her leg pains for the moment. She twitched her broad toes and thought she'd better get a pedicure.

✞   ✞   ✞

Next day, before Irene opened the wicket, busloads of Japanese waited to board the first run. It was a beautiful morning; a massive rainbow arched over the Falls and the mist rose like a giant white genie into the blue sky. The Japanese tourists milled about in yellow Maid of the Mist raincoats. Irene printed out ticket after ticket until

Joanna arrived at ten to relieve her. A red silk kerchief adorned her hair. She was always a little out of uniform, and somehow got away with it. But Connie dreaded a showdown with the woman, and who could blame her?

"So Irene," Joanna said, chewing a wad of cherry gum.

"Good morning to you too."

"Oh, yeah." Joanna frowned and stopped chewing. "Look, I'm sorry if I centred you out yesterday. My curiosity got the better of me. Anyway, accept my apology."

Surprised by her contrition, Irene let a hand rest on her shoulder. "You know, Joanna—it doesn't matter. The guy reminded me of my first. Are you surprised I had a first?"

"Of course not, Irene. I think you're a handsome woman."

"Handsome?"

After an awkward silence the two roared with laughter. Irene left the booth holding her stomach. She hadn't laughed like that for a while. In the crowded Table Rock food court, she purchased two cans of Pepsi and sat down at a table near the exit. She drank her first Pepsi in one go, and belched into her hand. Her sinuses rang. The food court buzzed with tourists and Parks employees but Irene recognized no one. Most of her colleagues took their breaks in the staff room. They loved to sit around gossiping and munching donuts or whatever else was around. Irene could only stomach so many of those conversations, their pettiness, their emptiness. She sipped her Pepsi and glanced at her watch. She had a few minutes left. She didn't want to be late or any good feelings Joanna had for her would be dashed. She was about to finish her Pepsi when a man in a red blazer asked if he could join her. She failed to respond for a moment, but snapped out of it in time to nod.

"Thanks," he said, smiling with very white but black-traced teeth, the veneers failing to mask the dark. "Place is crowded." He sat down and placed before him a lidded Styrofoam cup.

Heart pounding, Irene shrugged and almost giggled. What was this? She couldn't believe he was sitting right across from her. What were the odds?

He looked at her. "Forgive me, but have we met before?"

Irene smiled. "Yesterday. You were with the kids."

He locked eyes with her and pointed his finger. "Of course. You sold us tickets for the Maid of the Mist. Quite a thrill that was."

"Did you get caught in the storm?"

"Only the tail end. The lightning was brilliant. The children were delighted."

Irene smiled. "So you work with the kids?"

"I volunteer, yes, on my free time."

When Irene reached for her full Pepsi can she knocked the empty one to the floor. The man jumped from his seat and recovered it before it stopped rattling. He sat down again, stood the empty can beside the other one. She noticed that his red sleeves were dry and undamaged, as was the rest of the jacket. It had somehow escaped getting wet. She wondered if it was another one, identical to the first.

"You're not with the kids today?"

He smiled. "They're at the Butterfly Conservatory."

This made no sense to Irene, but she didn't want to be rude and press further. Besides, she felt strange in the hazy light of the food court, people shuffling in and out of focus, a muffled hubbub. She glanced at the man's face but couldn't fix on any of its details. Her heart continued pounding. For a second she thought she might faint—how horrible that would have been—but she sipped from her cold can of Pepsi and then held it between her wrists. This helped.

"Are you okay?" he asked.

"Yes, I'm fine," she said, unable to focus her eyes. She felt like a schoolgirl. It was ridiculous. What was she doing here? She glanced at her watch. She was late. But she didn't move.

The man pried the lid off his cup, the nails of his long fingers glossed and perfectly half-mooned. He pursed his lips and blew on the coffee, then sipped it with a soft sound. Streaked with silver, his brows and sideburns didn't match his thick black hair. How odd. Then Irene realized he was wearing a toupee. He was older than she had first thought. Beneath the collar of his black shirt lurked a wrinkled neck.

Under the table Irene felt his foot nudge hers.

"Well," he said, looking up from his coffee and squinting his eyes. "I see from your nametag that your name is Irene. Lovely name, Irene."

"Thank you," she said, taking deep breaths.

"Irene, Irene," he said, almost to himself. "Did you know that the name Irene comes from the Greek word meaning peace?"

"I didn't know that."

"Well, now you do." He flared his nostrils and reached his hand across the table. "Pleasure to make your acquaintance, Irene."

She stared at his hand. The ruby of his pinky ring shone like a little lamp.

Rocco

Rocco Schillaci regarded himself in the hallway mirror with some disappointment. Three years ago, at his son Johnny's funeral, the black suit was loose; and it fit perfectly last August when his father-in-law passed away. And now? It had been a long winter. He unbuckled his belt and let it out a notch. Yesterday, his cousin Joe Garzo died in hospital. Rocco had admired and respected Joe and had shared many fine moments with him and his family. Hard to believe he was gone. He'd been so fit for an eighty-year-old, sharp as a tack, even nimble. Then, a month ago, his abdomen swelled up. Tests revealed cirrhosis of the liver. The doctors could do nothing.

Isn't it cruel? Rocco thought, squatting and pulling at the seat of his pants. You dodge all the bullets of life, avoid the calamities, then you hit eighty and parts wear out, the machine breaks down. There's no escaping it. And if your body doesn't go, the brain turns to cheese. His maternal grandfather, Luigi, came to mind: he lived to be ninety-three but spent his last ten years counting and recounting a demijohn full of pennies. Rocco undid his belt another notch. Anyway, not likely he'd live to be ninety-three. He was fifty-five, smoked a pack of cigarettes a day, drank too much, and ate like a pig. He'd be happy to make it to eighty, he'd be lucky.

He smoothed his lapels and stepped out on the deck for a smoke. They'd be burying Joe the day after tomorrow. Why the wait? he wondered. Why the spectacle? Let him go already. Rocco expected his wife, Domenica, back any minute from Sunday mass. Only the second of May and the twin magnolia trees behind the wood shack had shed their blooms; now forsythia pushed up against the old stone wall and tulips crayoned Domenica's flower garden. The Schillacis had bought the homestead off Green's Road near Winona back in the spring of '75. It seemed they'd moved to the wilderness, but by the '90s Winona, Fruitland, Stoney Creek, and most land east of Hamilton had been developed. Rocco loved the big house and the three lush acres, a far cry from the postage stamp lots being parceled out now. A creek ran along the end of the property line, beyond a row of scrolling birches. Rocco used to walk down there to smoke and reflect. But after Johnny died he stopped going, less taken to reflection. The way he saw it, all riches and joys, poverty and sorrow, were meted out in this lifetime. And that was fine.

At Friscolanti's Funeral Home in downtown Hamilton, Rocco's brother Pepe greeted him and Domenica in the foyer. Pepe's wife, Petrina, in a drab purple dress, her black hair pinned back in a severe bun, didn't acknowledge them. She and Domenica weren't speaking; or rather she wasn't speaking to Domenica for reasons unclear. Four years Rocco's junior, Pepe looked it; the brothers came from the same mold. Yet they had little in common and seldom saw each other any more: each viewed the other's wife as shrewish and controlling. Rocco considered Petrina a sourpuss; nothing made her smile, and she had a way of spreading her misery. Pepe, who long ago had courted Domenica, thought her the ultimate opportunist. She had said at the time that he wasn't serious enough for her. Not serious enough? A year later she was married to his more "serious" brother.

"One by one they're dropping," Pepe said. "Petrina's Zi Tomasso died in Thorold last week."

"Sorry to hear. What of?"

"Stroke."

"How old was he?"

"Eighty-one."

Rocco sighed, passed a hand over his face. "Let's go out for a smoke."

"You know I don't smoke."

"Just step out with me."

Pepe rolled his eyes, put his hands in his pockets, and followed his brother across the foyer to the front doors. They exited into the fresh air. Rocco loosened his tie and lit himself a cigarette. "How are Caterina and Miccu doing?" He hadn't seen Pepe's children since Christmas.

"Good. They're good. Miccu just finished his third-year exams at Guelph, and Caterina is still with the City. And the boys? I saw Carlo at Maria's the other day."

"At my mother-in-law's?"

"Yes, I was dropping off biscotti my wife baked for her. Poor Maria. All alone in that house."

"And Carlo was there?"

"He was. He was clipping her toenails."

Rocco squinted and brought the glowing cigarette to his lips. He looked up at the sleek evening sky and exhaled a bluish plume of smoke.

A fire engine clanged and wailed in the distance. He glanced at Pepe's dull black shoes. Domenica wanted to take in Maria. His mother had been dead for years and, with the boys gone, rooms sat empty. But she hadn't asked yet, and he wasn't about to bring it up. Maria was a wretched hypochondriac. How ironic that her husband died first.

Ugo Troccoli, a friend of Joe Garzo's and Rocco's cousin by marriage, also stepped out for a smoke. He was a trim seventy-year-old, with cropped white hair and a raspy voice. "Rocco, Pepe." He gently shook their hands and took a drag of his cigarette. "The King is dead," he whispered.

"Yes," Rocco said. Ugo had given Joe the moniker during their poker-playing days for his knack of drawing kings.

"Rocco," Ugo's tone changed. "Isabella tells me you're getting rid of the Malibu."

Rocco grimaced at the thought of that rust-bucket. He had spent thousands keeping it roadworthy, yet neither he nor the wife ever drove it, and his sons had their own vehicles. "Yes," he said. "Cost me an arm and a leg this past year."

"My grandson Luca is going for his licence tomorrow. How much do you want for it?"

"Zi Ugo, I don't want anything."

"Is it certifiable?"

"I think so. The transmission's new, but the engine burns oil. It won't last the year. You can have it if you want."

Ugo seemed pleased. "How's your mother-in-law?" he asked.

"She's fine," Rocco said.

"But she was on her deathbed, no?"

The men burst out laughing.

"Ah," Ugo sighed, staring at the starry sky. "King." His black eyes moistened.

After the funeral home Rocco and Domenica stopped by her mother's house in Hamilton's East End. She had her hair in angry curlers and a trademark scowl pinching her face. She was eighty, always ill with one enigmatic malady or another, but Rocco suspected that she'd outlive them all.

"Hi, Ma," Domenica said, kissing both her cheeks. "We went to see Joe Garzo."

"He's joined Antonio now," she droned. "But that's okay. We'll be joining them too. We're all going there sooner or later. We're all in line. The other day, diarrhea. I almost died. When is it going to end? Tell me. All this suffering. When? Let me die. Let me die now. Rocco, you don't say anything?"

He shrugged.

"Yes," she said, "You too, my boy. You too. Don't worry."

Rocco endured her laments while Domenica made espresso. Maria and he had never gotten along. She didn't like him or his brother, considered them underachieving peasants. He had long ago stopped listening to anything she had to say. He shook his head as she went on. Life is a mess, he thought, watching her baleful mouth churn. It seems okay at times, but at bottom it's a mess.

When they got home, Domenica and he sat at the kitchen table. She peeled and sliced a couple of pears. He looked at his wife, at her pale familiar neck, at the thin blue vein faintly striping her temple, the soft cheek . . . He remembered the first time he saw that profile. His brother had just started bringing her around. She was all of eighteen, shy as a doe. Born in Serradifalco, Sicily, she had just emigrated to Canada. Rocco couldn't take his eyes off her. He hated coveting his brother's girl, but he sensed that she shared his attraction. And she did.

"What are you looking at?" she asked.

"You, bella."

But she frowned and stood up from the table. She moved to the sink, turned the tap on full. She was never good with compliments, he thought, as he chewed some pear and poured wine into a glass.

Later, Marco the second-youngest came by to borrow his mother's pasta-maker; he and his beautiful wife Giannamaria had invited friends over Friday evening for lasagna. She was five months pregnant. That girl was a miracle, a real mother's daughter. Her lasagna rivaled Domenica's. How she fell for Marco, of all people, was beyond him. He thought Marco the flimsiest of his five sons.

After one glass too many, Rocco started berating him for never going to his brother's grave site—he had skipped the funeral. Marco claimed he didn't have the strength. Didn't have the strength? What did that mean? There was no mystery to it, in Rocco's opinion. Marco's attitude reeked of self-absorption and cowardice. A man had to face up to his responsibilities. Rocco was curious to see how he would deal with fatherhood, and how he would measure up in the event of a *tragedy*. Tomorrow, May third, marked the anniversary of Johnny's death. Rocco had loved Johnny, his firstborn. Unlike the sombre, thin-necked Marco, Johnny could light up a room; Johnny had style.

"What did he ever do to you?" Rocco asked, his voice cracking.

Marco blinked.

Domenica put her hand on her husband's shoulder.

✤ ✤ ✤

Next morning, Rocco's hangover had fur and green teeth and was gnawing on his brain. He smoked a cigarette upon waking and moments later rushed to the bathroom to vomit. Oddly hungry after that, he went down to the kitchen and fried himself two eggs. Domenica had left a note: she'd gone grocery shopping with Carlo, and don't forget to shave, shower, and put on your black suit.

Rocco had booked the week off from his millwright's job at Stelco, using up accumulated lieu time. Twenty-seven years toiling with steel and it felt like it. His shoulder was acting up again—he'd injured it a few years ago in a fall off a scaffold. Given Joe's death and the anniversary of Johnny's death, it was a good time to take a break.

He ate his eggs with an end of Calabrian bread and some black olives, washing it all down with a half-carton of orange juice. He drank a shot of cognac, smoked a cigarette, and then felt better. He felt quite fine considering—that is, until Domenica returned.

"So you managed to get up, eh?" she said. "Didn't die in your sleep? Sounded like you might."

"Where's Carlo?"

"He dropped me off and went home. You'd better be planning to go back to work next week. I've had enough of you around the house. Want coffee? I see you already made yourself something to eat. You can cook when you have to, hmm? If you made a mess in the bathroom I'll cut your head off."

"Do you have to talk so loud?" Rocco pressed his fingertips to his temples.

Domenica brewed another pot of espresso and Rocco drank a sugar-thickened cupful with a dash of anisette. He smoked another cigarette. The telephone rang. Domenica answered. "It's Benny," she said.

Rocco covered his face with his hands. Benny was his youngest son and the brightest next to Johnny. But he'd been away at Dalhousie University for most of the last five years, and would be there for at least two more finishing his law degree. Rocco doubted he'd ever move back home.

"Your father's hung over."

"Dom—"

"Talk to him, Benny. Talk some sense to him."

"Domenica!" Why wouldn't she just let up?

She handed him the receiver. He glowered at her; he didn't feel like talking to Benny, at least not now. He put the receiver to his ear.

"Pa?"

"Yeah, Benny. How are you, son?"

"I'm good. Did Ma tell you I'm staying in Halifax for the summer? I got a clerical job with a big law firm."

"Yes, she told me. Good for you, Benny."

"Pa, are you okay?"

"I'm fine."

"Pa—"

"Don't worry about me, all right. I'm doing fine, kid. Anyway, I'm handing you over to your mother. Be good and call anytime."

Benny had something else to say, but Rocco returned the receiver to Domenica. She snapped it out of his hand and cut her eyes at him. He got up and went to the bathroom. He checked the floor for splatters. He blew his nose with tissue paper, flushed it down the toilet, watching the swirling water until it grew still. He flushed again. Then he studied himself in the mirror. His eyes looked ruined, heavy and bloodshot; his cheeks bulged and his skin was florid. He felt short of breath. The doorbell rang.

"Dom," he cried, "I'm in the bathroom!"

But the doorbell rang again: Domenica must have been out back. He dried his face and hands and hustled downstairs. He stubbed his bare toe against an umbrella rack and cursed. His brother stood there in a pale yellow jacket looking mournful.

"Pepe," he said, rubbing the toe. "I'm surprised to see you here."

"I'm on afternoons. Thought I'd pop by and pay my respects before I go in."

Rocco seemed puzzled.

"For Johnny," said his brother, frowning. "What's the matter?"

"Nothing."

"You look terrible. Are you ill?"

"You could say that."

Pepe shook his head. "You're drinking again," he said.

"Hey," Rocco snapped. "Did you come here to break my balls or what?" He felt his temper thrashing under the baggage of his hangover.

"Roc, I'm just saying . . ."

"You're always just saying."

Pepe's lips tightened.

"Anyway, forget about it," Rocco said, his head pounding. "Come on, I'll pour us an anisette."

"It's too early."

"Come on."

He led his brother into the kitchen. Pepe also worked at Stelco, as a crane operator. Rocco had helped him land the job after he signed on.

His relations with Pepe had never been close. Even as boys, Rocco had found his brother's stubbornness and lack of verve annoying. Yet these were predominant family traits. His father and uncles were mulish and dull, never in a hurry for anything or anyone. Rocco considered himself an exception, more like his mother and aunts who were attractive and shrewd. The brothers shared a resemblance, but Pepe was slimmer, his eyes heavy-lidded like those of their father and uncles, men who always looked half-asleep.

"Sure?" Rocco said, handling the anisette bottle.

"Yes," said Pepe.

Rocco poured himself a drink. In time Domenica joined them. She had been tending to her flower garden. Pepe hugged her and said a few quiet words.

"How are the kids?" Domenica asked.

"They're fine, Dom."

"Rocco, enough with the anisette!"

He looked up from the bottle, guilty.

"Coffee, Pepe?" she asked.

"Thanks, Dom. I will have a drop."

Domenica made another pot of espresso and they drank it in silence. It was different, a young man dying the way Johnny did; it

was different from breaking down in old age, or even meeting your
end in an accident. At least you understood the causes.

Johnny was thirty, entering his prime. The doctors called the
aneurysm an anomaly. Rocco imagined him standing in the hall,
waiting for an opportune moment to leap into the kitchen, hooting
and laughing. He saw himself jumping from his chair and hugging his
son, then grabbing his face with both hands and shouting at him,
Where the hell have you been?

But only the whirring of the refrigerator and Domenica's sighs
punctuated the silence; the kitchen remained unvisited, restrained.
Then even the refrigerator fell silent; Rocco found himself staring at
his wife, at his brother and, finally, at his hands.

After Pepe departed, Rocco returned to the bathroom for a shower
and a shave. This made him feel marginally better, so he popped a
couple of Valium and put on his black suit. The Valium was his little
secret. He'd convinced Domenica the pills were painkillers, for his
shoulder when it ached; but the truth was he relished their mindless
buzz, especially when he was hung over. He told Domenica he'd be
back by noon. He said he had to run a few errands, but he just wanted
to go for a cruise. He jumped into the pickup truck and headed to
Fruitland along Highway 8. The drive was pleasant, the escarpment
shagged with spring green, the sky a luminous blue. The Valium took
hold and he felt billowy and carefree. He stopped at a convenience
store outside of Grimsby and bought himself a package of mints. He
sat in the pickup for a few minutes sucking on a mint and feeling the
warm sun on his face. A blue jay flared by the open window, a cool
breeze gusted and he found the coolness delicious, hinting of pine
and the bright north, of freshness and hope.

He drove back toward Stoney Creek to his Aunt Carmela's house
off Grays Road. His Uncle Calogero was out buying lottery tickets.

"What would he do if he ever won?" Rocco asked with a chuckle.
The youngest of his mother's three sisters, Aunt Carmela was the
most beautiful. Rocco recalled what an elegant dancer she was. Time
had taken its toll, to be sure, but her sharp blue eyes still sparkled
and her carriage expressed a refinement and grace.

"I think he'd have an *infarta*," she mused.

Rocco laughed but his head felt thick, his face hot and damp. His eyes and nostrils burned.

"You look awful this morning. Coming down with something?"

"Today's May third, Zia."

She searched her thoughts for a moment, then her eyebrows arched. "Oh, Rocco," she put a hand on his shoulder. "I'm so sorry. I forgot—Johnny, of course."

He nodded. His aunt covered her face and wept. A moment passed. Rocco sat staring at the white tablecloth, a dull roar in his ears. Then his aunt, dabbing her tears, got up and prepared espresso.

All the strength seeped from Rocco's arms and shoulders. He had an overwhelming desire to rest his head on the table. He couldn't keep his eyes open. He just wanted to sleep for a while.

The doorbell—poorly installed by his uncle—issued a wounded carillon that roused Rocco from his stupor.

"Your uncle probably forgot his keys."

The doorbell clattered again. "Coming," she called, shuffling off to answer it.

Rocco stared at a framed map of Sicily on the wall. He had emigrated from Sicily when he was twenty, from the ragged town of Racalmuto. He had married his wife in Hamilton; his entire family now lived there or in Buffalo, except for a few distant cousins. He'd been back twice to his hometown but had found it stressful, too hot, too unfamiliar somehow. He didn't mind the seasons of Canada: even the long winters had their good points. Winona suited him just fine. He had endured the unspeakable poverty and corruption of the *miseria* in postwar Sicily, and the memory of it rankled. He had prospered in Canada, had raised five sons, had forged steel, and lacked for nothing. As far as he was concerned, Winona was God's country.

"Look who's here," said his aunt.

"Hi, Pa," said a familiar voice.

Rocco jerked his head around. His son Carlo, hand extended, stood there grinning like an idiot. He had on a burgundy costume that reminded Rocco of bellhops. All he needed to complete the ensemble was a little cap with a strap. Rocco blinked, automatically shook his son's hand. What was he doing here?

Carlo was an ambulance attendant. He'd bought a little townhouse in Stoney Creek, but Rocco saw him more than ever these days, and he had mixed feelings about that. He needs a woman, he thought. Or a hobby. Too much time on his hands. "No work today?"

"I've taken a few days off, Pa. Are you going to the cemetery?"

"I've got my black suit on, don't I?" he snapped, glancing at Carlo's tasseled black shoes. He didn't know what to make of this Carlo, his fair-haired middle son: he was a stranger. On the other hand, Aunt Carmela looked delighted to see him.

He presented a string-tied white box. "Canoli from Valentino's."

"How nice," said the aunt. "Will you have one, Rocco? More coffee?"

"No, thank you, Zia. I have to run."

"When are you and Ma going?" Carlo asked.

His tone annoyed Rocco, affected, perhaps insincere.

"One o'clock."

"I can't come at one. I'm going to Nonna's house to mow her lawn."

Rocco stared at Carlo. "Well, ciao, Zia, and . . ." he didn't complete the sentence, but nodded and departed.

✝ ✝ ✝

At Holy Sepulcher Cemetery, Domenica fussed around Johnny's grave site, picking off grass and bits of debris. She had brought a bouquet of yellow tulips and retied the crimson ribbon before setting them down by the headstone. She had on a pale blue dress and a white beaded sweater. Her eyes were dry, her movements happy and light. She didn't cry any more. She had cried herself out that first year.

Rocco felt lucky; the woman's heart was infinite, her loyalty and warmth, her concern immeasurable. Domenica's sons worshipped her. Mother's Day at their house was like a festival. Flowers, ribbons, cards, balloons, the boys spared no expense or novelty to make her feel special. On Father's Day they'd give Rocco lottery tickets or shaving supplies, as if he needed their gifts. But as he watched his wife kneel, eyes shut, hands folded to her breast, he knew she deserved nothing less. He gave the two of them some privacy; he lit a cigarette, and moved away between the headstones. He glanced over the names—he didn't want to know them. He popped a mint and screened his eyes. The sun blazed. He took off his jacket and loosened his tie. It's enough to know the names of your own, he thought. It's more than enough.

They left the cemetery and drove to their son Tony's house in Parkdale. Tony and his wife Barb had invited them over for a late lunch. Rocco was quiet throughout the meal, Domenica morose. They left Barb's cabbage rolls uneaten; usually they couldn't get enough of them. Tony, the second oldest, was a brooder, but there was something almost smug about him. He's content with who he is, Rocco thought. He's pleased with himself. Tony had the hooded eyes of Pepe, and Rocco's father and uncles. He had taken Johnny's death quite hard but hadn't dwelt on it and hadn't visited the cemetery in two years. But what was one supposed to do? Rocco already felt bad for chewing out Marco. Besides, he would never discuss these matters with Tony in Barb's presence.

Tony's bright blond son Julio injected some joy into the proceedings. Rocco thought the child all his mother, which could not have been a bad thing, Tony being so serious. He engaged Julio in a little game of peekaboo. When Rocco covered his face with his hands, Julio pointed and cried, "No, no, no!" When he uncovered his face, the child squealed with delight. If only everything were so easy.

They finished the meal with watery espresso and pastries.

Barb said, "Johnny used to love canoli."

Domenica forced a small smile and Rocco nodded. Barb reddened, concerned she had said the wrong thing, but Domenica reassured her, touching her wrist and saying, "Johnny was crazy about canoli."

When they got home, Domenica went straight to bed for a nap.

Rocco got out of his suit and put on a pair of loose-fitting pants and an old work shirt. He poured himself a brandy and took a seat on the front porch. The air had a pleasant bite to it. He sipped the brandy and swirled it around his mouth before swallowing. A bubble of warmth burst in his chest. He took a deep breath and shut his eyes. He could hear the breeze swishing through the silver maples on the other side of the road. An empty lot sat there, abandoned by a man who had bought it in the '70s but never built on it. Rocco didn't know why, though rumor had it that his wife had died, or divorced him.

Moments later Ugo appeared in his pearl-grey Buick, accompanied by a lanky adolescent whom Rocco recognized as the grandson, Luca. He forgot which of Ugo's four daughters was the mother. What a Lurch he was turning into.

Ugo got out of the car, but Luca stayed put. "Rocco," he said, approaching, "we've come to take that Malibu off your hands."

Rocco reacted with surprise. He hadn't expected him to collect it so soon.

"He got his licence this morning," Ugo said, jerking his thumb at Luca who looked on with his mouth agape. "I'm going to drive the Malibu back to my place and he'll drive the Buick. I'll get it certified tomorrow. Okay?"

Rocco started to say something, but stopped.

"Well?" Ugo said.

"Okay," Rocco said, suddenly bored by the whole thing. He had bought the Malibu for Johnny years ago. The kid needed a car, but what did that matter? Johnny had never liked it, not partial to the four doors and the dull brown exterior. He'd give Ugo the keys and be done with it.

Carlo pulled up in his dark red Saturn and tooted his horn twice. A startled Ugo swung his head around and cursed him in Sicilian. Carlo cried out apologies. Ugo turned to Rocco shaking his head. Rocco shrugged—what could he say? He wanted to weep and burst out laughing at the same time. Carlo waved to him. He sighed and nodded to his son, who had on sunglasses and was grinning. He was something that kid. They were all something.

Coop

"What do you plan to do with yourself?" I asked, staring at the youth's gap-toothed grin. "You turn eighteen tomorrow."

"I plan to party tomorrow."

"If you get busted you'll do adult time."

"I can do it."

He could do it all right. Ever since he was a toddler he'd been in and out of foster homes and group homes and hospitals and detention centres and high-risk youth facilities. I had no answers for him. I told him to sign a form.

"What is this?"

"A release of information statement."

"Why?"

"Just sign it, Coop."

He inscribed the spot with a childish scrawl.

"Happy now?"

"I'm not happy, Coop."

"What do you mean, you're not happy?"

"My wife left me last night."

"That sucks."

"It does. She left me for another man."

"I'd smoke the motherfucker."

"I know," I said. I put away all the paperwork, shut the filing cabinet and escorted the youth to the foyer.

"This is where we part company, Coop."

"It's been real."

"When you go back in, get them to fix those fucking teeth of yours. I hear they've got a great dental plan in adult prison."

"Yeah, right on. Maybe we can talk about it when *you* go in. I'll get them to give you the cell beside mine."

"Very funny, Coop. Very funny."

"Later, boss." He stalked off through the doors and out into the harsh sunlight.

The Dog Went Out and Sat in the Snow

A clear sky promised less grey that day, reason to crack open a bottle of champagne perhaps, and somewhere in Niagara Falls this might have been going on. Niagara Falls was all about what bubbled and foamed. I felt somewhat tingly, my skull, my skin, my heart, but kept my ebullience in check. February had just begun. We weren't out of the woods yet. Not by a long shot. A blizzard could strike at any moment and bury our optimism. Still, caught up in the dazzle, I found myself fighting back a smile. When was the last time the sun appeared? Maybe in November. I drank coffee by the living room window, watching people trundle back and forth across the frame, their faces all lit up. There were so many of them and yet I knew none of them. Maybe they were doing a loop, bit players recur in the movies. Watch the crowd scenes closely. Some change hats or coats. But here they never doubled their roles. In itself surprising. You'd grant at least one redirect to the source, to the home place, mission complete, reward or refreshment awaiting. But not insofar as I could see, though at times my eyes glazed over and the faces blurred together and I could not distinguish one from the other.

I heard a sound in the bedroom and wondered if the wife was waking up at last. The woman could sleep. I wished I could sleep like that, but I've never been good at it. Even as a child I had trouble sleeping, fearing the dark, fearing the strangeness of dreams.

I listened for another sound from the bedroom but only heard myself breathing.

The cream in my coffee congealed soon enough. The house was cold, but I wouldn't turn up the heat just yet. A big red sweater with a charcoal moosehead, black sweatpants, white tube socks: these kept me warm enough. The dog scratched at the side door. I let him in. He looked at me and yawned. I pulled his ear, he ducked his head, good boy. Stark contrast to yesterday's reaction, snapping at my hand. Lucky he misjudged. Had he bit, well. His was the good life. What did he want for? Not food or exercise, not toys or cuddles. The wife provided most of this. But I contributed to his life and his well-being in my way, walking him around the block, but not so often now. I hated walking now. At two hundred kilograms I was bursting at the seams and growing by the day. Bad food and my gluttony! More than anything I dreaded getting so big they'd have to bury me in a piano case. That would take the cake. Going out like that, mammoth, monstrous. Had I eaten more vegetables, more roughage, and so forth, things may have gone differently. But it was too late. I accepted that. I envied the dog in many ways.

Eventually the wife emerged from the bedroom in a loose red robe. She was shrinking.

"You're even smaller today," I told her.

"Thanks," she said.

"But it's something we should discuss," I said, and I meant it.

She dismissed me with a wave of her small blue hand. What was I to do? The woman had an iron will and a quick temper. I knew better than to push her. I could see her tiny feet under the robe, thrashing like hairless, emaciated mice. The dog howled like a wolf and the wife responded in kind. They howled for several minutes. I never joined them when they did this. It was their thing.

"Pick your poison," she said later, in the kitchen. Rashers of burnt bacon and sausages beside runny eggs. The dog simpered under the table, waiting for whatever fell his way. I chose sausages that squirted when I stabbed them with my fork. The wife crunched a bacon bit and mopped up slithery yellow yolk with a crumb of toast. The sausage smelled too porky for my liking but I ate it anyway. The wife would have taken offense otherwise, turned beet red and opened up on me. She had a mouth when she lost her temper. I knew she didn't mean all those things she said, but they stuck in my skin.

"Is it good?" she asked.

"Delicious," I said.

I excused myself and hustled to the bathroom. I tried to bring it up quietly but my system betrayed me with horrible gargling sounds and something akin to barking. My stomach squeezed and heaved. It all came up in the same order I'd swallowed it. I returned to the table ready to give it another go.

"Are you in a funk?" the wife asked me, dwarfed by her high-back chair, her voice a trill. When I failed to reply she leaned forward and said, "Tell me what's the matter."

But what was I to say? Your shrinkage horrifies me? But when did it begin? I found it hard to recollect. Things sneak up on you. Day by day you notice nothing changing—but, in increments large and small, everything changes. I thought about the weight I had put on and how suddenly, one day, it occurred to me that I was *obese*. Not just plump or fat, but morbidly obese. The dog emerged, baring his teeth, one blackened by a cavity, a visit to the dentist imminent if the dog lived. I would do that for him, if he lived. He studied my wife. Unsure of his intentions, I banged the table with my fist. He glared at me.

"Bad dog!" I shouted.

"He doesn't know any better."

"On the contrary," I said. "On the contrary." I tossed him a sausage and he snatched it out of the air like an acrobat; he could do that for food but not for sticks or frisbees. His will matched that of the wife. He would not cur to me, not this dog, and despite the rancour it sometimes stirred in me, I found that admirable. He gulped down the sausage without chewing and sat there licking his chops, waiting for more, then looking almost puzzled. He tried his puppy face. The puppy face worked for years to solicit whatever he wanted, but it had lost its efficacy. With no more sausage forthcoming he dropped the act. Moments later he scratched the door to get out.

"You know better than to feed him sausage," the wife cried from the folds of her red robe. "It repeats on him."

I had to be delicate with her, my pinkies extended. She looked as fragile as a china doll; the slightest force might fracture her. No, I kept silent while she chewed on a crumb of bread, chewed and chewed. My heart ached for her at that moment. We had been through so much together, so many ups and downs, so much joy and sorrow. Fill yourself up, I thought, do it, honey. Eat until you're bursting. And she gave it hell. But she was getting small, smaller, smaller, exponentially diminishing. Her tiny jaws worked. Her little peep eyes blinked and blinked. Her pinhole nostrils glistened. Such effort she put into it, a simple act like eating. She tried so hard. What a fighter, fierce in her way, but so delicate, such a flower. She tired, poor thing. She told me she needed a nap and excused herself, dragging the robe behind her like a parachute.

Sunlight poured like corn syrup through the east-facing window, and once again I found myself smiling and fighting off the smile. I had no reason to be smiling. But I truly felt that somehow things would sort themselves out, that the presence of the sun alone guaranteed a positive outcome, as it often does. Maybe all I had to do was go back to bed and fall asleep and when I awoke the queer dream that this was would be over, the wife would be normal again, and life would be better than ever. But as I said, I was never much of a sleeper. I rapped my knuckles on the tabletop. Then I bit the base of my thumb. I pinched the fat of my left upper arm. This was no dream. I returned to the food. My egg had congealed on the plate and I refused to touch the fleshy sausages, but I ate bread and drank more coffee and soon felt that I could get through the next few hours without fainting.

I went out with the dog. He sat on a pile of snow. Red tongue flopping, he fixed his gaze on something in the tree. "What are you looking at?" I asked him. Maybe a squirrel perched in the snow-covered branches mocked him, and he'd have none of that, not from a squirrel, but I saw nothing. The dog often reacted to things not there, or things invisible to me. "What's that, boy? What is it?" But he reveals nothing. Not pleasant to imagine he could sense things I could not. Not pleasant to observe him staring at the tree in that fashion, trembling, no, not trembling, like I in my massive body trembled, studying something there that I was not privileged or sensitive enough to see. Maybe that was my problem, my inability to see things right before my eyes. They had to sock me in the nose for me to see them, to acknowledge they were there. This came as a grim self-revelation. This told me I was not just a gluttonous man, an oaf, a lout, a sloth, an unmotivated lay-about, but I was selfish as well, so self-absorbed I couldn't see the trees for the forest.

The dog suddenly lost interest and led me to the snow pile near the shed where he had puked up the sausage. His eyes drooped on cue. Good dog, that's right. Bad sausage. So what are we gonna do about it, dog? Puke it up, move on. Everything should be that simple. Go through your progressions, make a throw. Don't hang in the pocket too long and take a sack. Chuck it away if nothing is there. You'll live to see the next play. I threw my hands in the air as if I had just scored a touchdown. Yes! I am the champion! I am the champion of the world! These gymnastics tired me. But what a fine day it was. To have all these thoughts. To be alive, thinking and witnessing the wide world around me. The dog snuffled the snow, rooting out a grey vole and then watching as it shot across the ice-crusted path and under the neighbour's privacy fence. The dog looked at me. And if he had shoulders, the dog would have shrugged and then gone on with his business. It was what it was. Still, I felt too tense to appreciate the pale blue sky and the light scudding clouds and the sparkle of icicles melting from the eaves of the bungalow. The cold air nipped my hands and ears, and loud and mournful barking from down the street made me go inside sooner than I wanted, and then I had no choice but to deal with the vanishing wife.

She lay on the pillow fast asleep, her tiny naked body covered only by a handkerchief. I gently touched her abdomen and she stirred. "How are you feeling?" I asked, for I could only imagine. Her eyes popped open and then her mouth issued a squeak. I couldn't help but chuckle at this sound, to which she took offense, shaking her little

fists at me and squeaking some more. Regaining my composure, I
asked if I should call a doctor, but perhaps I should have suggested
this long ago; that she hadn't mentioned a doctor herself eased my
conscience, though I knew that some form of punishment awaited me
nonetheless.

What can I say? She was strong-headed. Very much her own person. She never changed her last name when we wed. We kept separate
bank accounts, held different religious beliefs, and—except for
breakfast—ate vastly different things at different times of the day.
That being said, even after seven years of marriage, we still managed
to make love once or twice a month. Not bad when you think about it.
Now lovemaking was out of the question.

"I would ask you," I said, "how this transmogrification came to
be, but frankly I'm afraid of what you'll say, so I won't."

She squeaked.

"Honey," I said, "keep calm, no need to get in a tizzy. I'd take you
to the hospital, but don't you think it's a bit late for that? Don't you
think we should have moved on that earlier? I would have taken you
myself, or at the very least called a cab. Now what? Eh?"

She squeaked.

I prayed for divine intervention. I shut my eyes and prayed. I
waited several seconds, hoping that when I opened my eyes everything would be back to normal. Please God, I pleaded, please. Fix
what is wrong here. Perform a miracle for us. I who never prayed for
anything beg you to . . . I heard a squeak before I opened my eyes and
my heart sank for I knew what that meant. God wasn't there for me. I
prayed and He did nothing. Now I knew why I never prayed. But perhaps there was nothing metaphysical about the transformation.
Stranger things have happened than people shrinking. A neighbour's
cousin was a victim of spontaneous combustion. All they found of the
poor bastard were his charred boots and an ankle bone. But thinking
of these anomalies, these freakish occurrences, did not mollify my
growing anguish.

How would I manage on my own? I mean, without my wife's
help? For instance, I had trouble getting in and out of the tub, and

her assistance proved invaluable. She would push my buttocks over the lip of the tub and facilitate my entry. Then when I was done, I'd call her and she'd come and grab my arm and pull with all her might and somehow yank me out of the tub. And she gave me fabulous foot rubs, my God, she could turn me into jelly when she worked over my feet. My weight had doubled since we married, but she swore it made no difference. A fellow could get self-conscious, but other than calling me a lard-ass on occasion, something I deserved, she tried very hard not to offend me and not to make me feel terrible about being so fat.

The dog bayed and I raced out of the bedroom, stumbling in the hall, knocking down a portrait of my mother-in-law and a green vase on a table that shattered into a million pieces. Jesus Christ, I thought, everything is held together with spit. In the yard, the dog and a black squirrel squared off by the maple tree. The beady-eyed squirrel made a strange rattling sound. The stiff-legged dog snarled and humped his back. And as much as I wanted to see a good scrap, I feared for my dog's eyes. Squirrels must be ambushed to be vanquished without injury. They have a genius for gouging out the eyes, they go right for them. This one readied to spring, ogling the dog's corneas like they were candies. The dog stood no chance. I clapped my hands and whooped. The squirrel climbed the tree and then sat on a branch glaring at me. I picked up a stone and flung it but missed completely. I picked up a second stone and pulled back my arm but the dog jumped me before I could hurl it. "What's wrong with you!" I cried. He pointed his nose at a stone bigger than mine. I dropped it, picked up the bigger stone and once again pulled back my arm.

The squirrel escaped a direct hit, but the stone struck an overhanging branch and knocked snow down upon the startled critter. Fury best describes the reaction, but what of it? What a sunny day it was! The sky so blue you wanted to eat it. Birds chirped in the branches. Cats stalked around. Soft white mist swelled and swirled from the cataract like a pleasant, benign tornado. It wasn't spring yet, but the air held forth cool promise.

After all the stress, the dog drowsed by the shed with the sun warming his matted fur and highlighting the foxy red in his tail. He was a handsome dog, and for the most part not annoying. The snowmelt tinkled down the drains and vapours rose from heating snow piles. But despite this winter beauty a black cloud hovered over me, over us. I was sad my wife couldn't be out here to enjoy the beauty. Then an idea occurred to me. I went back inside and took a wicker basket out of the pantry. I layered it with cotton batting and linen napkins. I carried it into the bedroom and set it beside the wife. She squeaked, and I didn't know if she was happy about it or not. I gently picked her up and lowered her into the basket. She was so small her gesturing signified nothing to me. Anyway, I transported her to the yard. The dog jumped to attention.

But the cold air must have affected the wife; I heard a couple of tiny yipping sounds that I realized were sneezes. Poor little thing. And I had no tissue to offer. I leaned down to her and spoke in my softest voice. "Do you want to go back in?" I asked, but she squeaked. I had to squint to make out the features of her face. She was either smiling or grimacing, same difference. But I felt the bottom falling out of my life. And I could do nothing about it. This was beyond me. The dog sniffed under the basket and then presented his tongue. What did he have in mind? What was he feeling at that moment? Did he understand what had happened to his momma, no bigger now than the vole he startled earlier?

Maybe I have never been a grounded individual. There is a fine line between normalcy and deviance. Well, that's just it. Veer one degree to the left or to the right and in time you are irrecoverable, skirting distant galaxies, alone and afraid. I fear nothing now, having lived through that day. And later on that evening, as I stoked the embers of the fireplace and gave the dog a nudge and peeled a few roasted chestnuts and sipped a goblet of port and watched the basket where the wife slept, I felt at peace. Then the dog started scratching to go out again and I went with him to take in some air. Orion's belt glittered like rhinestones in the black impasto and the moon loomed like a giant Pierrot's head. The dog scuffed around the shed and peed while I listened to the world and what it was telling me.

Grassy Brook Trail

Josh Grenier squeezed on his red parka and hesitated for a moment in the doorway of the Port Robinson Youth Centre before he stepped out into the frigid air. It had snowed all day, but the roads remained unplowed for the most part, the going slippery. Screeching children tumbled and tobogganed in the nearby park. A cone of smoke ascended from the stone chimney of the ancient toll building at the end of the street, a structure of historical significance, occupied by a shadowy custodian. All good but for the thick white blanket. A ghost town like Port Robinson fell last on the snow-remover's list.

With great difficulty, Josh climbed into the waiting white van. It smelled like burnt hair in there. One of Josh's counsellors, Marty Bush, sat in the driver's seat sucking on a lollipop and tapping together his steel-toed boots. He glanced at Josh with his sharp blue eyes, and gestured for him to do up his seatbelt. Josh's ample girth complicated the task. The van rocked as he worked the belt around his belly. Marty glared at him with annoyance. Finally, Josh managed to secure the seatbelt.

The van crunched out of the snow-banked parking lot and skidded into the street. A discarded Christmas tree laced with tinsel jutted out from the curb. Marty steered around it and tapped the brake pedal as the tires caught a patch of black ice. The van swerved through the black ice and hit the salted intersection, coming to an abrupt and gritty stop.

"Where are we going?" Josh asked.

"For a drive in the country," Marty said. "It's part of your therapy."

"It's almost dark out."

"Yeah, I know."

Josh's plump fingers drummed his thighs as the van sped by stands of snow-capped trees and the white monotony of the surrounding landscape. Low, leaden clouds filled the sky, promising more of the same. Josh pushed his thick glasses up his small nose and sniffed.

Bothered by the icy windshield, Marty blasted the defroster and rubbed the back of his gloved hand on the glass to no effect. He gnashed his teeth and slammed his palms against the steering wheel. Then he raised the volume of the radio, set to a call-in sports station. He listened for a minute, tilting his ear to the speaker and sucking on the lollipop.

"So, Josh," he said, turning to the youth, "I've been wanting to talk to you."

Josh could barely hear him over the radio chatter. "About what?"

Marty lowered the volume. "Hey, man," he said, removing the red lollipop from his mouth and pointing it, "have I ever treated you badly?"

Josh frowned and pushed his glasses up his nose. A smattering of acne reddened his wrinkled forehead.

"I'm talking to a wall," Marty said to himself.

"No," Josh said. "You've been okay. Why? What's this about?"

"What's this about?" Marty pulled the lollipop from his mouth again. "Josh, let me ask you something. Why don't you ever hang out with people your own age—fifteen-year-olds like Ryan and Jesse? I mean, why is it that every time I see you in the recreation room or in the hall, or near the washrooms, you're hanging out with little punks like Daniel?"

"Ryan and Jesse are bullies. Daniel's my friend."

"That's nice. Daniel and Josh. Like Beanie and Cecil . . . okay. I've seen you two wrestling around. You must be four times bigger than Daniel, swear to God. I know he's twelve, but he's more like an eight-year-old. You could crush him."

"He likes to play-wrestle. He starts it."

"Bet he does. Daniel's not all there, is he?"

"He's just different."

Marty crunched on his lollipop. "I know, I know, Josh. *Vive la dif-ference*, is what the French say. Ah, those French. I love Montreal! Love it. Some day I'll visit Paris, mark my words. I want to learn French proper before I do that, though. Maybe I'll go to night school. Your name's French, but of course you don't speak French, do you Josh? Didn't think so. That's a shame. Look at me yakking away like there's no tomorrow. And I haven't asked you how you're doing, Josh. How *are* you doing? Fine? Okay. I can see that. Hale and hearty. Fit as a fiddle, except for the asthma, right? Still on the puffer? How about a refreshment? How would you like a nice hot chocolate. I know you like your hot chocolate, boy."

Josh said nothing as Marty pulled into a drive-through donut shop. He placed the order into the box on the post and eased the van forward into the pick-up circle. The woman serving Marty retracted her lips, showing dead front teeth. Ball-bearing earrings pulled down her yellow lobes and her hair looked scorched. A strange crush of people dressed in black crowded the space behind the woman, argu-ing, clanging metal objects. Were they other workers? Patrons? She handed Marty two beverages, and a box of donuts. He paid, grumbled something—not thanks—and she made a gurgling sound. This amused Marty and he clapped Josh's knee. The knee smarted for some time.

As the van exited the coffee shop, a slushy compact car cut in front of it. Marty slammed the brakes and palmed the horn. The blue-haired woman piloting the compact froze upon hearing the honking and remained that way until Marty inched the van right up to her rear bumper and hit the high beams. Then she lurched ahead, just missing an oncoming Coca-Cola truck. Marty swung his head around with his teeth bared.

"She could have died right there and then, man! Holy shit! It wasn't her time though. See what I'm saying? It wasn't her time." He pointed to the donut box. "Help yourself."

"I'm not supposed to eat stuff like that."

"Hey now. I'm the one calling the shots here. Like I said, this is all part of your therapy. If I say it's okay for you to crush a few donuts, what the hell."

Up ahead a blue-lit tow truck yanked a car out of a ditch with a steel cable. The owner of the car, a man with a flowing white scarf wrapped around his neck, stood there clapping his hands and jumping up and down. Marty waited for the tow truck to pull the car closer to the shoulder before he passed. The tow truck driver gave them the finger. Josh burst out laughing.

"Funny stuff, eh?"

Wheezing with laughter, Josh nodded.

"Good, laugh it up. Laughing's good! And eat the donuts. Go on, don't be shy."

When he settled down, Josh reached into the box and selected a honey-glazed. His pale fingers held it to his lips and his nostrils quivered as he bit off half of the donut and chewed. He finished it and took another out of the box. He made short work of that one too. Sugar crusted his lips. He gobbled three more, spilling oily crumbs over his chest. Marty nodded and smiled as though he knew exactly what was happening and how good, how incredibly good, Josh felt at that moment.

"It's nice to see you in your natural element. Swear to God. It's cool. Complete license. Eat till you drop. Fucking-A. I would have taken you to a Chinese buffet and let you vacuum down some chow mein and egg rolls but this is way better. This is pure. Sugar and fat, that's what it's all about."

"You're talking a lot of garbage."

Marty chuckled. "I know, I know. Way to go, man. You're cranking those things down good. Hey, save me one or two—just kidding! I don't go for the donuts, my cholesterol. But you don't give a shit about that. You're grooving right now. Nothing else matters."

Josh gulped his hot chocolate. He reached for the donut box but withdrew his hand at the last moment. Marty had turned off the main road.

"Where are you going?"

"Ever been to Grassy Brook Trail?"

"Yeah, with my father once. We went horseback riding. Along the river."

"That's right. There's stables. Pretty country. Must be picturesque with the snow. I saw horses out there the other day. Nice."

"Are we going horseback riding?"

"Have another donut, Josh."

"I've had enough donuts. I want to return to the Centre."

"What? And miss the surprise?"

"What surprise?"

"Wouldn't be one if I said what it was, would it?"

"Take me back to the Centre."

"Not now, pal."

"I don't like this. I'll file a complaint."

Marty wasn't smiling. "Shut the fuck up and eat another donut before I clobber you."

Josh resisted for a moment then grabbed a double chocolate and crammed it into his mouth. His cheeks and the blubber folds under his chin trembled as he chewed. Sweat streamed down his forehead. Snot flowed from his nose. Sugar and fat coursed through his veins. He drank more hot chocolate, took deep breaths, his heart thumping.

Snow blanketed the new golf course and grey ice plated the still active river, walled for long stretches by tall grey reeds. They passed red stables with black horses steaming in front of them. A series of beautiful ranch-style homes hugged the riverbank.

Marty drove past the buildings and turned down a deserted stretch of road. He pulled the van over and parked by a snowy field but didn't kill the engine. A flock of black birds rose up from the fence and clamoured in the twilit sky before setting off en masse across the river. Josh tried to undo his seatbelt but couldn't worm his hand to the release. Marty sat there gripping the steering wheel, humming a tune. Josh wheezed. His hair dripped with sweat. He reached into his pocket, took out his puffer and inhaled a blast. He rolled down the window a little. Cold air gusted into the van.

"Feeling better?" Marty asked after a moment. "Thank God you remembered to bring your puffer. Imagine if you had forgotten it. Jesus. And I don't know CPR—just kidding! I'm certified, I know it well. I would have saved you. It's warm in here, eh? Undo the seatbelt. Take off the parka. Relax. This is pretty country, no one around for miles. It's therapeutic. Here, let me help you." Marty unlatched Josh's seatbelt and then with considerable effort pulled off his parka. Sweat blotched Josh's grey sweater; a sour milk stench filled the van.

Marty switched on the radio and the sports guys continued blathering. He found a classical station, sat back and spread his legs. Nice listening to this stuff now and then. Violins and oboes soothed a body. Snow fell, large lovely complex flakes, feathering the windshield. Marty chuckled to himself, switched on the wipers, and sipped his coffee. What a perfect moment. Everything harmonious, in rhythm. He shut his eyes and listened. What else? A million things. He could talk about a million things right now with the right person. He turned and looked at Josh.

Josh shifted his haunches. Sweat trickled down his ass. Marty kept staring at him with his mean blue eyes. What the hell did he want?

"Christ, you're humongous," Marty said, "and only fifteen! I remember when I was fifteen. That's when I started getting interested in girls. Are you interested in girls, Josh?"

The youth frowned. "Why would I be interested in girls?"

"I mean, you know, sexually. You're not gay, are you?"

"I'm not gay."

"Well, Josh, I'm not trying to pry, but I can only help you if I know where you're coming from. I know you're self-conscious because of your obesity. But you must have sexual urges by now. I see a bit of facial hair sprouting, I hear the deepening of the voice. It must be happening, no? Help me to understand you." Marty waited.

"Girls are cruel," Josh blurted.

"Cruel, eh? Yeah, they can be. Boys, too. Make no mistake. Boys too. Josh, just one thing, I noticed that you like drawing stick figures in your sketchbook."

"I'm not very good. So?"

Marty leaned closer. "No, but you *are* good, Josh. That's the thing.

There's a very expressive quality about them. Look, I brought one with me." He pulled out the sketch and held it up. "This was the coolest one. I want you to explain what it means. Is it a dream or something?"

The sketch consisted of a stick figure and a larger, rounder shape joined by a thin line.

Josh stared straight ahead with his arms folded over his gut.

"See, Josh. It's not just a stickman like the others, there's also that big balloon thing, eh, with the string. But my, that balloon is big. And it's not really floating, is it? Like it was too heavy or some-thing."

"I don't know what you're talking about."

"The balloon man, silly. I was looking at it and boom, it came to me. Swear to God. Check this out: the stickman is Daniel, and the balloon man is *you.*"

"You're crazy."

"Not so crazy, Josh. Come on, it's me. Marty. I've been good to you. I want to *help* you. That's my job. So tell me about Daniel."

"Daniel's my friend."

"No, Josh. He's out of it. He's fucked. He lacks affect. He's not capable of true friendship. He's like a doll. Or a puppet. But you know that." Arching his eyebrows, Marty mimicked a diabolical laugh. "I am not afraid of you, Dracula! Just kidding! Come on now, Josh. 'Fess up! Be real! Bare your soul to me, brother, let the healing begin. I know you know the difference between right and wrong, but you can't help yourself. Is that it? I totally understand. I *empathize.* Believe me, Josh. I feel you, man."

Tears filled Josh's eyes. "Daniel and I are friends."

"Aw, touching. I'm touched, really. Young love. It's fucking Shakespearean, I tell you. And maybe in some world, in some sick, fucked up, degenerate, madcap world, such a union would be sanc-tioned, even encouraged, but not in this one, Josh. Not in Marty's world. I am not—I repeat—I am not a horse's ass. Do you think I'm a horse's ass, Josh?"

The youth shook his head.

"Good answer, boy. You saved yourself a slap in the chops. So, the question is, what do we do with the young monster? Do we train him to be civil, to repress his ugly urges? Or would this just teach him how to blend in, how to mask who he really is and who he will always be? Because let's face it—Josh will never change. He hasn't changed thus far. If all interventions and therapies have failed, what can anyone expect Marty to do?"

"You're talking garbage."

"Is that right? I've been at this for a long time, boy. One thing I know. If it walks like a duck and quacks like a duck . . . See what I'm saying? Now get out of the van, Josh."

"What?"

"Get out of the fucking van."

"I won't do it."

Marty punched Josh hard in the ear then punched him again, knocking his glasses off his face. Then he hauled Josh out the van, flung his legs out from under him, and started kicking him with his steel-toed boots. One of the blows cracked Josh's ribs. He grunted in pain, unable to draw a breath. Marty continued the assault, pumping his thighs, digging his boots into Josh's body. Gasping for breath now, Josh pitched himself sideways. He tumbled into a deep snow-bank, bleeding from the nose, his mouth gaping. He didn't even try to get up; a light layer of snow covered him. Marty watched for a moment, grinning. Then he returned to the van, climbed in, shut the door, and roared away.

The wipers thwacked back and forth. The headlights illuminated nothing but a whirling wall of white. Crosswinds shook the skidding van. Marty leaned on the steering wheel and strained his blue eyes for the main road, but didn't see it or anything else for that matter.

The snow whipped down, big fat flakes.

Outside

Larry Ostrander's latest counsellor, this guy named Miguel, took himself too seriously. When they first met, Larry didn't like him. He struck him as a bit of a blowhard. He swore a lot and seemed to have a bad temper brewing underneath the surface, a temper that took every ounce of his self-control to contain. He looked powerful, big forearms and a football player's neck. He had done some time, he admitted, but had seen the light. Larry had sat through five sessions with the guy—or "modules" as they liked to call them. He didn't feel any better or different for it. Anyway, during the sixth module Miguel said something that struck Larry. He said that each random act of kindness yields two more acts of kindness in return. Larry had to think about that and its implications for a minute. Was it true? No, it couldn't be true.

Larry didn't believe that if he did something kind for his mother, say, she would go out and do something kind for two other people. She hated everyone. If Larry did something kind for her she'd ask him what the hell he was up to; she'd be sour. But he went to the local groceteria and purchased a bouquet of white carnations for her anyway. When he entered the apartment, she was draped over the coffee table doing lines of coke from a small mirror. Where'd you get the money for that, Ma? he asked her. She blinked her red eyes and told him to shut up. Her hands shook as she rocked a credit card over a bluish lump of cocaine. I know where you got the money, Larry said. She didn't look at him, continued with her business. He went to his room, threw the bouquet on his bed. Then he opened the window and lit a cigarette.

But it wasn't enough to be kind. Larry thought Miguel had over-stated the case. Even when you were kind, it didn't mean anything, it didn't change anything. People were dogs. If you threw them a bone they'd fight for it. And something told him Miguel understood the truth but refused to admit it, maybe as a matter of policy. They put together these programs, hired compassionate goons to run them, then forced young offenders like Larry to sit through them. And for what? Last thing he wanted was to be like Miguel, barely containing his true self. Miguel was dishonest about the world and about himself, and his message to Larry suffered from a lack of conviction. No matter how Miguel put it, the premise of random acts of kindness multiplying fell flat.

Downtown, near the new library, Larry ran into Toby, a bum who always asked for money. Larry figured he'd throw the stiff ten bucks for the hell of it, enough for a bottle of something to drown his sor-rows. Unlikely he'd spread the grace. Larry walked up to Toby, who was bent over a trash can. Toby pulled out a half-eaten pizza slice and sniffed it before taking a bite. He started at the sight of Larry and dropped the pizza. What the hell do you want? he asked. Larry moved closer. Remember me, Toby? Yeah, Toby said, I sure do, you cheap bastard. Hey, Larry said. He flashed the ten-dollar bill. Toby's demeanor changed. He got real close to Larry, smiling with black-studded grey gums. Larry winced. Did you shit yourself or some-thing? he asked Toby. No, the bum said. He thought about it. Then he said, Well, yes, I did a few days ago.

Then Larry went down to the park near his flat—Duke and Cayuga stood near the swings, selling crack. Duke saw him first and slapped Cayuga's shoulder. Cayuga looked over with his fake ferocity. He didn't scare Larry. He was a rat. Whenever he got pinched he ratted out the whole neighbourhood. And Duke was a punk. They knew Larry had been in for beating up a guy from Niagara Falls—put him in a coma. It was over an ounce of weed. The guy, this big mouth bastard, accused Larry of selling him a bad count. Larry didn't sell bad counts. Big mouth had it coming. Cayuga had it coming, but the act of kindness for him today was sparing him a beating. Hey, bro, Duke said, his greasy hair shining in the sunlight. Cayuga, in torn and tar-stained dungarees, put his hands on his hips and tilted his shoulders. What's up, Larry? he asked. You're fucking lucky, Larry said, pointing at him. They kill rats inside, you know. Kill them. Taking a step back, Cayuga said, So what are you saying, man? He's calling you a rat, Duke chirped. Larry turned to Duke and without pausing a beat slapped him so hard flakes of dandruff flew off his head and shoulders.

Lacking fear gives you freedom in some respects. But fear serves to protect you. Bam-Bam and his son Darcy took turns on Larry one night in front of Duffy's Billiards. Larry had just stiffed this sap for fifty bucks playing snooker and was heading out the doors to go score some weed when he ran into the pair, both of them wired. Larry used to hang with Darcy. He had the triangle face happening now from using crack. Darcy asked him what was up and Larry said nothing much. Red-eyed and drooling, Bam-Bam looked fucked. Larry was about to split when without warning they jumped him and knocked him to the ground. Bam-Bam kicked him in the head. Darcy worked his torso, front and back, really reefing to impress the old man. Blood poured from Larry's torn mouth. Bam-Bam tired, wheezing, bending at the waist. Are we going to kill him, Dad? Darcy asked. Bam-Bam gave him a backhand to the teeth and told him to shut his fucking mouth. Bam-Bam then took out a pipe and cooked up a rock of crack right there, over Larry's motionless body. Darcy watched the spectacle with his head tipped almost sadly. Fuck you, Bam-Bam said, hauling. His eyes spun in their sockets and he started drooling. He forgot about Larry and his son and staggered off down the street. Darcy kicked Larry in the face one more time and then went through his pockets.

☦   ☦   ☦

How long was he in hospital? A few days? His mother didn't come to see him. When he got home she wasn't there. A note taped to the refrigerator said she took off to Florida for a week with a *friend*. Bruises ringed Larry's eyes and a white cast encased his right hand

and forearm. They stitched up his lips and gums pretty good but it hurt like a bitch. He checked for telephone messages. Miguel left three. He sounded pissed off. He said that if Larry didn't call him within twenty four hours he would issue a letter of non-compliance. That message was two days old. Great, Larry thought, now my P.O. will breach me—MacKinnon didn't take any shit—and send me back inside to complete my entire sentence—one year. His brain couldn't get around that: *one year*. He couldn't do it—he couldn't do another year. He'd kill himself first. He called Miguel's number, got the machine and left a message explaining his situation. Miguel wouldn't doubt his story once he saw him. Miguel was a reasonable man.

Miguel was not reasonable, or sympathetic. Anger thickened the veins in his neck and heightened the dark intensities of his eyes; he cracked his calloused knuckles and flexed his forearms. He acted as if Larry had committed the assault. He said that Larry had put himself in place for the beating. If he had used his large human brain he would have stayed away from Bam-Bam and Darcy. Miguel knew Darcy very well. He had tried to run him through the Program but Darcy stopped coming after two sessions. Why didn't you press charges? Miguel wanted to know, flexing his forearm muscles. Get serious, Larry said. He had to live in this town. The Criminal Justice System offered little protection and less solace. So you'll let them get away with it, Miguel said with a sigh. But Larry never said he'd let them get away with it.

Early on Miguel insisted that the only thing the Program could do was make him *think* before acting, and before talking. Too often people rush into action, or blurt out whatever comes to mind. It only takes a few seconds of thought to change the course of history, because everything you do comprises your history and stays with you one way or the other. Did Larry want to go back inside? He was fifteen now, he'd be charged as a youth and serve three years. He couldn't do three years. He didn't think he could. He'd be eighteen when he got out.

And if it was something he could do, three years, why should he not get even? The modules preached non-violent solutions to all problems but this seemed unrealistic, even dangerous. Showing softness left you vulnerable, open to attack. At the heart of the Program throbbed the idea of a benevolent, peaceful, and lawful society, where everybody scratched each other's back, but in Larry's estimation such a society could never exist. Miguel talked a good game—and appeared empathetic. You were raised fatherless, he said, you have no positive male role models. An attentive father would have nurtured your strengths, turned all that mayhem into something powerful, for the good. You're smart, Larry. You understand what I'm talking about— you know the difference between right and wrong. You don't suffer from a cognitive disorder. And even though you've had it rough— remember you're not the only one. Larry, I was the son of immigrants, poor, despised, beaten down. And I fought. I fought like a tiger. Made a name for myself. Don't fuck with Miguel, my homies would say, he's loco. That's right, Larry. So I was a tough guy for a while. But for me it wasn't about that, it was about right and wrong— but only how I saw it, not the way society did. We live in a society, man. If we can't follow its rules then we get erased from the picture. I stood up for myself, yeah, with my fists. And it got me a good chunk of time. And during that time I came to understand that violence only leads to more violence and that when I thought about it, my . . . is any of this sinking in, Larry?

✝ ✝ ✝

So his arm would heal and his face would come around. His mother had returned from Florida accompanied by this tall dark guy with a pencil-thin goatee and chocolate eyes. He called himself Jean-Guy. Jean-Guy is staying with us for now, Larry's mother informed him. Jean-Guy pretended not to speak English. Larry couldn't believe his mother spoke French as well as she did. Who could have known? He wished that she had taught him some of it. Comes in handy in a bilingual country. Grandma was French, she explained while she mixed a pitcher of martinis. What did you do to your arm? she asked. I fell, Larry said. You were always clumsy, she said. Jean-Guy laughed. He rested his Cuban heels on the edge of the coffee table.

He had very white teeth. I suppose the bruises on your face are also from the fall, his mother said. Yeah, Larry said. Jean-Guy laughed even louder this time.

Miguel picked him up at the apartment and drove him to his office. He ran module seven of the Program with a PowerPoint presentation that he projected onto a wall. His use of imagery and narrative impressed Larry. This wasn't as dry as the other modules. This one dealt with the Power Equation. It suggested that the powerful often win battles and wars. Implied throughout the module were two ideas Larry found disagreeable: one, that we were obliged to feel empathy for the underdogs, the victims, the powerless; and two, that the victories of the powerful were somehow tainted. One doesn't naturally feel empathy for weaklings; often one hates them. And if the powerful win contests, if the scales always tip in their favor, why not go with power?

Jean-Guy insisted they find a new apartment. He was willing to pay for the upgrade. Jean-Guy turned out to be a decent guy. You can never go by appearances. He treated Larry's mother better than her other boyfriends. He didn't slap her around or get her to do bizarre sexual things. And he wasn't into cocaine. The man liked his grass, smoked it all day, but he hated the white stuff, called it an ego drug. He liked to sit around smoking herb and listening to Brazilian music. Larry had no idea what the man did for a living, but it must have been shady—he never kept regular hours. When Larry asked Jean-Guy why he liked his mother, Jean-Guy thought about it for a moment and said, Your mother is very sad, very deep. When we met it was sexual— forgive me for saying it. But I feel something else now, something deeper. She needs to get out of this shit-hole and start fresh. You too.

✝   ✝   ✝

Larry asked Miguel about revenge during one session. Miguel's eyes lit up at the mention of the word. He paused a long while before giving his answer. It is my belief, he said, that in some rare moments—for instance if someone grievously injures a member of your family—a man has to do what a man has to do. That being said, I don't want you to get the impression that I condone violence. I do not. I repeat, I do not condone it in any way. In no way do I condone or encourage violence or any other criminal activity. Perpetrators must be prepared to face the full brunt of the law. But as I said, in some instances . . . never mind I said that. Miguel grew uncomfortable with the subject and asked Larry how things were going in general, if his injuries were healing. He looked better, and so on. But Larry had only one thing on his mind and this made it difficult for him to suffer Miguel's tactics. I don't like you, Larry blurted. Miguel looked surprised at first, then hurt. You give me mixed messages, Larry said. That's a sophisticated term, Miguel said. No it's not, Larry said. Don't condescend me, I'm not stupid. I've got a legitimate beef and I plan to do something about it. Miguel sighed and cracked his knuckles. Then I'll have to make a report, he said, opening a drawer and pulling out a form. Do what you gotta do, Larry said.

The park near the new apartment spared Larry the likes of Duke and Cayuga. The last he heard, Duke had stabbed Cayuga over money and was back inside. He punctured Cayuga's liver—the guy almost died in hospital and wasn't out of the woods yet. Larry thought he'd go visit Cayuga and find out what went down, also to mock him a little for letting a bitch like Duke fuck him up like that. It was funny. Larry went to the hospital, found Cayuga's room. He was in no mood for a visit but Larry brought chocolate bars and a porn magazine. They ain't feeding me shit, Cayuga bitched. And the nurses are mean. He grabbed a chocolate bar, tore the wrapping off and chewed. This relaxed him. Larry asked him what had happened. I stole twenty bucks off Duke, Cayuga reported. He didn't have to stab me. It did seem extreme to Larry. But twenty bucks was twenty bucks, and the last thing you wanted to do was to start a trend with Cayuga. And what happened to you? he asked Larry. Bam-Bam and Darcy, he replied. Cayuga grimaced. After a moment he said, Thanks for the stuff, man.

Larry spotted Bam-Bam in the mall one day without Darcy. Tattoos riddled his arms and big gold hoops dangled from both ears. He was missing a few teeth and scared people just being in the vicinity, but combine that with cocaine psychosis and a penchant for hyper-violence, it didn't take him long to clear a room or turn it upside-down. He started screaming at an old guy in a plaid vest near the fountains about something and Larry thought for sure he was going to hit him. Mall security—two porky guys in wrinkled white shirts with walkie-talkies—hastened to the scene but slammed on the brakes when they saw the perpetrator of the disturbance. They came to a halt a safe distance away but that didn't stop Bam-Bam from closing in on one of them and clobbering him across the neck. The guard went down in a heap. The other tried calling for back-up but at the last second lost his nerve, dropped his walkie-talkie and turned on his heels.

Darcy too was busy. Larry observed him one day in a schoolyard beating a skinny kid senseless then taking his Blue Jays cap. When the cap didn't fit his big head, Darcy threw it down and stomped on it. Larry wanted to do something but was afraid that Bam-Bam might come around. The beaten kid got up, badly shaken and bleeding from the nostrils. He retrieved his battered cap, then turned on a smaller child standing there watching. Larry walked home. He had a bigger bedroom now. He spent a lot of time in there thinking, weighing things in his mind. A room. That's all it was, then, a room. He could do three years.

✝   ✝   ✝

Bam-Bam must have been inside again. Darcy was spotted roaming around alone. His mother, a stripper, lived in a nice little house near the canal, prim and clean, with a white picket fence and a rose garden. You wouldn't think a peeler would live like a schoolteacher. Darcy tried to burn down his mother's house once, on Bam-Bam's orders, so he wasn't exactly welcome there. Darcy was up for trial soon—he'd be going in for a long stretch. He said he could do it. No one would fuck with him inside. Everyone knew Bam-Bam. He used to ride with Hells Angels, he used to be a hit man for the mob. He was a crackhead now, but that made him even more dangerous. On his own, Darcy was nothing. He probably wanted to live a quieter life, but it was too late for that.

And it went down like this one night, not far from Duffy's
Billiards—Hey, Darcy. Even though the voice expressed cheer and
frankness, Darcy cautiously turned around. His eyes widened when
he saw the cast coming for his face. He dropped to the ground with
his forehead cracked. Larry fell on top of him. He beat Darcy with the
cast and his good hand until his face turned pulpy and he stopped
moving. Then Larry sprang to his feet and raised his throbbing hands
in the air. Blood dripped off his elbows. What, Darcy? he shouted.
What? He kicked the body, just visible in the dim alley. He kicked
again. Then he went through Darcy's pockets, pulling out two hundred dollars or so in twenties and a baggie of crack cocaine. He threw
the cocaine into the gutter. As he walked away, he thought he heard
Darcy groan. He stopped and looked over his shoulder, but Darcy
wasn't moving or making any sounds.

Bam-Bam went inside for putting an off-duty cop into a coma.
Bam-Bam would later die in his cell, allegedly from self-inflicted
head trauma. Larry followed Miguel's advice and reflected on his
crime—but no matter how he tried to humanize Darcy, he failed to
draw a drop of remorse from his heart. He even tried to imagine his
stripper-mother bawling her eyes out. But Darcy would have probably
given her more grief had he lived. He was a chip off the old block, a
growing menace to society. The three years went by as well as they
could have. Larry suffered, but he came to know himself better. He
read the classics, built up a fine physique. He even learned some
French. He planned to attend university when he got out and study
journalism, or law, he wasn't sure yet. His mother never came to visit
him, but Jean-Guy showed up one day with a tin of cashews and some
magazines. He didn't have much to say, only that he was leaving her,
she was back on the blow, and this didn't surprise Larry. Despite
everything, he felt strangely happy near the end of his term.

He rarely thought of Darcy, except when it got damp and his
hands ached.

The Fishhouse

I killed the headlights of my black Cadillac as I inched down the dead-end to Tommy Sardo's place on the wharf. I could barely see a thing, most of the streetlights blown out or busted except for a small blue lamp shining at the end of the pier. Tommy lived in a converted fishhouse, a soulless and impersonal edifice, the windows uncurtained, the glass sheathed with filth. A dark blue van sat near the entrance, manned by a guy in a Maple Leafs sweater. His face looked encased in pale blue hosiery. He ignored me—or maybe he was sleeping with his eyes open. Maybe he was dead.

I parked in front of the van and put on my black leather gloves, pressing them slowly down between the fingers as I checked myself in my rearview mirror. My eyes looked bloodshot. I took out my drops and applied a few to each eye. That helped. I climbed out of the car. Debris littered the street: crushed cans, broken bottles, fluttering plastic bags. A mangy dog came trotting by, ears pinned back, a fugitive look in its eyes, and hurried down the street, abruptly veering off into a dark alley. Against a wire fence leaned a discarded clothes rack, a dress of pink taffeta still clinging to its bar, an eye-catching garment.

"I'd like to try on that dress," I said in a falsetto. "The pink one."

"Oh, what a beauty. It happens to be a size . . ."

I wondered if someone was watching me through a peephole. I stepped toward the van, and the fellow inside it remained motionless. I went around to the driver's window and tapped on the glass with my car key. Nothing, even though his eyes looked open, or his John Lennon glasses created this illusion. Then I could see from the steady rise and fall of his chest and the drooling mouth that he was sleeping. I tapped harder on the glass. Nothing. I went around the van to the fishhouse entrance, a frame of heavy, water-logged timbers. I walked up to the door, a thick wooden number with an opaque portal window. I searched for a doorbell but didn't see one. When I knocked on the door, no sound issued. I neared my nose to the glass and opened my eyes wide but saw only vague shapes moving around in the interior's yellow half-light.

"Tommy!" I shouted. "Tommy!"

I waited a second, then stepped back and glanced up at the windows. I cupped my mouth with my hands and shouted Tommy's name again. A frog in my throat spiked my voice to a pitchy screech. Pathetic, I must have sounded pathetic. I cleared my throat and retried, keeping in mind what I represented. No one came to the windows. For all I knew Tommy wasn't around. I felt foolish standing there. The damp cold chilled my bones; I clenched my stomach muscles to keep from shivering like a child. I had on my khaki trench coat, a handsome garment, but one unsuited for the damp. I'd have worn my black leather coat had it not been ruined the week before during a messy operation. The mark in question bore a resemblance to a siphonophore, his face a swollen sac of cysts, his hair like jellied tentacles.

Something thudded behind the great door. Then it slowly started opening. I braced myself. When it opened fully I saw a piston-like device attached to the doorknob, maybe an automatic opener of a design unfamiliar to me, industrial in sturdiness and power, perhaps necessary to move such a heavy door.

A small bald man in a tight black suit appeared in the doorway, sallow, serious. In addition to the clean, smooth head, the man lacked eyebrows and lashes, giving him a peeled or parboiled look. A crimson pouf flared out from his breast pocket. His tiny black shoes shone as though they had just been polished. He stared at me with large, moist black eyes.

"Where's Tommy?"

The little man blinked once. "Who's asking?"

"Tell him it's Charlie."

"Charlie who?"

"Charlie Bacala."

"You're Charlie Bacala?"

"That's right. Tell him I want to see him."

"What's the nature of your business?"

"That's between Tommy and me."

The little man smiled and leaned forward, looking at me with the tops of his eyes. "Tommy's not taking any visitors at this time. Maybe you'd like to schedule an appointment." He pulled out a small black book, licked his thumb and flipped through it. "Sorry," he said. "But Tommy's booked solid till next month."

Funny, I thought. Amusing. "Just tell Tommy I want a word."

"You don't listen too good, do you?"

"Tell Tommy what I said."

The little man sniffed and thought about it for a minute. Then he pushed a red button on the wall that released a whoosh of hydraulic pressure; a noise of sucking water commenced, and the door slowly shut.

I wondered how long this would take. I had tried to contact Tommy previously with no luck. He was a man of mystery, difficult to pin down. It took some serious arm-twisting and palm-greasing to gather any information about him, truly testing my resolve. After months of probing, my sources determined that Tommy resided in the fishhouse, a structure not unfamiliar to me. It seemed strange; but when I tried to find out why Tommy lived in the fishhouse no one could say. Maybe I'd soon discover for myself why he lived there.

The air was colder now; stars glimmered in the sky like beige diamonds. A nearly full moon, unusually luminous that evening, hung there like a hideous mocking clown face. Lunatics must have been beside themselves. A dull metallic clanging issued from the dark docks. I stretched my neck to spot its source but could make out nothing. The clanging stopped. The light from the lamp on the pier hovered there like a small blue cloud the breeze could not diffuse. A treat for the eyes in the gloom. I kicked a pile of salty slush and described a circle before the door, concerned that when this day ended, my shoes would not regain their shine. Salt wounds leather.

After a moment I heard the door opening again. I took a deep breath and steeled myself. The little man reappeared, carrying a small white envelope. He held it out to me.

"Well?" he said, shaking the envelope.

"This is Tommy's response?"

"That's what it is."

I heard something creak above my head but did not look up. "How can I believe you?"

"Tommy wrote it, okay. And if I were you I'd read it."

"You would, eh?"

"You're a touchy sort, aren't you?" he said.

"If you were me, you would be too." The creaking above me continued.

The little man shook the envelope again.

Glancing up and seeing nothing out of the ordinary, I took the envelope from his hand.

"Step back," he said.

"What?"

"Step back."

By then he had pushed the button that triggered the door, issuing a hydraulic whoosh and then the liquid sucking sound as the door inched shut. The creaking I heard earlier continued. I looked above the entrance and saw the end of a lead pipe jutting out of a window. Someone or something was turning it, hence the creaking. Puzzling. I stared at the pipe for another moment then held up the envelope and tried to read the writing on it—worromot—but it made no sense. Then I realized the word was *tomorrow* written backwards.

Did Tommy want me to return tomorrow? This sounded odd. I ripped open the envelope and pulled out the slip of paper inside it, hopeful that it would provide a more comprehensive explanation. But on this slip of paper appeared the same handwritten word: *worromot*. It meant nothing to me, much as tomorrow meant nothing to me, if that's what it meant. I was not about to wait until tomorrow to meet with Tommy. *My* schedule would not permit that. And I suspected he understood that all too well. The situation demanded expediency, like fish heads waiting for the bouillabaisse. Delaying a conference by a day served no purpose whatsoever, to my mind. It merely delayed the inevitable. I glanced up again and saw that the pipe had been withdrawn.

I walked along the wharf, breathing in the cold harbour air. I liked it near the water, even on a chilly December evening. Snow on the sidewalk resembled heaped ashes, and black slush frothed in the gutters. I felt disoriented, somewhat detached from my surroundings. Things changed as focus and perspective changed, my skull shifting this way and that, my eyes thinning shut then popping open. A block of desiccated blood became a fire hydrant. A Santa Claus with his back to me turned and flashed a pair of bulging D-cups. An undressed mannequin lying by a trash bin jumped to its feet and started sprinting toward the water. Jesus walking an elephant yielded nothing but a snuffling pug and a teenaged boy in a silver costume with spikes poking out of his head. I wanted to hate him for being so young, for being so bizarre, but hate takes time and energy. It is not a simple emotion. Hate must be laid down brick by brick for it to take hold, for it to be strong. Something splashed, something black and slick, a scuba diver—no, some kind of fish, huge. My eyes blurred over; the cold air raked them. I took out my drops and squirted.

When my eyes cleared I looked at the black water and considered how cold it would be if I fell in. I could swim, but not well, given my weight. I had ballooned in the past year, a glandular issue. I detected no movement among the blocky shadows and heard nothing but the distant traffic and machines of night, and the water.

I needed to find a quiet place to sit down and sort this out, drink something hot, warm up. I couldn't think straight in the cold; my ears ached, I could not feel my toes. I walked up from the wharf to a street lined with Christmassy boutiques and candle-lit cafés. I ducked into a place with multi-paneled leaded windows. I sat by one of the windows, beside a blue aluminum tree strung with tiny white lights, and tried to make myself at ease, removing my gloves and stretching my legs. Xylophone music tonkled a gentle Christmas groove over the speakers, and I found myself nodding to its rhythm, feeling it in my bones.

A red-vested waiter, a man with gaping nostrils and a moustache drawn in with eyeliner, approached the table, crossed his arms on his chest, and stood there without saying a word. His head was square in shape with bloodshot eyes edging toward the temples.

"Hook me up with a hot toddy," I joked, but the waiter didn't flinch. "I'll have a coffee and a snifter of Grand Marnier, okay?" Unimpressed, the waiter slid off.

Other patrons occupied tables in the back, and though I heard the muted tones of their conversations and the light tinkle of their glasses and cutlery, and though I smelled their perfumes and colognes, their sweat and their breath, and felt their mild scrutiny thrashing like snakes in the shadows, I made a point of not looking at them.

The drinks arrived; I creamed my coffee and took a sip. A rich, nutty brew, it pleased me, and I am not easy to please when it comes to coffee. I grind my own beans and so forth. Not that I pretend to be anything but what I am—a working stiff—I do like a nice cup of coffee. I swirled the Grand Marnier around in the snifter and I felt quite light and happy for a moment, almost in a swoon. I sniffed the orange bouquet and let the liqueur trickle into my throat where it burned going down and settled in my stomach like a cool flame.

The waiter returned.

"I'll have another snifter of the juice," I said. But the waiter lacked affect. "Is something wrong?" I asked.

"What could be wrong?"

"You look—I don't know—disgruntled, depressed. Not the best face to put forward to the public. You think?"

"Are you some kind of smart ass? I'm just saying."

"See. Hostile. What if I were to crack you across the face with a karate chop? Or rip your throat out? Would that discourage your rudeness? I'm just saying."

Why wait tables if you can't give a customer a little smile, a bit of poetry, some song and dance, whatever? Especially during the holiday season. Why piss in *my* egg nog? Many people get depressed during the holidays, it's *normal*, we've all *been there.* So, when all is said and done, it's absurd to continue doing something that makes you unhappy. Life is very short. In the past, I had been a heedless young man, roaming around without a plan, without a thought in my head, a maniac, a brute. I had come a long way since then—but it had not been an easy road. I had to get the pick and shovel out and break things down, then rebuild, brick by brick. Was I happy now? Well, perhaps not ecstatic. I was not walking around wearing a simper or an expression of beatitude. I was not handing out free balloons and jellybeans at a corner. I had been happier in the past, likely, at some point—I draw a blank but blame that on a memory shot full of holes for many reasons, and not on the past. The past is an elephant: it forgets nothing. It is like the Incarnation, forever in place as time speeds toward the future—or gives that illusion. I was neither unhappy nor labouring at something I hated with my entire being, like the waiter for instance.The waiter sniffed.

"I hope I didn't offend you," I said, noticing his chafed, scaly hands.
"You did."

"But you still brought my drink." I wondered if he had stuck his finger in it, or worse. Angry waiters like this one had a million tricks up their sleeve.

"Yes. Yes, I did."

"Well, thanks. Professional of you. It's admirable. I was starting to lose faith. And it is the *holiday* season, after all. Isn't it? But, seriously, you should cheer up. Probably hurts on the tips with the sourness."

"My mother died yesterday."

This took me aback. "Geez—I'm sorry to hear that, man. Your mother? Well, when is the funeral?"

"She lives in Greece. I can't afford to fly out."

My mouth fell open. I didn't know what to say. Life is a bastard sometimes, a real cocksucker. But we had a point of contact here, a shared human thing occurring. "I've also had a situation arise."

The waiter did not reply; instead his eyes filled with tears and his chin quivered.

"I'm sorry," he said, blowing his nose into a large, checked handkerchief. "I'm afraid you've caught me at a moment of great weakness, what with the Christmas holidays and so on. It's been rough. You were saying?"

"Nothing," I said, watching him fold up the handkerchief with those hideous hands. He must have doubled as a dishwasher. But anyway, why bother going into details about my situation with this poor guy? I thought. Nothing was for certain. Despite the simplicity of my objective, an octopus of intangibles clouded my clarity, wrapping its tentacles around my head and dragging me along like some kind of mindless meat-puppet. What could I do about it? Sometimes intangibles trump common sense and steer you to dark corners. And yet, without intangibles the world would be a boring place. "It's not important," I said to the waiter. "Believe me. And I'm real sorry about your mom, there. I truly am."

"Thank you," said the waiter, dabbing his nose with the folded handkerchief.

"Hey," I said. "Not to change the subject—but I have a question for you."

"Yes?"

"You must know this neighbourhood, eh? I mean I used to know it well when I was a kid. Oh yeah, used to come down here all the time with my mates and horse around. My buddy Turkey Mancini fell into the water one windy November day way back when—I remember like it was yesterday—and drowned beside a docked cargo ship. That's right. But tell me, what's up with the fishhouse these days?"

"The fishhouse?"

"Yeah, the fishhouse down on the wharf."

The waiter shrugged.

"No, no. Come on. Don't play dumb, now. You must know what I'm talking about. The fishhouse right down the street. Some big shot lives there. Yeah, the fishhouse down on the wharf. Real ugly looking building."

"I'm sorry, I can't help you."

And with that he turned and walked off. Son-of-a-bitch.

I glanced at the blue Christmas tree flanking my table and while it pleased me, with its little white bulbs glowing so prettily, it gave me no Christmas feeling whatsoever. Even the vibraphones, now soft-hammering a moody rendition of *We Three Kings* left my Christmas spirit unmoved. I had grown too cynical perhaps, too hardened, too conscious of the commercial propensities of the season. To think that not so long ago Christmas filled me with ticklish ebullience, with joy. The sight of a twinkling Christmas tree or a diorama of the Nativity would bring hot tears to my eyes. I would sob with delicious self-pity watching *It's A Wonderful Life* and almost be overcome with emotion when I heard Vince Guaraldi's soundtrack to *A Charlie Brown Christmas*, for it summoned all my childhood Christmases. Yes, quite a softy when it came to Christmas. What happened? What happens to everything. It gets old.

The patrons in back erupted with laughter. I looked but saw only shadows. The laughter continued, surging and withdrawing like an ocean wave. Well, at least someone was having a good time of it, and that was key. I finished my coffee.

As I headed back to the fishhouse, a high-gloss black Hummer pulled up in front of an antiques shop. I wondered if Tommy had sent some of his boys down to further press home his message. But what was his message? To come back tomorrow? That wasn't going to happen. Two Frankensteins in black leather overcoats jumped out of the Hummer. They carried dark green cases and neither took notice of my presence. I could have nailed them right then and there and they would not have seen it coming. They stiffly moved to the shop entrance and one of them removed a key from his pocket. He dropped it and when he bent down to pick it up his mate did the same, and their foreheads clunked.

I kept walking and soon realized I was lost. The structures, many windowless, abandoned, or serving as sets for American film production companies, looked unfamiliar. Comical this, for me to lose my bearings in a neighbourhood I could have called my own. As a youth I had spent so much time near the water, on the docks, by the wharf, that I felt quite at home, quite easy in my feeling there.

Clouds blocked the starlight and fishy odors swept through the street arousing my disgust. Acid burned in the back of my throat, cheesy and scalding. I swallowed. Despite the cold air, sweat beaded my forehead, and my limbs trembled.

I continued toward the water, guided by the winking harbour lights and the sloping shadows of the wharf. My legs moved of their own accord, or at least I wasn't conscious of guiding them. Tommy—I had almost forgotten about Tommy. I wondered what he was doing at that moment—with an inward chuckle I imagined him and his little man decorating their Christmas tree. Not likely, but in this life one should presume nothing.

By the time I found my way back to the fishhouse my face felt like a mask of carved ice, my feet like frozen cinderblocks. The fishhouse stood dark and silent—abandoned? The blue light on the pier floated there like some kind of plasmic phantasm. Had Tommy and his boys left the premises? I shouted out his name several times with no response. I neared the door and banged my fist against it.

After a moment, the door thudded and started opening. The little man reappeared holding a lantern and wearing a black fedora.

"If you really have to see him," he said, "I'll take you. He's around back."

"Around back?"

"Yes, follow me."

He led me down an auxiliary dock next to the blue-lit pier to a loose row of wooden planks roped together haphazardly and jutting out on the water. He said something under his breath, gave me a sidelong glance, and stepped across these planks as nimbly as a tightrope walker, the lantern swinging back and forth, its greenish light washing over everything like a dash of chartreuse. Below us, black water gurgled and splashed. I walked with a wide base and my arms spread for balance.

The little man flashed the lantern beside the planks, and I saw a wooden rowboat bobbing in the water. He planted his polished shoes, bent his knees, and jumped into it, gesturing for me to follow suit. A man of my size doesn't just jump into a rowboat. My days of jumping into rowboats were long gone. With great exertion, I flung my left leg over, my foot hitting like an anvil, and then when my right leg crashed down, the boat almost tipped. It rocked for a moment, threatening to toss the little man, who clung like a lemur to the bow, eyes gleaming, his free hand clawing for purchase. When the boat stopped rocking, he attached the lantern to the bow with a rope catch and then grabbed the oars.

"Need help?" I asked.

"No, I can manage, it's not far."

The lantern cast an emerald sphere of light around the boat as it rolled through solid black. I heard clanging from the docks and dogs barking. In garish whiteface, a mocking moon gaped down at us, its reflection shimmering in the water like pooled milk. The little man rowed with sharp grunts and heaves and shortly pulled up to a dock. He got out of the rowboat and helped me out. Then he tied the rowboat and seized the lantern. As he turned, his hat flew off his head and fell into the water. Without hesitation he handed me the lantern, removed his shoes, and leaped into the water. He went in without a splash. I couldn't see him. I waited.

After some minutes he still did not appear. I peered at the dark water but saw nothing. Where could he have gone? It had started snowing. At first a few big fat flakes whirled around like lackadaisical moths, then more and more fell, more and more until the air became a swirling mass of white. It fell so thickly I could no longer see the water. In moments snow blanketed the dock. Teeth chattering, I hugged myself to keep warm. I felt concern for the little man, but not so much that I would jump into the cold water after him, not with the sudden onset of a blizzard. That would have served no purpose. Not knowing what else to do, I staggered through the blinding snow toward what looked like an entrance in a large wall of corrugated steel down the dock. As I drew closer, a rubber-coated handle came into view: a door of some sort, I conjectured. I pulled the handle, and a section in the plate wall swung away from the structure, slipping from its stanchions and slamming to the dock with a great metal slap.

I entered the building and found myself standing in a concrete entranceway with a caged blue lamp shining from the ceiling. Blue sticky puddles gleamed on the floor and I stepped over them. Christmas music murmured from deep inside the building, Frank Sinatra's *White Christmas*—scratchy and quavery as if being spun on an old-fashioned hand-cranked phonograph. I walked down a dim hall that reeked of fish entrails. At the end of this hall shone a pale yellow light. I heard strange sounds, like wood being chopped.

"Who's there?" a thin voice cried.

"I'm looking for Tommy."

"Is that Charlie?"

"That's me."

"Come in so I can see you."

I followed the music to a chilly cinder-block chamber aglow with strings of red and white Christmas lights and flickering votive candles. A concrete slab sat in the middle of the chamber with a sluice-channel running under it. A mahogany handkerchief table flanked the slab; on top of it rested a small phonograph with the turntable spinning a record:

> May your days be merry and bright
> And may all your Christmases be white.

On the concrete slab sprawled an enormous beheaded fish, a marlin, or a tuna. Tommy stood behind it in a gore-splattered leather apron and rubber gloves, holding a blood-greased cleaver. A veil of fine black mesh covered his face, and on his head he wore a brass helmet of sorts. Tommy has his vanities, I thought, as he yanked a stretch of viscera taut.

"Tonight is my gutting night and normally I take no visitors." He reached his hand into the cavity of the great fish and pulled out intestines. They writhed and wriggled like skinned snakes. He tossed them into a barrel and reached into the fish again.

"You're a hard man to get a hold of."

"Apparently not." He yanked. "So, tell me, Charlie. What brings you here?"

"I think you know why I'm here, Tommy."

He slammed the cleaver down with a clang, wiped his gloved

hands on his apron, and nodded. "I know why you're here, Charlie. I know. Did you have to come tonight, with Christmas just around the corner?"

"What can I say, Tommy? Nothing personal on my part."

Tommy waved his hand. "I know, I know. This has nothing to do with you, Charlie. Nothing at all. Listen, I have a small, a very small favour to ask."

"Go ahead, Tommy."

"Can we play the song one more time? Just one more time."

I thought it wouldn't hurt to let him hear the song. "Go ahead."

"I've loved this song ever since I was a kid," he said, going around to the phonograph to restart the record. "Doesn't feel like Christmas without it."

I couldn't disagree. "It's snowing outside, Tommy."

"Well, how about that. And look who's here to join us. Come right in, Bruno."

The little man stood in the entranceway sopping wet and trembling, clutching his crumpled, dripping fedora.

"Little accident, Bruno? Too bad. You'll have to get out of those wet clothes later, eh. Charlie, you don't mind if I sing along, do you? You're welcome to join in. Bruno, you too."

"That's okay, Tommy. Let's just get this over with."

He lowered the needle and the music started up:

I'm dreaming of a white Christmas . . .
Just like the ones I used to know . . .

Tommy sang along with a high sweet voice. He wasn't half-bad. The little man, Bruno, surprised me, crooning in a rich baritone. They sang their hearts out. It was a beautiful thing, touching. But it gave me no Christmas feeling whatsoever, it did not move my spirit. I had become too cynical perhaps, too hardened. To think that not so long ago Christmas had filled me with joy. Yes, I used to be quite a softy when it came to Christmas. What happened? What happens to everything. It gets old.

ABOUT THE AUTHOR

SALVATORE DIFALCO was born and raised in Hamilton
Ontario, the son of Italian immigrants. He attended the
University of Toronto, and won a Canada Council Doctoral
Fellowship, completing an M.A. in English. He continued
on with PhD studies in Modern Irish Literature and is the
author of one volume of poetry and one chapbook of stories,
Outside. Mr. Difalco has had numerous stories published in
journals and literary magazines in both Canada and the U.S.
He currently lives in Niagara Falls.